ORANGES
AND
LEMONS

For Juliette,

ORANGES
AND
LEMONS

With a big curvy smile,

Paula.

X

Paula F. Andrews

Matador
9 Priory Business Park,
Wistow Road, Kibworth Beauchamp,
Leicestershire. LE8 0RX
Tel: 0116 279 2299
Email: books@troubador.co.uk
Web: www.troubador.co.uk/matador
Twitter: @matadorbooks

ISBN 978 1838592 066

British Library Cataloguing in Publication Data.
A catalogue record for this book is available from the British Library.

Printed and bound by CPI Group (UK) Ltd, Croydon, CR0 4YY
Typeset in 11pt MinionPro by Troubador Publishing Ltd, Leicester, UK

Matador is an imprint of Troubador Publishing Ltd

For my Four Family

"Oranges and lemons," say the bells of St Clement's.
"You owe me five farthings," say the bells of St Martin's.
"When will you pay me?" say the bells of Old Bailey.
"When I grow rich," say the bells of Shoreditch.
"When will that be?" say the bells of Stepney.
"I do not know," said the Great Bell of Bow.
Here comes a candle to light you to bed.
Here comes a chopper to chop off your head.
Traditional nursery rhyme

JESSIFER JORDAN

2019

S O COLD. AND TOO SMALL AND FRAGILE. HAVE you ever felt it? When a little kid slides their hand into yours? But this was no ordinary kid clutching my hand. This one was dead.

Fear shot through me, yet, when I looked down, there *was* no kid. I gazed at my palm as if I'd find it there, the hand. Ridiculous.

Clunk-clank. The muffled sound grabbed my attention. I drew in a breath. Trembling, I crossed the room to the glass cabinet containing the old weighing scales, said to have come from the kitchen when Mulberry Hall was a Victorian family home. The brass pans were tipping and rising, yet the scales were in a sealed cabinet. I looked around. I was alone, waiting for my great aunt who was paying our bill in the café upstairs. The low drone of chatter drifted down with the tang of coffee.

"Come with me."

The voice came from the cabinet. It was clear and insistent. A child's voice. The scales continued to see-saw. My hands shook as I placed them on the glass casing.

Immediately, I drew them back, scowling at my skin, expecting to see ice burns. The glass was freezing cold.

"Jess, shall we go home?"

I turned to see Aunt Ruby, stepping softly down the carpeted staircase, then I glanced back at the cabinet. The scales had come to rest. I rubbed my frozen hands. My memory had taken a snapshot of those tiny fingers.

"Are you cold, darling?" Aunt Ruby asked.

I nodded but couldn't speak. My throat was dry and my mind was spinning like a Catherine wheel. Could the story possibly be true?

"I hope you're not coming down with something," she said and began fussing with my scarf, before fixing her own.

We stepped out of Mulberry Hall into the January afternoon, leaving the shop's bell jangling behind us.

*

We approached our house as the last feeble talons of daylight clung to the horizon. A smoky-grey cat stood by our wrought-iron gate, its green eyes fixed on us. I clicked open the latch; it stared briefly then turned away, bored. A little bell around its neck tinkled softly.

"Who does that cat belong to, Auntie?" I said, closing the gate behind us. "I've never seen it before."

"I don't know but it probably smells Jupiter on you."

Jupiter, or Joopy as I mostly called him, was my pet rat. He'd be fast asleep in my room right now and probably wouldn't wake until supper time.

While Aunt Ruby delved in her bag for the key, I stamped my feet, trying to warm up. I turned at the sound of a child's voice. Singing, growing steadily louder.

"Here comes a candle to light you to bed…"

"D'you hear that, Auntie?" My voice shook and I tugged my aunt's coat sleeve as she fumbled with the lock. I stared at the low wall at the end of the sparse garden.

A child sat there, her legs swinging. She hadn't been there seconds ago. She wore a white party dress and little dark lace-up boots but no coat. A pale ribbon was in her fair hair.

I gasped. She'd freeze. Without thinking, I rushed towards her.

"Go home to your mummy. Where's your mummy?"

She smiled. Then she turned, clambered over the wall and ran off, laughing. Her mum must be waiting along the path, hidden from view by the privet hedge of the house next door. I shivered.

"Come on, Jessifer," shouted Aunt Ruby. "What on earth are you doing?"

*

I began to warm up once we were inside and Aunt Ruby had made a pot of tea. I checked on Joopy and smiled at the mound of shredded paper, his bed; it rose and fell. He was definitely sleeping, then.

In the lounge, cradling a steaming mug, my mind drifted back to the weighing scales in Mulberry Hall. Had I *imagined* them moving? No. They really had been. They had swung up and down. It had looked wrong. Then there was that tiny hand. I put my tea down and examined my fingers. They looked normal but when I touched them to my lips they felt like ice pops, in spite of the hot mug. A tremor of fear filled my tummy again.

"Get a grip, Jessifer," I murmured. I huffed and lifted my tea again.

"Talking to yourself, Jessifer, darling?" said Auntie as she walked into the room with her cup and saucer. Auntie was so refined. She didn't like drinking from a mug.

"Nearly spilled my tea, that's all, Auntie."

"I still think you're coming down with something. Early night for you tonight," she said as she sat across from me in her favourite chair.

"Okay, Auntie. I'm fine though; just tired." I paused and looked at her. *She* didn't look as if she was coming down with anything. Her fossil-grey eyes caught the soft light and her pumpkin hair, though silver-streaked, shone in its side-swept chignon. She was always so clever at piling and pinning her hair artfully and she oozed health. I hoped I could look as good as her in *my* sixties. "Auntie, something weird happened today. At Mulberry Hall."

"Oh?" Now she frowned.

"Well, it was nothing much. You know the old weighing scales in the cabinet?"

"Yes, you were gazing at them when I came downstairs."

"They were moving. On their own, inside the cabinet. How could that happen?"

"They weren't moving when I saw them, darling. Are you sure you're all right?"

"Maybe it was just a... you know... like an optical illusion then," I said, rubbing my cold fingers again. But I couldn't dismiss it. I knew the stories, legends, folk tales, whatever. This town was stuffed with them. I mean, bulging, like a fashion victim's cabin bag. One of them concerned Mulberry Hall China Shop and Café: Aunt Ruby's favourite place in York for a sandwich and mine for hot chocolate and toasted teacakes. And that was the one everyone was talking about right now: the little Victorian ghost of Mulberry Hall. I could still feel her tiny fingers in my hand.

*

I woke in the middle of the night; it was pitch black and a cold draught cut through my cotton pyjamas. I sat up, switched on the light and heard what had woken me: a thrashing and banging in the corner of the room. Joopy was hurling himself about his crate. It wasn't like him. His night-time sounds were usually gentle roamings around the obstacles and 'rooms' of his big metal house and were so familiar to me I mostly slept through them. He'd had supper earlier and a good play in my room before bed. Perhaps he was frozen, too. Had I left the window open? I crossed to the curtains and pulled one aside to check.

"Oh." I flinched. That cat, the smoky one, was staring right in at me. Creepy. How had it got there? We lived in an old Georgian townhouse split into three apartments and we were on the top floor. My room, like the lounge, faced the street and a cat must be practically magic to get up this high. But then, cats are a bit like that, aren't they?

Joopy went crazy-manic, squeaking and bolting about his crate like a lunatic.

"Shh," I urged, "you'll wake Auntie." I stood back from the window, daunted by the cat's soulful gaze. Then, it blinked and twisted into a jump, down into the inkwell of the night. I yanked the curtain shut. Joopy was scuffling but his squeaking settled to a murmur and I watched his pale tail disappear into his snug, tangled nest.

I did an almighty full-body shiver and decided to check the thermostat in the hall. Auntie didn't mind me adjusting it sometimes. Perhaps she'd forgotten to turn it up when we'd got back from town. I padded out of my room and found it much warmer in the hall. I'd make hot chocolate to help me sleep. I tiptoed into the kitchen and shut the door carefully. Auntie was a deep sleeper but with Joopy's clattering and me prowling about, I wouldn't have been surprised if she'd been disturbed.

While my milk heated on the stove, I sat at the kitchen table, shivering. I began to feel sleepy and wondered if I really needed hot chocolate. I gazed at the saucepan and my eyelids began drifting shut until movement from the windowsill distracted me. Unthinking, I turned my droopy eyes that way. They shot wide open. Our little old weighing scales, like a mini version of the ones in Mulberry Hall, had begun to swing up and down. Clunk-clank, they went; clunk-clank. Then, right there in front of me, growing out of nothing, sitting on the work surface, swinging her legs, appeared the same little girl I'd seen outside on the wall.

I tried to breathe and I tried to speak and I tried to still my hammering heart and I just stared and my eyes began to fill with tears. Nothing came to mind. No thought. No words. I just sat and stared at her. Stunned.

"Will you come to Stonegate?" she said in a little-girl voice. "Will you come to Mulberry Hall? Will you come? Will you be my friend? Will you?"

I gripped the edges of the kitchen table, paralysed, still staring, even though I could see the milk boiling over. I couldn't speak. My heart was pounding painfully. She didn't seem to mind that I didn't answer. She smiled at me then slid off the work surface like a breeze and landed silently in her little dark boots even though the drop was too great for such a small child. She walked right past me and drifted through the closed door.

I came to my senses. Something absurd had just happened. I should be terrified but there was nothing terrifying about what I'd seen: a small, pretty child in a frothy, white dress, swinging her legs playfully and smiling at me. What was there to be frightened of? I looked around the kitchen through teary eyes, turning, hugging my arms around myself.

"Oh my God," I whispered. "Oh my God... what... just... happened?" I slowly bent my neck and peered through the kitchen door into the hall. I could see as far as Auntie's door and everything looked normal. The framed botanical prints; my babyish grin beaming from my Year One photograph, too many coats and jackets bulging from the wall hooks. I heard the hiss of the hall radiator but otherwise the house was silent. I stepped out of the kitchen. She was there. Standing in the entrance to my room. Facing me and smiling. Then she turned and disappeared inside. I followed her, mesmerised, and watched her part the curtains, climb onto the windowsill and vanish. I edged forward, pulled the curtains wider, peered down and saw her... in the dark, her pale dress illuminating her. She stood, waving and smiling, a few paces beyond our gate. Something about her made me keep wanting to look. What was it? And then it hit me. She was like my sister. The same round face. God, she was beautiful. A little angel, like my big sister, Judith, who died, so long ago, aged six. I was only four then but I remembered her better than I did my parents. Of course, I had the photographs Aunt Ruby had given me, which were my greatest treasures. Strangely, I felt like the *older* sister now. I'd lived so much longer than she had.

Movement caught my peripheral vision and I saw a boy, much bigger than the girl, appear from behind the hedge. He smiled up at me too, a big, round-faced, jolly smile, then he took the girl's hand and off they went, him walking and her skipping. They crossed the road and, like snuffed-out candles, vanished into the black of the night.

I stood in my room, trembling and frozen, confused thoughts tumbling all over in my head, until I smelt the scorched milk. I ran to the kitchen to find it foaming up like a ghostly potion all over the stove.

2

ADELINE

YEARS AND YEARS AND YEARS

"ORANGES AND LEMONS..." I SANG, MARCHING up and down the nursery. Clementine watched me from the windowsill and I watched Nanny clear away the toys. She was putting them all in boxes, closing the lids and tying them up with string. Now and then she looked at me sharply and frowned and frowned but she didn't say anything. I tried to sing louder and faster and I spun around and around until I was dizzy, trying to make her laugh, even though I didn't feel like laughing. I knew, even though it was my home, I didn't really belong here any more.

"Nanny, Nanny," I called but she just reached for her woollen cloak and pulled it around her tightly and fled from the room. I saw something on the floor by the window, so I went and picked it up. Clementine was very interested. It was an envelope. It must have dropped out of Nanny's apron. I opened it and pulled out an invitation from the party. Then I remembered it was the one Mama had given me to keep;

a spare one. I'd propped it on the nursery windowsill in its envelope so that I could open it and look at it every day because I'd been so excited about the party even though I wasn't allowed to stay for the whole thing.

*

I held the invitation in my hand until Nanny left for ever. I held it until Papa went away to America and Mama went back to the country to live with my grandparents and I still held it after I made friends with Tom. I played in the houses and shops because there wasn't much else for me to do. Sometimes, Clementine slunk in and out after me but she always went back to her hole in the wall. I counted up years and years and years and then I lost count. The houses of Stonegate all turned into shops and the shops of Stonegate turned into different shops. The printer's changed into a bookshop and the ironmonger's changed into a shoe shop and then a clothing shop and the toy shop changed into a soap shop. My favourite thing was skipping up behind the shop men and ladies and tugging on their funny clothes, which weren't as thick as the ones the grown-ups used to wear when I was alive. The shop people frowned and shivered but mostly, they couldn't see me. I knew the ones that could. My favourite was a lady called Freda who worked in the tartan shop opposite Mulberry Hall. The first time I saw her, she was in her office at the very back. She was writing on a page that said '1980' at the top. I think that meant that I was very, very old but I didn't feel very, very old. Just a bit fed up because people thought I'd died because of an accident, but I didn't.

Freda was kind and I think she liked me and she didn't seem frightened like the others. The first time, she jumped and said where did I come from and she didn't understand when I said I lived in Mulberry Hall. She said I should go back to my mummy which I think meant Mama. I told her my mama was dead but she didn't understand, again. But after that she did understand and blew me kisses, nearly always. I began to sit beside her when she was at the counter putting garments in bags and taking money from the customers. One day, she wasn't there any more and, eventually, the shop started selling only confectionery and not garments. I was sad she had gone and I wondered where to. I would always go back to Mulberry Hall though because that was where I lived my whole, whole, whooo-le life.

*

I was still holding onto the invitation when, finally, the lady came. Then I knew it was time to do something.

*

I decided to go and play with the scales. They had been moved out of our old kitchen, into the new shop. The people called the shop Mulberry Hall, like our house, but now it was called a china shop. The scales weren't used for weighing things any more. The new people had put them in a big glass box. Customers liked looking at them. They were in the room that used to be our big entrance hall and they were surrounded by cabinets full of platters and cups and saucers and teapots that the new people liked to buy. Mostly, when I played with them, people didn't notice me but there was a lady here today who was watching. I'd seen her here before. She was tall with long black hair. She might not have been a full lady but someone a bit like Tom who was sort of a man but not quite old enough yet.

"Hello," I said but I don't think she heard me. I would have to try harder. I watched her put her hand on the glass but she pulled it away again. I began to make the scales tip, just like I always had in the kitchen. I liked the way they went: clunk-clank, from side to side. Clunk-clank. Clunk-clank. Cook hadn't minded me playing with them and she'd nearly always given me biscuits when I'd gone into the kitchen.

The lady kept watching and I thought she could be my new friend. She would like Tom too because everyone liked Tom. I moved next to her and took her hand but she pulled it away, which made me sad. But then she looked right at me, which made me smile. I don't think she really saw me though, so I dropped the envelope in her bag and then an old lady came and they left.

I followed them all the way home and sat on their wall. When I sang the nursery rhyme, she heard me. Then later, I went into her house. I didn't think she was very happy about it; a bit like when Nanny hadn't liked me being in the nursery. She didn't run off like Nanny though. She watched me and she followed me. I think she will look for me and be my friend. She might be able to help me.

3

INVITATION

"**D**ID YOU PUT THIS IN MY BAG?"

"What?"

"This." I held out the cream card envelope, browned at the edges. "For a party at Mulberry Hall."

We were sitting on a bench in the PE changing rooms waiting for the bell for first period.

"What d'you mean?" Caroline said, chucking her trainers on the floor. "Jess, they don't have parties at Mulberry Hall. With all the china – they'd be mad. It'd be like a Greek wedding or something."

"No. From back then, I mean. Y'know? When that wee girl died."

"What? When?" she squeaked. Like I was a complete nutcase.

"Victorian times. The ghost. The six-year-old that died in Mulberry Hall. You know the story, how she fell from the second-floor landing. Everyone does." I was getting exasperated. Caroline's mum worked there for goodness' sake. She must know about the little ghost.

"Oh. Her. Well, *story's* the word. It's just legend, Jess. You can't believe all that stuff." She took the envelope from me and pulled out the invitation. Her brows arched as she read it. "Where did you get this?" she said.

"Well, that's the thing. I thought you must be playing some sort of spooky trick on me."

"Don't be daft, cheeky cow. I never put it there. Don't know anything about it." She handed it back to me.

"Well, somebody does," I said, flouncing off to the toilets.

*

I joined Loopy-Lou and Rachel in the canteen at break. Loopy was scrolling down her phone and Rachel had one hand in her bag, checking hers but trying to hide the fact from the teachers. I pounced on her, putting on a deep voice.

"I'll take the phone thank you, Rachel Bosworth. You can collect it at the end of the day."

"Aargh! You!" She picked up her bag and swung it at my stomach. I deflected the bag and sat down, laughing. I looked at Lou who was so absorbed in her phone she hadn't even noticed what had happened.

"Everything okay, Loopy?" I asked.

"The usual," she said, without looking up.

Rachel shoved her phone deep in her bag then we looked at each other with scrunched faces. Lou's home life was difficult. Her mum had cheated on her dad. It had ended in a horrible marital break-up. Lou had gone with her dad while her little brother and sister, Luca and Katie, had stayed with their mum. Yet Lou was always having to care for Luca and Katie after school, while her mum did whatever she fancied. It wound Lou up something rotten but while she couldn't stand her mum, she loved her brother and sister like mad and wouldn't leave them at the mercy of their petulant cow of a mother.

"Have you seen this?" I said to Rachel, pulling the Mulberry Hall invitation from my bag.

"What is it?"

I told her and she read it, in silence, her bottom lip curled out.

"That's weird," she said. "It looks really old. Where'd you get it?"

"Well, that's the thing. I found it in my bag this morning. Don't know who put it there." In my mind's eye, I saw the little girl standing in our hall last night. I shuddered. She'd looked so like Judith. I knew it wasn't Judith because Judith was born with only one hand. She'd had a prosthesis. We still had her spare one tucked away in a cupboard because Aunt Ruby couldn't bring herself to throw it out. Though ghostly, the little girl last night had both her hands. When I'd woken this morning, the whole episode had felt like a dream. I'd wondered if it had really happened. Yet, I couldn't stop thinking about her; that little pale face with a sweet smile; her thin, high-pitched voice asking me to go to Mulberry Hall and be her friend; her disappearance through my window. It had been *real*.

Nevertheless, it was inexplicable enough to put down to some sort of sleepwalking experience.

"Maybe it was Caroline?" Rachel asked.

"Caroline what? Who's taking my name in vain?" Caroline sidled onto the seat next to Loopy, facing me.

Rachel held up the invitation.

"Oh, not that again," said Caroline, snatching it from her and scrutinising it. "Jess accused me, this morning, of playing some trick on her."

"Isn't it like, a kind of retro event, celebrating the history of Mulberry Hall or something?" Rachel asked.

"Well, then it'd have a future date on it. I mean, look at this," Caroline turned it round to show us the date, which was already burned on my mind. *Saturday 23rd May 1863.* "Unless the management have special time-travelling skills, that's not possible. Jess, *you're* having *us* on. It's you playing the trick. Bet this is like that time your drama club asked you all to pretend you were someone else for a whole day."

"No, it isn't."

"Anyway, isn't Mulberry Hall where that little ghost is meant to hang out?" asked Rachel. "Cos, people are talking about that a lot these days. My next-door neighbour was in the coffee shop recently. She was telling my dad people have seen that little girl. Did you know she's meant to have fallen from the second floor when that place was her house? Can you imagine?"

"It's tragic," I said, shaking my head.

"For God's sake, listen to you two. It's just a story."

"It might not be," I said. And it made me think about Judith. She was real but sometimes she felt like a story, too. Because, although Aunt Ruby and I talked about her from time to time, and about my parents, they weren't an everyday part of our lives and they didn't feel so real any more. And that made me feel bad.

"Well, even if it is just a story," Rachel said, "it seems to be all over school now, too. Everyone's talking about it."

"You're not wrong," said Caroline. "It's like a virus. Spreading all over. But it's ridiculous. It's just a story. Nothing more. That's why no one knows what really happened. Because nothing did. It's all made up. My mum says she wishes people would shut up about it. It's been around for, like, forever, and nothing's changed."

Caroline was right about one thing. It *was* like a virus. Affecting everyone.

"I don't agree," I said, though. "Something *has* changed." I paused. "It makes me feel sad," I said, not meaning to speak aloud. My eyes filled up.

"Aw. Are you okay, Jess?" Rachel asked, frowning.

"I'm fine." I sniffed and tried to divert the attention back to the invitation. "This *is* weird though, isn't it?" I tapped one corner of the yellowed card.

"Not really," said Caroline, rooting in her pencil case. "Has anyone got a spare pen? Mine's run out."

I was annoyed she wouldn't take it seriously and scowled at her. She gave me a familiar look that said: *Don't think about arguing with me*, so I decided to change the subject.

*

By the time I'd had tea that night, I was yawning my head off. I was about to go to my room when Aunt Ruby stopped me.

"I forgot to tell you, Jessifer, darling," she said, "I'll be out all day tomorrow. I'm meeting my old friend, Lynn. Remember Lynn? We're shopping in the morning then doing lunch followed by the new exhibition at the Art Gallery."

"Good for you, Auntie," I replied. "Hope you enjoy it. Night, night."

I was in bed by ten o'clock.

4

UNDER THE LAMPLIGHT

IT WAS ONE TWENTY-FIVE WHEN I WOKE. MY curtains were flapping and snapping like flags in a storm. I sat up and heard a car shooming by on the dark street below; its headlights fanned across the ceiling and glinted off the mirror on my wall. I knew for certain my window had been shut when I went to bed last night. How could it have opened? As I stepped out of bed, the little girl's face swam into my mind. I had to see what or who was out there, in the street. And I knew, really, that it was her. Holding my breath and shivering, I stepped to the window.

"Hey, Joopy." The dark shape of my pet rushed to the front of his crate, his nose ghostly in the gloom; he began squeaking when I reached the curtains, which slapped my face. I pinned them back and peered out.

Then I found her. Spinning and dancing in the road in her little white dress. She saw me and stopped moving. She smiled and beckoned to me. When I kept staring, she let her hand drop and closed her eyes. A dark patch, like blood, appeared on her forehead. She seemed to be floating in the air like that and her dress looked longer, more like a nightie. When she opened her eyes, her appearance looked exactly as it had before, and she seemed, once again, to be standing in the road in her party dress. She began to curl her palm repeatedly. She wanted me to go to her.

I turned from the window and wondered what to do. I clenched and unclenched my fists, turning this way and that, feeling panic unfolding inside me. Why did I keep seeing this child, the same girl who had sat on the wall and on our kitchen counter? A little Victorian. She'd said: "Come to Mulberry Hall." She seemed so small and so young. Like someone who needed protection. Yet, she didn't seem to be unhappy or even vulnerable. That made me feel unsettled but intrigued. Why did she keep showing up? Why me? And what would I find out if I responded to her invitation?

I shut my window. The curtains had stopped dancing and I drew them closed then quickly swapped my pyjamas for leggings, a jumper and some socks.

"Come on, Joopy," I whispered, scooping him up into my bag. I grabbed a torch and my coat, inserted my key in the lock with slow precision, making the minutest of clicks, and tiptoed downstairs to the street.

*

I followed the little girl. The closer I got to Lock Woods, a stone's throw from the house, the fainter she became until, eventually, all I saw was a weakening splodge of light.

I entered the woods. I wasn't unhappy or troubled here. I loved these trees. They were a guard of honour, stretching ahead in my bouncing torchlight. Weirdly, they seemed like companions to me. I remembered woodland forays from nursery school; the babble of my playmates, clear, crisp and echoing. I used to play hide-and-seek here at dusk, too, with my cousins from Pateley Bridge. Uncle Jack's vibrato whistle, signalling time to leave, always disappointed us. And I smiled at the memory of my first kiss, here, three weeks ago. I bet I could find the actual birch I'd leaned against when Stefan told me he loved me. We'd met up a few times before that, but I'd rejected him a few days later. I hadn't been ready for a boyfriend, as much as I'd enjoyed a few dates with him.

Yet, it was different here at night. Then it struck me. What if Aunt Ruby finds my room empty? I grimaced. It'd be just my luck if this was the night she developed insomnia.

"Have to do this," I muttered and tramped on, looking for the blob of light, but it had petered out altogether. My steps were muffled by the damp, leafy carpet underfoot. The only sound was the remote murmur of cars on North Road, filtering through the sparse wood.

An owl's hoot set me on edge a little. Then a puff of wind teased my hair and the chill snaked around my neck, fingering its way to my collarbone.

"Should've worn my cosy wool scarf." I stopped to button my coat right up to my chin, but my ears pricked up as I heard a voice, singing.

"Say the bells of St Clement's..." A child's voice, high-pitched. The nursery rhyme 'Oranges and Lemons'. Aunt Ruby used to sing it to us, me and Judith, when we were small, jiggling us on her knee in turns, and Judith protesting that she was too big but laughing anyway. I remembered my aunt telling us they used to play a game with the same title in her school playground. And it always ended with someone being trapped when it came to the final line: "... here comes a chopper to chop off your head.".

The owl hooted again and the voice was cut short. Then a draught blew against my face. The dim light from my torch confirmed the bird's silent flight across my path, a pale spectre. I wasn't alone.

My skin tingled. Was she still here? I wasn't sure. A twig snapped, sending a judder of fear through me.

Not going to let my woods scare me, I thought, then jerked as something brushed my side. My heart pounded.

Warmth swept my cheek.

"Oh! Joopy, it's you!" Relief flooded me.

He'd abandoned the safe comfort of my bag and now sat on my shoulder, his warm body quivering.

"The owl must've startled you too." I stroked his neck.

"... You owe me five farthings..." the song continued. Was it her, playing with me?

I scooped Joopy up, eased him into my bag and felt him settle compliantly into a sleepy coil. I realised that anything might happen next, but something drove me on, out of the woods and into town.

*

I glanced both ways on Church Road, the street that separated our suburb from the city proper. It was as dead as I'd expected. I peered at my watch under the glow of the street lamps. One fifty. The pubs and takeaways would be long shut and all the shops would be dark and desolate.

As I drew near the oldest part of the city, it was like stepping back in time. I saw the town I had always taken for granted in a new way. There was this invisible line of change beyond which the ancient buildings jostled together like a huddle of schoolchildren trying to protect one of their own from the new modern constructions of the wider city outside.

Passing the Minster, solid and silent, its Gothic beauty out of reach in the darkness, I went down the narrow alley of wonky old houses and entered Stonegate. A weird feeling, like a sad thrill, came over me. What was wrong with me? Should I go back?

"Don't be ridiculous," I whispered to myself. My logical brain was trying to reassure me that the story of the little ghost was nothing but folklore, but I'd seen and heard things that left no doubt in my mind: that little girl was real.

I looked towards the half-timbered Tudor building which housed the china shop. As I approached, I imagined it lit from within as if it were daytime. I stared between the stands of crockery and saw a woman standing at a counter using a cash register. There, beside her, stood a small girl in indistinct dress, her hand on the woman's arm. I watched the woman glance down at the girl, then the image, formed from a combination of my imagination and what I'd seen recently, faded. I'd heard the stories. Everyone in York had. How, in the shops of Stonegate, a ghost-child was said to tug at shop assistants' clothing or to sit on shop counters while staff worked the tills. I stood right up against one of the large windows. A face stared back at me making me gasp but I soon saw the familiarity of my own pale skin and strands of my straight black hair escaping my clip. My dark eyes were wide and my expression looked haunted. I shuddered and turned to face the street. No one about.

Jupiter was restless again. His pink nose poked out of the bag.

"Hey, Joopy," I whispered. He began squeaking and fidgeting. He must have sensed my unease. I looked around. Not a soul to be seen. I walked past all the windows of Mulberry Hall and wondered where the child had gone. Had she really wanted me to come here? I gazed into the inky depths of the shop. I knew I'd get a fright if she appeared in front of me suddenly, but nothing happened and nothing changed.

Joopy's squeaking became more frantic. This wasn't fair. Something was upsetting him. Perhaps it was just the lingering smell of the busker's dog who sat here with his master every day. Even so, this was plain weird. I began to feel the rising fizz of uncertainty in my tummy. Time to go home.

I turned away from the shop. I'd only gone a few steps when I heard a voice calling.

"Miss?"

I spun round, expecting to see a police officer. Perhaps he'd cut through Mulberry Lane. My eyes widened.

A boy, about fourteen, like me, was waving. Was this the lad I'd seen with the girl last night? He wore old-fashioned clothing, with a white-spotted neckerchief and clumpy boots. He seemed to think he knew me. Light from the street lamp caught his eyes, which sparkled. His face was wide and cheerful. Then, I noticed the petal-like stain seeping through his jacket. Was it blood? It looked more black than red, but it was spreading. He looked down, then looked back at me and smiled.

I grimaced.

"You need help," I called. "You're bleeding!"

"Ah, just an argument with a scythe on t' farm," he said, as if he was talking about a scratch on his hand.

I glanced down because Jupiter's agitation was making my bag bounce. When I looked back at the boy, he'd vanished. I checked all around the dark street, but he was nowhere to be seen.

Suddenly, I felt exhausted. My feet felt as if they contained magnets, pulled by an underground force; my legs felt as if they'd been filled with concrete. With enormous effort, I shuffled away from Stonegate, only picking up speed as I crossed Church Road. By the time I reached Lock Woods, I couldn't help questioning what I'd seen and heard. Did that really just happen? Did I just speak to a ghost boy? Am I going crazy? I'd always had a vivid imagination; even Mrs Fortiver, my English teacher, had remarked on it. But I knew it. This was no imagination. This was real. Even so, by the time I was home, I could barely get my pyjamas on before I fell into bed and a deep, deep sleep.

5

Heavens Above!

"Ow!" I groaned.

"I said, are you okay, Jess?" Caroline was emphatic. I was sure her finger had left an impression on my ribs.

"Keep your hair on," I glared at her. "You didn't need to poke me."

"I'd already asked you twice."

"Woohoo, yeah!" Loopy Lou bounced off my right shoulder, knocking my bag to the floor before sailing past us, punching the air.

"Augh!" I gasped, stumbling forward. "What did you do that for?" I stopped to pick my bag up.

"Because, I, Louise Gordillo, brand new captain of the junior girls' footie team, am celebrating, that's why!"

"Great," I said, without enthusiasm.

"Thanks," Loopy said. "Love you too."

"That's brilliant, Lou," said Caroline, "I told you you'd get it."

"Miss Towers said I was her favourite all along! I hope I can live up to her expectations. What's up with you, grumpy chops?" Louise scowled and hooked her gaze up to look at my downcast eyes.

"Nothing, just a bit tired. And, sorry, but you gave me a fright. I'm pleased for you. I know how much you wanted it." I saw a look pass between my friends as we went upstairs to the library. It was our last period before lunch and we were supposed to be doing some research for a biology project I had no interest in. Worse, I was both knackered and starving. After my weird night last night, I'd struggled to get out of bed this morning, so breakfast hadn't been my priority.

In the library, I slumped at a table and let my bag fall to the floor, then I put my head on my arms until Miss Pugh came along and spoiled my fun.

"Someone's letting social media rule their night times." She gave my arm a rough nudge. I groaned and thought how wrong she was.

"So, you all know what you're looking for. You can work in your groups, or individually if you want; just make sure you communicate, so we don't find out on the day of the presentations that you've all covered the same section." She clapped her hands and continued: "Get on with it then; I want to see books flying off the shelves. We're equipped with an excellent science section in our library. Make use of it." Her speech was followed by a series of groans from around the room.

"Which bit are you doing, Jess?" said Caroline.

"Just tell me what to do and I'll do it," I said, yawning.

"Okay, then, you can do variation. I'll do DNA and Loopy, will you do biodiversity?"

"I'll try," said Lou, sarcastically.

"You can do it. You're good at biology."

"Am so not," said Lou.

Caroline huffed. She was such a bossy organiser at times, but it suited me now.

I waited for the rush to settle and went and picked out some books. There was a small table at the far end of the library, near the connecting door into the Home Economics block, where I could sit and work in peace, away from everyone else.

I'd begun to look through the first book when I heard whispering, in a sing-song voice. It was like the sound I'd heard in the woods last night:

"… said the bells of St Martin's…" Was it that nursery rhyme again? But it stopped. I looked around and, of course, the library looked exactly as you'd expect it to. Some people were working but most were chatting, sniggering, mucking about with stationery and generally being annoying until Miss Pugh shushed them and threatened detention.

I carried on working, trying to ignore my stomach. I scribbled and scribbled. Caroline would be happy.

It was nearly time for the bell and I was pleased with how much I'd got done. No one had bothered me back here.

Then the whispering started again and grew more insistent. It was coming from the corner, by the door. I stood up. I looked straight ahead. Nothing. I turned around to face the rest of the library; some people were still working but most were returning books to the shelves, waiting for the bell. I turned back.

"Say the bells of St Martin's…" It was getting faster and faster. "When will you pay me…" I put my hands on the table and looked up: there was nothing there. Then I looked down and nearly knocked my chair over as I fell back into it. The whispering had stopped. She looked awful. She was lying between a bookshelf and the door, spreadeagled. Her head was crusted with dark, dried blood and she was very still, unseeing. Her face was pale and her long white nightie, with a gathered neckline, looked how I imagined a shroud would.

My heart was thumping and I couldn't move. And then the lunch bell rang.

The vision snapped away, like a screen powering off. My breath snagged in my throat and I kept staring at the floor, where she'd been.

"Are you okay, Jess?"

The voice belonged to Lorraine, a girl in our class. She was staring at me, her face a mixture of surprise and delight.

"I've just seen a ghost," I blurted, then immediately realised my mistake. Lorraine's lip curled scornfully, before she twisted away.

"Jo! Emma! Guess what?"

I looked around. Checked the floor again. I saw bare carpet, nothing more. I was trembling. I was now the only person at this end of the library. Everyone else was either packing up or edging towards the door at the other end of the room.

Then Caroline was beside me, one hand on my arm.

"Jess," she said. "Jess? What's wrong?"

I felt stunned and couldn't seem to get myself together until I heard Lorraine, the idiot, passing on what she no doubt considered unexpected, yet delicious, news:

"Jess just saw a ghost." Then louder: "Everyone... Jess just saw a ghost." A clamour began to build and people who'd been about to leave the library began bundling back inside, searching me out.

"Leave the books," Caroline said, "come on. Grab your stuff. Let's get out of here."

I came to my senses, shoved my notes away and shrugged my bag onto my shoulder. The noise was growing and I kept hearing the repeating phrase:

"Jessifer's seen a ghost, Jessifer's seen a ghost..." People were starting to shriek and I could hear one of the lower classes on the landing, through the open door at the other end of the library. High-pitched voices getting wound up.

"Jess?" said Loopy who had appeared just as Caroline and I made for the door. "You okay? What are they on about?"

"Nothing," said Caroline. "Come on, Lou; we're going this way."

"No, I have to go back and see Miss Towers," said Loopy, "so I'm going down the other stairs. See you in the canteen."

Of course, everyone else had gone down the other stairs, too, because that's where all the commotion was, so, as I shut the door behind us, I shut out the noise with it.

"Jess, did I hear right?" said Caroline as we descended the stairs to the canteen. "Lorraine said…"

"I know… I heard her," I said, tonelessly. "No… yes… it was weird. There was…"

We'd reached the ground floor and Rachel came bounding up to us.

"Here, you two… watch my bag will you… I'm starving… I'm going for chips." She chucked her bag onto the first table in the canteen and I pulled it onto the bench beside me as I slumped down.

I crossed my arms on the table and laid my head on them. Hungry as I was, I now felt sick and needed a minute before I went to get food. The awful scene flashed into my mind. The same little girl I'd seen in the kitchen and in the street. But not the same. Rather, dead. Dead and shocking. Was that how Judith looked when she died? Or worse? But I had to quash the thought; it was too awful.

"So, what happened, Jess? Up there?" Caroline asked.

I didn't want to talk about it, so I kept quiet, my head still resting on my arms.

"Jess? Are you okay? Do you think you're ill or something?"

"No, I'm all right." I turned my face towards her. "Think I'm just tired. Didn't sleep well last night." My brain was moving into gear again. Now, I needed to manage this conversation and somehow steer Caroline away from the subject of the ghost. Otherwise, who knew where it would lead? It was all too confusing.

"So, why did Lorraine say that? About a ghost or something?"

"Cos she's an idiot?" I said.

"Fair point. Well, if you're all right, can we discuss the project? Did you get much on variation? I got tons on DNA. We'll need to put it all together."

Knowing Caroline, it was only a matter of time before she demanded I hand over my work. She'd want our group to get the best mark out of the whole class and the only way that was ever going to happen was by her taking over. So, I leaned down to my bag with a groan and pulled out the notes I'd made.

"Here," I said. Caroline snatched them like she was four years old and they were her favourite teddy that some other kid had had the nerve to play with. With my head back on my arms, I watched her through one eye. She spent the next few minutes in silence, devouring the top page, then turning it over, soaking up my scrawl.

"This is perfect, Jess. Nice job." I had to smile. Caroline was so brainy, and she just loved schoolwork. Not much made her happier than studying and getting good marks. She was weird. She sighed with contentment, slid my notes into her bag, then stood up.

"Will you be all right then, if I go and get my lunch too? Oh, hang on a minute, there's Loopy." I lifted my head and saw Loopy skirting round a group of fifth years, half sprinting, half skipping, towards us.

"It's all gone crazy," Lou called. "The first years are..." but she was cut off by a high-pitched squeal. It came from around the corner, where the corridor led to the gym, and was instantly followed by a roar of many voices and thundering feet. It sounded like a stampede and was quickly met by Mr Bendrigg's booming tones and Mrs Mills' screeches.

I shifted in my seat and watched a group of first years come bundling across the open area towards us. They were a jostling sea of bug eyes, hooded frowns and trembling lips. Despite the horror I'd just seen, their fear was slightly catching.

I looked at Lou, who said:

"Our class was getting them all wound up upstairs, trying to spook them, saying there's a ghost in the library. Jess, I take it you didn't really see a ghost?" she spluttered.

"What?" I muttered, frowning.

"Ridiculous," Lou said. "But they're just young kids… I suppose they might believe something like that. I know what Luca and Katie are like."

The first years began talking all at once. They were animated and excitable and lots of them looked terrified.

"Someone saw a ghost in the library just now, that wee Victorian girl everyone's on about, she was just hanging there in mid-air," spouted a sturdy boy, his neck like a stalk bearing his gabbing head, his arms out behind him, penguin style, for balance. He rolled out his speech rapidly like one multisyllabic word.

A tiny, skinny girl took over where he left off:

"It was in the toilets just now and it touched Michaela's hand. She ran out screaming and now she's crying in the cloakroom!"

I thought how easily tittle-tattle started flying about and it made me hot and irritable. I was beginning to think of that little girl as my ghost, even though I didn't understand what was happening to me, or why, and I didn't want stupid untruths spread about her.

A hoard of kids surged into the hall, joining the crowd out of curiosity, shepherded by Bendrigg and Mills. Mills was wearing her usual high-fashion, too-short, stretchy skirt.

"Heavens above!" screeched Mrs Mills.

She planted her hands on her hips.

"Half our first years… hysterical."

From under hooded brows, her eyes scorched the canteen.

"Influenced by the third years, evidently."

Her gaze rested on our table.

"Who ought to know better."

She raised her eyes to the ceiling.

"I want every third year in this school to go to the assembly hall… right now."

I couldn't believe it. She actually glared at me, stalked over, took my arm and pulled me off my seat.

"You three, Jessifer Jordan, Caroline, Louise, you can lead on. If you see any third years on the way, tell them to drop whatever they're doing and follow you."

"Rachel's just gone to get some food, Miss," said Caroline.

"Well she needn't bother." Mills then screeched like a brawling feline across the lunch hall.

"Rachel Bosworth, get yourself over here now!"

Rachel turned maroon as everybody in the hall looked at her. She put down her plate of chips and raised her palms upwards, questioning us with her eyes.

I grimaced and sluggishly waved her over.

*

The last fifteen minutes had been a waste of time and my body was so tired and heavy it wanted to slump like a de-stuffed scarecrow. Not only that, half our year had escaped to the local shops for lunch, so as usual, it was just the people who were in the wrong place at the wrong time that had to put up with Mills' wrath.

Lou's face was beetroot with indignation and she kept huffing and muttering curses against Mills. She wanted to eat and get out on the pitch. Of the four of us, she felt injustice the most. Unfortunately, it frequently led to her speaking her mind at times when silence was clearly the better option. I hoped she would calm down before she brought trouble on herself.

Mrs Mills wouldn't let us go until someone owned up to "inciting hysteria over some ridiculous story of a ghost." I couldn't stand it any longer. Lou's explosive temper was a time bomb and I needed to sit down and eat. Robotically, I raised my left arm and found myself admitting to something I hadn't done.

"Okay, Mrs Mills," I said, "it was me."

"What?" Caroline shrieked, beside me.

"Jess! You idiot," Lou hissed.

*

As the rest of the kids disbanded, I trudged along behind Mrs Mills to her office, too tired to care what people thought. On their way back to the canteen ahead of us, my friends stopped and watched me trailing behind the deputy. Caroline pursed her lips; Rachel shook her head and Lou's face was scrunched, clearly indignant at Mrs Mills' staccato steps and look of disgust. I couldn't see it through the back of her head but I knew it was pasted thickly across her hammily garnished face. I knew they were all on my side even though I'd been daft to say it was me.

"Shut the door," Mrs Mills said.

I obeyed and turned back to face her.

"I'm disappointed in you, Jessifer Jordan," she said in calmer tones. "Now, who are you protecting? I saw you in the Refectory..." (Why did she always call it that? No one else did. To every other normal person living in this century, it was the canteen) "... and you had your head on the table, so unless you can be in two places at once..."

"It doesn't even matter," I mumbled.

"Don't you dare mutter under your breath at me, Jessifer." Her tone was ugly. "Speak up and tell me what's going on."

"Oh," I sighed, stalling for time while my stagnant brain came up with something. "Well... we're doing a ghost story at my drama club. I wanted to see how people would react if I started a rumour of a ghost, that's all. I thought they'd be a bit jumpy and then just forget about it. I didn't think they'd go and spread it among the first years." I shrugged.

I was surprised how easily the lie came but I just wanted out of there. I needed to eat but even more, to think. Besides, she'd hardly believe me if I told her what had happened in the library. Moreover, I needed to protect that little girl from the likes of Mills. There had to be a reason why I kept seeing her and if I explained the whole caboodle – the moving weighing scales, the tiny fingers, the child in our kitchen at night and so on – our bolshie deputy would have a priest in here pronto, armed with robes, candles and a Bible. Well, either that, or referral to the school psychologist.

"Well, I can't say it surprises me, with your dramatic abilities but, heavens above, girl. First years are impressionable and vulnerable. They look up to you third years. You know how easily a bit of gossip spreads. In addition, there could have been a terrible accident on the stairs. We can't have that sort of carry-on. We can't, do you hear?"

"It's not as if it's a new idea, Miss. Everyone's been talking about that little ghost." It was true. Which was why I hadn't minded saying it. Everywhere you turned in school these days, people were talking about Mulberry Hall being haunted. As if to make up for there being nothing else exciting happening. I was stumped for anything else to say. I shivered and my eyes began to fill up. The same helpless, weepy feeling I'd had last night.

The girl's sweet face and the image of the bleeding boy floated into my head, only to be replaced with the scene in the library: a tiny, lifeless body, right there on the floor. I felt myself swaying.

"Are you all right, child?" came Mrs Mills' distant voice. Her hand was on my head. One long, varnished nail scraped my left ear. "You're frozen."

*

"What happened there?" I muttered to myself a bit later. I remembered Mills escorting me to the sick room where I'd flopped onto the medical bench, but I'd lost the intervening time. Now, there was a tap on the door and in walked Aunt Ruby.

"Hello, darling Jess," she said, stepping towards me. "I've a taxi waiting outside. Let's get you home. You must be coming down with something, as I thought."

*

At home, I climbed into bed and slept soundly. I woke and grabbed my alarm clock. Four thirty. Aunt Ruby's head poked round the door.

"How do you feel, angel?" she asked. Her face was etched with worry as she pulled on her crumpled velvet hat.

"I'm okay thanks, Auntie. Oh, and I'm sorry if you had to cut your day short. Y' know, with Lynn?"

"Don't be silly. We saw the exhibition and, anyway, Lynn wanted to miss the evening rush at the station. I'm going to pop out for some Lucozade, darling. Will you be all right?"

"M-hm." I returned her smile. It always amused me that Lucozade was her cure-all for illness. I hated its weird, metallic taste but usually sipped a bit from my glass to please her and drained the rest down the sink. Inevitably, Aunt Ruby would guzzle the rest of the bottle. I reckoned she had a bit of a habit with it. She used any old excuse to buy it but never seemed to notice she was the only one drinking it.

I heard the front door click shut and eased out of bed. Man, I was hungry. I lifted my phone and clocked the message box with a '3' beside it. I did my blind walk to the kitchen, head down, gaze fixed to the screen, fingers working.

Rachel: *You ok? Poor Jess Sorry you ill x*

Caroline: *Hope you ok Just to let you know Mills is mad Thinking of you Asked mum re party Mulberry Hall... no such thing Talk later x*

Eng dept: *Critical Essay due Thurs. Counts towards final marks for year.*

I'd need to fine-tune my essay tonight. I hoped Mrs Fortiver would like it. English was my best subject along with drama and art and I knew Mrs F had high expectations. Plus, I liked her. She was my favourite teacher in the whole school.

I stepped into the kitchen and looked around. It was three nights ago that I'd seen the little girl here. The memory was surreal. The kitchen looked just as it always did. Aunt Ruby kept it clean and tidy. I was messy which, sometimes, she got on to me for but mostly she dealt with. Right now, the blind was down to shut out the dark. The surfaces were all sparkling clean; the draining board was empty; everything was in its place. I crossed to the counter where the child had sat, dangling her legs, and ran my hands over the surface. I shook my head then turned, grabbed a mug from the cupboard and went to fill the kettle. As I skimmed the fridge for something disgustingly comforting to eat, my phone pinged. This time it was Lou:

You feeling ok Jessy? Mills is pain in a### Just finished first game as captain Awesome 5-2 to us You be at school tomorrow? Might call but at mum's tonight You know what like x

Brilliant Loopy! I bet she's feeling fab after getting her first win as captain.

A short while later, curled on the couch, munching mouthfuls of molten cheese on toast, I messaged my friends back.

Time, sleep and food had slightly dimmed the horrible image of the child's body in the library but I knew I'd never forget it. Rather, I felt there was now a purpose in what was happening to me. I didn't know what was coming or how I'd handle it. But I did know that child brought back powerful memories of my sister, Judith; I'd barely stopped thinking about her these last few days and now, my imagination kept drifting back to the idea of Judith's mangled body when she died. That was something I'd never considered before. So, yes, that child had grabbed my attention. She was trying to tell me something and, though I tried to suppress the feeling, I was scared. I mean, really scared.

6

BLEEDING BOY

APA TELLS MAMA TO LET NANNY RAISE ME but I love being with Mama. Mama smells good and her hands are always warm like Clementine's tummy. Papa's are cold and Nanny's are in between. I was playing with a doll Papa had brought me from London. I smoothed down her pretty silk dress and wondered why her felt boots wouldn't come off.

"Why does Papa say Mama mustn't read to me?" I asked Nanny.

"Your papa doesn't mind, Adeline," Nanny said then smiled. "It's more that Papa pays me to care for you." She leaned down and whispered, "I think he likes to get his money's worth."

I pushed the doll away. I knew it was polite to pretend I liked it, but it wasn't interesting. I ran to Nanny who had moved to the other end of the nursery, tidying as she went.

"Mama said she would read her new book to me."

"Oh? What's it called?"

"*The Water Babies*. It's by Charles Kingsish. Mama says he's clever and he teaches the Prince of Wales."

Nanny laughed.

"You mean Charles Kingsley. He has a good reputation, I think."

I heard loud shouts through the open nursery door, so I clapped my hands to my ears.

"Goodness, what can be going on?" came Nanny's muffled exclamation. Her skirts swept the floorboards as she hurried out to the landing.

Why can't we have the nursery at the front? I thought, lowering my hands. The windows faced the back courtyard where nothing ever happened. I often heard clip-clopping echoing in Mulberry Lane but I could only ever see the horses' pointy ears sticking up above the wall. If the nursery was at the front, I could watch the carriages and carts rattle by on the big road, Stonegate. I hurried after Nanny now and grasped the shiny wooden banister. Clementine leaped up the stairs with a meow and made a dash for the open nursery door. I wondered what she was hiding from and stood on my tippy-toes to stare down into the hall. I felt as if my eyes grew as big as apples.

There was a man lying on the floor all covered in poppy-red blood and the staff were shouting for Papa. He came rushing into the hall from his medical room. The man didn't look old like Papa but more like a boy and he was wriggling and groaning.

*

Papa was giving instructions, but I couldn't hear them. It was all over quickly. Mr Partridge, the butler, and the servants lifted the bleeding boy and carried him to the medical room with Papa following. The boy looked a bit broken, but Papa would be able to fix him. Nanny grabbed my hand and pulled me back to the nursery.

"Poor lad. I hope he's all right," she said.

"Will Father take him to the hospital, Nanny?"

"I expect so, Adeline. That will just leave us at home. Apart from Cook."

"And Clementine," I said.

"Yes. Clementine too. The maids are all off duty by now. Your father will need the men to transport the patient."

I was used to this kind of thing. People often brought sick people here for Papa to help. Papa said most of them ended up going home still poorly because it was a lot, a lot of money at the hospital and they didn't have a job to pay for it.

There was so much excitement at this house and I was mostly kept away from it. I felt bored and fed up. I wanted Mama to start reading *The Water Babies* to me. I could snuggle up in her lap and listen to her rock-a-bye-baby voice.

"When will Mama be home?" I asked.

"After bedtime, Adeline. Run down to the kitchen now and ask Cook for your milk and biscuits."

Mama sometimes went to places to tell people about things like Sunday School and especially things about helping poor people. She was at the big museum tonight. I would have to wait and see her tomorrow.

If I ran downstairs quickly, I could have a peek at the hurt boy. I pushed through the nursery door, skipped towards the staircase and jumped my boots together. Then I rushed down, pitapat, pitapat, nearly all the way.

But when I got near the bottom, Papa called to me, waving.

"Good night, Adeline. And please *walk* down the stairs. You are a little lady, not a ruffian."

"Good night, Father," I replied. I watched him march towards the open front door. He was following Mr Partridge and another man, who were carrying the injured boy on a stretcher. A red and white spotty cloth hung down, trapped under the boy's arm. I watched them all leave so that I could run down the last few steps. When the door shut, I took a huge, big, enormous breath. Then I launched myself onto the hall floor just because Papa wasn't there. I made a wonderful loud bang.

*

A short while later, I was sitting at Cook's big kitchen table, clunk-clanking the big brass weighing scales. Steam from my hot milk was drifting onto my face, wetting it. I was confused. Nanny was wrong. Not all the maids had gone home. One, Miss Betsy, had been talking to Cook. I had hung outside the kitchen door and listened. Her words hadn't made sense, but they made my tummy wriggle about as if it was full of caterpillars.

"Never 'eard 'im speak to Mistress like that before," Betsy had said.

"Oh, Betsy, yer so young yet. 'E's like most men. Thinks she's 'is property. 'E seems to want to control 'er more these days. Never used to but 'e's allus been the serious type. Think e's worried she might get 'er 'ead turned by some nice young man while she's out doin' 'er talks an' that."

"Well, the mistress shu'n't put up wi' it," Betsy said, moodily.

I knew they were talking about Mama. When I walked into the kitchen, Betsy's face was like a jug being filled up with tomato juice. It went red from the bottom to the top. I knew from the way she looked at Cook she was talking out of turn.

"Right, let's be 'aving ye, Betsy. Time ye went 'ome," said Cook and Betsy scuttled past me to the back door.

In bed, I twisted and rolled like an itchy cat, but I pretended to be asleep when Mama came in to kiss my head. I heard her bedroom door shut and wondered if Papa was still at the hospital.

7

Family, Friends and Facts

I woke on Wednesday morning and felt something stuck to my face. It was a photograph of Judith I'd taken out of my drawer before going to bed. I must have fallen asleep still looking at it. I smoothed my fingers over her cute little face and smiled, but there was such an ache in me. I'd been so young when my parents died, with Judith, but I'd never fully learned to accept the loss. Perhaps if I hadn't been able to remember them at all, it would have been easier, but I'd spent my school years always being reminded of what I didn't have, and I'd go home and talk to Aunt Ruby and we'd get the photo albums out. Every Mother's Day, every Father's Day, when all the other kids were making cards for their parents, I'd made cards for Aunt Ruby.

"You've done it wrong; you're supposed to write *Mum* on it," kids would say to me, or, on sports day: "You can't do this race cos it's only for dads and kids." Then when my classmates' brothers and sisters who'd been in Judith's class were moving up to the high school, I remember thinking she should've been going too.

I shook myself out of my reverie before I went and got my breakfast, then I texted Caroline before I left the flat:

Meet me corner as usual.

"Bye, Aunt Ruby," I called as I pulled on my boots. I heard her shuffle towards her bedroom door.

She appeared, looking bedraggled as she always did in the mornings.

"Are you sure you're fit, angel?" she asked.

"I'm fine." It was true. I'd slept well and wanted to see my friends. I gently teased out one of my aunt's loose amber curls and hooked it over her ear. "Looking grand, Auntie," I said, pleased with my sarcasm. Even so, I loved the way she could transform into a picture of elegance within minutes. "What are you doing today?"

"Well, you'll think it a bit indulgent but I'm going to put on my best things and I'm going to meet Ali Butler. Two days of lunching in a row but it's the only day Ali could make it for a while."

"Oh. You deserve it, Aunt Ruby. You don't spoil yourself often enough. Have fun then. Are you going to Mulberry Hall?"

"Yes. Ali's off today. We've been saying for a while we'd go and try their new lunch menu."

"Isn't that what they call a busman's holiday?" I asked.

"I suppose it is, but they do things so nicely, I don't think she's complaining," Aunt Ruby said, then laughed.

"Say hi to her from me then. And tell her that her daughter's still the biggest brainbox among us all! But she can't tell Caroline I said that!"

"I think Caroline Butler's too nice to think you could possibly mean it, darling."

"Oh, and Auntie, would you mind changing Jupiter's water for me? I didn't get time."

I dashed for the door, pulling my coat round me and shrugging my bag higher onto my shoulder. I ran down the steps to the front door of our building, thinking about Caroline and her mum, Ali.

I got on well with them both and I was proud of my friendship with Caroline. We'd known each other since we were at nursery school together when we were three. It's where I'd been when my family died, killed in a gas explosion that also destroyed our house. Judith had been off school that day with a fever. If I'd had the same bug, I'd have been killed too. Anyway, Caroline and her family lived in a bungalow in the estate behind Aunt Ruby's street. We'd lived just down the road from her. After the explosion, Aunt Ruby dealt with everything and took me on as her own child. Now, I could barely remember living in a modern house. Aunt Ruby's eclectic flat was slightly nearer school than Caroline's, so we'd been meeting on the corner of my road, Hawthorn Road, and the main road into her estate, Gable Road, since we were nine. Lou usually met us a bit further along but only when she was at her dad's. Rachel lived on the other side of school, so she met up with us there.

"It's just us today," Caroline said as I joined her on the corner.

"I know. Loopy texted. She said she'd try and call me from her mum's last night but it's no surprise she didn't manage."

"Her mum's such a cow. She probably left Lou in charge of the little kids again last night while she was out bagging her next bloke."

"It's a wonder Lou agrees to go over there, but I think she feels sorry for Luca and Katie. If it wasn't for them, she'd probably tell her mum to get lost," I said.

"Anyway, are you okay? What was the matter yesterday?"

"Don't know. Must've been Mills. She can have that effect on people. I went dizzy and the next thing I knew, Aunt Ruby was in the sick room."

"Why did you say it was you? You know, getting the first years wound up 'n' all? And, what really happened in the library? You were being weird."

"Well, no one else was owning up to it and I wanted to eat. No big deal. The truth is, I didn't feel well in the library; I wasn't sure why, but it seems like it was a virus after all. Auntie thought I was coming down with something at the weekend so I suppose she was right. Anyway, it doesn't matter, does it? I'm fine now."

"Unless Mills has got some juicy punishment waiting for you," said Caroline, nudging my arm.

"Mm. Never thought of that. I can just imagine it: *'Heavens above, Jessifer Jordan! You must hit your knuckles one hundred times with this ruler!'* I mocked. "Do you think she'll make me do detention or something? I can't do tomorrow! Thursdays are sacred... that's my drama night."

"Like I don't know already!"

I chewed the inside of my cheek. Caroline would just laugh if I said anything more about the ghost. I'd thought she was about to press me on the subject and I'd already decided yesterday that I'd make something up if she did. I mean, who's going to believe you if you tell them you've seen a ghost? They'd have to see it themselves to believe it, wouldn't they?

We walked in silence. I began to think about the invitation again. How did it end up in my bag? Could I have somehow knocked it off the counter when I was in the café with Aunt Ruby on Saturday? But I couldn't remember seeing anything like that on the counter. The alternative was just too freaky: that the little girl had slipped it in my bag. The thing was, the way things were going, I couldn't rule out anything. My life had started to become distinctly abnormal. Decidedly spooky. Discernibly, downright unsettling.

Loopy interrupted my thoughts.

She ran up behind us both, squeezed between us and with one hand on each of our shoulders, launched herself forward.

Caroline and I turned to each other shaking our heads and grinning. Loopy was always so full of energy. A moment later, as we turned onto the road school was on, we saw Rachel arriving. Her handsome dad rolled up in his little sporty motor. Before Rachel got out of the car, we watched him lean over her seat and give her a peck on the cheek.

"Aw!" the rest of us all went, then burst into raucous laughter.

"Your dad's lovely," I said, when we calmed down. I wondered how it must feel; having a proper, supportive mum and dad like she and Caroline had. Even though my life was privileged, and Aunt Ruby was the bee's knees, that hole would never be filled. It was weird, missing your parents when you'd been too young to really properly know them. I mean, things like their mannerisms and tone of voice. Oh, Aunt Ruby told me what my mum's favourite colour was (lilac) and that she'd always dreamed of going to America but never had; she'd told me that my dad and Uncle Jack were going to set up in business together one day and that they wanted to learn to sail and take a yacht around the British Isles. But what would Mum's hugs feel like? And would my dad tease me about my (often) weird choice in clothes? And would they have let me have a pet rat? I wondered what Judith would sound like now. Would her voice be like mine? Would she be kind, like Loopy is kind to her little brother and sister, or would she resent having a younger sister who got in the way? Or, what would it have been like if I'd been the eldest and she was still a little six-year-old? I'd love to have had a little brother or sister.

I went to my locker and shoved my coat in. Then Rachel came and grabbed me.

"Come on, dreamy. What are you thinking about?"

"Nothing much," I said. "Just stuff."

*

Throughout the day, I waited to get a summons from Mrs Mills.

At break, Caroline caught up with me in the corridor.

"You look okay," she said, linking her arm through mine. "No detention then?"

"Well, she hasn't sent for me, so hopefully not. If she wants me, she knows where to find me!"

As I turned to grin at her, some second years pushed past us and turned to look at me then turned back, giggling conspiratorially. One of them looked over her shoulder at me and then they all began whispering and giggling louder: "It's her, it's her."

"You're a celebrity round here now," Caroline said, pulling me towards her with her linked arm. "You and your stories of ghosts lurking in libraries."

"Huh. I could do without it, trust me," I said. "Come on, quick. There's Rachel. Let's get a seat before the canteen totally fills up." I jumped in beside Rachel, and Caroline sidled onto the bench opposite. She'd barely sat down when a bag landed on the table between us, with a thump.

"Aaah!" Rachel yelled.

I flinched, more from Rachel's squeal, and then I heard Loopy Lou's cackle.

"Got you!" she proclaimed, sidling up to Caroline, practically wetting herself. "Should'a seen you lot jump! Here, give us my bag, will ya? Aw… remember when we were on that residential in first year?"

"Oh, yeah, yeah," I said, excited by what she was going to say. "There was that mouthy girl from that school in Leeds…"

"Her and her gang. What a racket they made," said Caroline.

"I know. Their dorm was *right* under ours," said Rachel.

"Yeah, and us lot couldn't sleep for the first two nights cos they were so loud," said Loopy. "So we got our own back. It was just brilliant."

"They *actually* thought someone was trying to break into their room in the middle of the night. Ha, ha-ha," said Rachel.

At once we all began to laugh at the memory and our hands were covering our mouths at the thought of what we'd done.

"And the best thing was, the teachers never found out what upset them," I said, trying to compose myself.

"No. Ha-ha-ha." Lou wiped her eyes, she was laughing so much she was crying by now. "You and Rachel crept down and spied on them, while me and Caroline hung out the window dangling my key on a string. And we swung it against their window."

I noticed that other people in the canteen were looking over to see what we were laughing about. Now, *we* were the loud ones because the memory was so ridiculously funny.

"D'you remember, we kept stopping for a while, and then starting up again?" said Caroline. "And every time, we were laughing so much we had to stuff pillows in our faces in case they heard us."

"What was our code, though?" said Rachel. Remember? Every time we saw them after that in the centre, we said it?"

And all at once, in unison, we spat it out:

"LOBSTERS!" That was it. We could hardly control ourselves, we were so hysterical. A teacher passed by our table and smiled but said:

"A bit less noise, please, girls?"

Then Emily and Kaitlyn from my art class came over.

"What's so funny?" Emily said, obviously miffed she wasn't included in the hilarity.

And we all sobered up.

"Nothin'," said Lou and then we all squeezed together across the table. This was our joke and it wasn't to be shared with anyone else. I could feel Rachel's shoulders shaking next to me and Caroline's head was bobbing up and down.

At times like that, we four felt as if we could take on the world together.

I had a sneaky peek over my shoulder at Emily and Kaitlyn's faces and you'd think they were chewing lemons.

*

At lunchtime, though, I remembered I was some sort of celebrity and it got even worse, with kids pointing and then running away. I bunged my bag in my locker and went for a walk around the frosty school grounds to clear my head. My hands were stuffed in my pockets and I nearly went crashing to the ground when Loopy came up behind me and leapt on my back, her legs looped round my middle. I staggered under the sudden weight of her and she dismounted and sprang round in front of me.

"Jess, do you have any idea how popular you are? Have you heard the kids in there?"

I scowled at her and kept quiet.

"There's ghost hunts going on all over the place. The teachers are goin' bonkers. Kids are looking in storerooms and chasing each other, trying to build up a whole scene of horror or something. I heard your name mentioned three times between maths and getting out here."

"How did that even start?" I asked.

"Well, obviously, Lorraine heard you in the library yesterday and then *everyone* heard Loudmouth Lorraine."

"Heard what?"

"She said you said you'd seen a ghost."

"Did I?" I honestly couldn't remember what I'd said, or even if I'd spoken at all. I know I'd felt shocked and dazed.

"Well, it's the topic of the moment anyway... the Ghosts of York... ooh." As she said that, she did this sort of spooky wiggle with her hands and body. Then she laughed.

"Don't look so serious, sister. It's a load of old crap."

She was right. It was. What was happening in school and the things I'd seen were two separate things. I'd been haunted. The kids in school were just hysterical gossips and babies looking for a bit of excitement. I switched my mood and changed the conversation.

"Let's forget all that. How are Katie and Luca?" I asked and we walked back inside, huddled together to keep warm.

*

Later, I walked home from school on my own because Caroline had the dentist and Loopy had a football match.

That night, after tea, I realised it would be good to ask Aunt Ruby if she knew anything about a party at Mulberry Hall. I showed her the invitation and she just frowned and shook her head.

"No," she said, "I'm sure there isn't anything happening, Jessifer. Just as Caroline said, I don't think it's the right environment for a party. This is rather lovely though, isn't it? It's a very good representation of bygone times: a little fusty but intriguing." She lifted the tea-coloured card to her nose and smelled it. "It smells of my old grandmother's house. You'd have loved it there, Jess; full of ancient books and curiosities. I think that's how I developed my love of history." She handed it back to me. "Perhaps it was done by a schoolchild and they dropped it. Maybe you should hand it in next time you are there? Some little one might be looking for it. Do you remember when you were about eight and you made that beautiful old letter from a child evacuee in the Great War? We stained it with coffee and burned it a little at the edges to make it look time-ravaged. Or I could drop it in for you?"

"No, it's okay Auntie, I'll take it. I might show it to Mr Lloyd in history today."

It was true that Auntie loved history and our house was shaping up to be like her grandmother's. Our lounge was crammed with bookcases and Auntie's bedroom was bursting with the overspill. She had a wealth of knowledge about York. She'd lived here most of her life. I was so curious about the Victorian girl and all I'd heard so far was the same: her parents were wealthy and frequently held parties at the large house, Mulberry Hall, in Stonegate. They had always allowed their small daughter to watch the guests arriving before she went to bed but, sometime in the 1860s, she died after an accidental fall from a high landing. Of all the old stories and legends about York, this was one of the vaguest.

I went to my room to put the invitation away. I'd attached an importance to it that I couldn't explain, and I felt I had to it keep it safe. Joopy was clattering around his crate so I lifted him out.

"Come on, Joops," I said. "What's up with you tonight?"

He snuggled inside my clasped hands, seemingly happy to be there.

"I suppose I haven't let you roam the lounge for a while, have I? Let's ask Auntie if she'll let you."

"Are you all right, darling?" Aunt Ruby peered over her glasses as I walked back in. She was planted in her favourite chair by the window, book in hand. I read its title: *Health Provision in 19th Century Britain*. A glass on the table beside her glowed orange from the dregs of Lucozade in it.

"Fine thanks. Auntie, can I let Jupiter free tonight? He's restless."

"Mm, okay darling, but shut the doors please."

"See Joops? She loves you really," I cooed to him.

"I would call it toleration," Aunt Ruby replied, pulling a sickly sweet smile. "And no chewing, Ratty!" she added.

I let him down and he immediately scuttled off towards the hall door, which I sprinted to shut, beating him by a whisker.

I slumped across the other chair, my legs dangling over its arm, swinging. I admired the sparkly claret polish I'd applied to my toenails last week.

"Auntie, do you know about the ghost stories of York? You've got such good knowledge of the city, haven't you? I was wondering how true all the legends are."

"Well, there are many of course," Auntie replied. "It's hard to know how much is true and how much is hyperbole. It's human nature to embellish but it certainly helps to make a story more engaging. Why do you ask, Jess?"

"Well, didn't Mills, I mean, *Mrs* Mills, tell you what happened yesterday? I wasn't just ill you know."

"Whatever do you mean, darling?"

I sighed then said: "I owned up to something I didn't do." I felt my face flush deeply. Until recent events, I had always been straight with Aunt Ruby. We didn't keep secrets from each other. I loved the way she treated me like an adult and I considered ours a special relationship. It was different from my friends' relationships with their parents, where they were just the kid and their parents held complete authority on every little thing. Rather, Aunt Ruby always consulted me about things and she never talked about me in my presence, something which made me squirm when I heard other adults doing it to their children. It seemed so disrespectful.

"I'm sorry, Auntie, I haven't had chance to tell you but I thought Mrs Mills would have."

"Noooo," Auntie drew out the 'oh' sound, questioningly.

"Okay, well…" I swung my legs round and sat up properly, facing her. "It was lunchtime and the first years went berserk. There was all this screaming and stuff. It was a bit alarming. Anyway, Mills came yelling into the lunch hall, wanting to know what was going on and someone must've said something about the third years because, next thing, we were all sent to the assembly hall and made to stand there like babies until someone owned up to causing hysteria among the tiny, impressionable first years."

"And did you know who the perpetrator was?"

"Well, not really. Everyone just stood there like dummies and I was tired and hungry so, I just kind of wanted to end it. It was such a pain. Mills was glaring at us, making us all feel bad, as usual. So, I stuck my hand up and said I did it."

"Oh Jess…"

"She marched me along to her office." I cast my eyes down, remembering the awkwardness of following behind her to her office, everyone gawping.

"Did she punish you?"

"Well, no." I looked up and frowned at my aunt. "She just made me feel stupid with her usual, you know… heavens above, I'm disappointed in you girl… kind of thing. Then I felt faint and she took me to the medical room and then you arrived."

Aunt Ruby nodded her head, patiently waiting for me to finish.

"Anyhow," I continued, "I'm pretty sure she didn't believe me. That's why I never got a punishment today, I bet."

"She has good reason to disbelieve you, darling. You are not the kind of girl that goes around causing a fuss. Yes, you can be rather dramatic at times but you are still a sensible sort, aren't you?"

"Well, kind of. Yeah, I am, aren't I?" I said then smirked.

Aunt Ruby smiled. Her eyes glittered with love and trust.

"So, the whole thing was about that little ghost, you see, Auntie, the whole school's talking about her, even some of the teachers." I huffed. "To be honest, I can't stop thinking about her myself." My eyes began to water again, inexplicably.

"Mm-hm. It's the same in town. People *are* talking about that little child. It makes you wonder, doesn't it? But Jess, I can't add anything I'm afraid. I don't know any more than you, darling. I tend to take the legends of the city for what they are. I'm more interested in the way history shaped the city and its people. The ghost stories interest the tourists, of course they do, but I'm sure they're mostly based on silly old myths."

"What about Ali? I mean, she works in Mulberry Hall. Do you think she's ever seen anything?" I began to shiver unnaturally. I hugged my cardigan round me.

"You're freezing, child. Do you think you're still ill? Perhaps you should stay off tomorrow." She stood and fetched the plaid blanket from the back of the couch then gently pushed me back in my seat and cosied it around me, tucking it in. She continued talking. "Ali dismisses it I think. She listens to all the other talk but she doesn't seem to get involved. Sensible, I'd say."

The trill of the phone startled us. Aunt Ruby jumped up. She was sprightly for her sixty-five years.

"Jess, angel, watch out for Jupiter while I get the phone, will you?"

"Joops," I called, digging in my pocket for a granola nugget, his favourite treat. "Here, boy."

He shot across the door, ignoring the granola.

"That's not like you, Joops. You love this stuff."

He began squeaking and ran under the leather footstool and then quietened again.

It sounded as if the weather was turning wild outside. I crossed to the window and peeped through the drawn curtains. A sudden shot of wind-blasted rain crackled against the glass and I flicked the curtains shut again.

I glanced down at Auntie's book, lifted it, tumbled into her chair and let the book fall on my lap. I gazed at the bottom of the footstool and Jupiter's nose poked out.

"Here, Joops," I enticed him with the granola again. He scuttled over, scrambled up my leg, took the treat and snuggled into my cardigan to feast on his prize. I began to browse through Auntie's book, flicking the pages. A sudden hot flush filled my head when my eyes picked out the familiar words: Mulberry Hall, Stonegate.

I was so engrossed in the text I didn't notice Aunt Ruby come back in.

I read:

"Dr Jonathon Laythorpe, of Mulberry Hall, Stonegate, York, spent many years undertaking research on the new drug. It became somewhat of an obsession for him, well situated as he was to observe its effects, being an esteemed practitioner of anaesthetics and part-time surgeon at the York City Hospital. With the introduction of the new hypodermic syringe and needle, his research escalated rapidly."

Abruptly, I noticed Aunt Ruby was in the room and was strangely still and quiet, her back to me.

"Aunt Ruby?" I said. "Is something wrong?" I put the book down.

She turned to me, her hands at her chalk-white face.

"Aunt Ruby? Who was on the phone?"

"Oh, just Lynn," she said, looking over her shoulder at the lounge door.

"Has something happened to her?"

"No… it's not that…" she frowned. "I thought… I think I…" She inhaled deeply and her colour began to change again, back to her normal slight flush. "No, it's fine," she said. "Must have been something else…"

"Aunt Ruby… what just happened?"

"What, darling?" she said, looking over her shoulder again. She came and sat down. I could see something had really shaken her, but she didn't want to tell me, whatever it was.

"Can I get you anything, Auntie?"

She shook her head and settled back in her seat.

I had never in my whole, entire life seen Auntie behave so strangely. My calm, collected, wonderful auntie. What the heck was that all about?

8

PARANORMAL

"SO, IT'S DRAMA TONIGHT," AUNT RUBY SAID IN the morning. "We need to get tickets for the next play, don't we? I think Uncle Jack and Auntie Kath will want to come."

"Auntie, the tickets won't even be printed yet." I paused and looked at her. Her face was a bit tight-looking, her lips drawn in. "Are you okay?" I asked. I was starting to think she was losing it, after last night. It was like she was making conversation just to avoid talking about something else. Something she was keeping from me.

"Yes, but we don't want to miss out. Especially if we need tickets for everyone. Your cousins might want to come too."

"Doubt it," I muttered. I liked my cousins from Pateley Bridge but we had grown apart over the years and I only saw them every few months. I probably wouldn't feel that comfortable performing in front of them. Uncle Jack, though, he was the best. He was my dad's brother and he always asked about my life as if I was actually interesting or something.

*

I met Caroline on the corner as usual, along with Lou. They were both blowing clouds of breath into the frosty air and I was careful not to skid on the glistening pavement as I joined them.

"Does anyone want to go into town this weekend?" Lou asked, her voice a bit muffled through her bunched-up scarf. "It'll have to be Saturday though. I've got a match on Sunday. If it doesn't get cancelled, with this weather."

"I was going to ask that too," I said.

"Yep, I'll come," said Caroline. "I need to get a present for my dad's birthday."

"Great. Listen you two. I want to find out more about that wee ghost. We could go to Mulberry Hall for hot chocolate and look for her!"

"Are you serious, Jess?" asked Loopy, nudging me. "Like a ghost hunt, d'you mean?"

"Yeah," I said. "Why not?" But I couldn't help biting my lip.

"Are you okay?" Lou asked, noticing.

"Yep. Sure am. I didn't get a punishment from Mills, I got my essay in and Mrs F said it's great..." I took a run-up, executed a masterful skid on the frost, then turned to my friends and wiggled my hips until my bag fell off my shoulder, "... and I've got drama tonight. Life couldn't be better." I was looking forward to drama, as always, but the last bit was a major overstatement. Life was weird at the moment and I'd been feeling gloomy with all the thinking about Judith and my mum and dad, but I was well practised at putting a brave face on. Audrey, my brilliant drama teacher, taught us to always smile, no matter how you're feeling inside.

"Oh, and by the way," I said, spinning back to face the same direction as them, squeezing between them, "my friends are fantastic!"

"Well, flattery gets you nowhere, JJ," said Caroline, "and I'm not going on any sort of ghost hunt. That stuff really creeps me out."

"Anyway," said Loopy, "what's happening with you and Stefan? Aren't you going to go out with him again? He's hot!"

"No, I'm not. You're right, he is hot, but football comes first for Stefan *and* he's allergic to pets!"

"Ooh, I'll have him then!" said Loopy.

"Cool," I said. "I'll see if I can set the two of you up! You should get on well, actually."

"Yeah," said Caroline. "Both sport mad."

*

At morning break, I got myself a big chocolate muffin from the school café and joined Caroline and Loopy Lou at a table.

"Caroline, do you think we could ask your mum about the little Victorian girl? She must've heard things at work."

"You can if you want, Jess. She might not have much to say though. She doesn't really get involved in all that."

"What's this?" asked Rachel, sidling up to Caroline with her own muffin. She began tearing hunks off the cake and stuffing them in her mouth.

"We're meeting in town on Saturday," Lou said. "All of us. Can you come?"

"Uh-uh," said Rachel, shaking her head and talking through a mouthful of crumbs. "Trumpet exam on Saturday. Grade six. I'll be practising all morning. Exam's at two. Can't we do the following week?"

"No. I want to go to Mulberry Hall and find out more…" I glanced sideways at Caroline who cut me off mid-speech.

"You know, Jess, if you started that ghost thing the other day, for whatever reason, like, as a joke or something, you've got a problem. You're being a weirdo. Maybe the whole being ill thing was just a pretence, too. I mean, I don't know what to think." She sighed.

"Caroline!" I rebuked, aghast that my best friend thought I was a liar. I scowled at her.

"Well, she's a super good actress if she can fake looking that ill," said Loopy. "I saw her in the library and she looked positively rank."

"Well, I just don't see what's so interesting about that fake invitation and some stupid legend," said Caroline.

"I think it's interesting," Rachel said, wiping crumbs off her face. "There must be something in it if everyone's talking about it."

"Urban myth," said Caroline, flouncing up. "And Jess is obsessed. I'm off to the toilets. See you after."

"Bit tetchy," I said, raising my eyebrows questioningly to Rachel. "I can't help being interested in the history of our town." I lunged at the top of my muffin and ate it as if it had offended me.

*

I got home from school to an empty flat. Aunt Ruby had left a note saying she'd be home by six. I wanted another look at her book. It was still on the table next to her chair.

I read more about Dr Jonathon Laythorpe. I knew the story went that the small ghost haunted several shops in Stonegate, but it was generally believed that Mulberry Hall had been her home. The book said Dr Laythorpe lived at Mulberry Hall and the dates seemed to link up. He was doing research in the 1860s and that was around the time the child had lived, wasn't it? They must've been related then, surely.

I heard a scratching, scraping sound and glanced around me. I was alone but I'd left my bedroom door open and I could hear Jupiter moving about his crate. Maybe that's what I'd heard.

Jupiter was normally quite lazy but these days he was always on the move, darting about, scraping up his bedding into a new bundle at one end or other of his black metal house. I was beginning to wonder if there was something wrong with him. I would give him a good check over before drama tonight. Aunt Ruby might not be too chuffed if he needed the vet. Last time it had cost her a fortune! There was a small closed box in my brain which held the idea that he might be sensitive to ghostly goings-on. Yet I didn't want to consider that right now. The box would remain firmly shut and padlocked.

I turned back to the book, shivering and pulling the plaid blanket round me.

Jonathon Laythorpe seemed to have been the first person in York to administer opium injections using the hypodermic syringe. The author claimed that he had a laboratory in his home where he experimented with dosages and apparently also gave treatment to people who came with injuries and health complaints. The book went on to discuss opium addiction in Victorian Britain as a bit of a scourge of the time. I found it interesting and thought I might ask my history teacher, Mr Lloyd, about it next week.

*

I realised it would be a good idea to start cooking, as Aunt Ruby would be back soon. We had a tradition of bacon butties on Thursdays before drama club. I usually made them because I was fussy about how my bacon was cooked.

I began cutting the rind off the bacon, leaving just enough for a taste of that gorgeous crispy frilled edging, which I liked almost black. It was when I switched on the grill that I heard a gentle tinkling sound. Just for a couple of seconds: a tinny, metallic rattle, then silence. I stood stock-still in the middle of the kitchen and listened again. It was vaguely familiar but could have come from all manner of things: jangling keys; teaspoons clanging; in fact, it was like a decoration we'd had on our Christmas tree just weeks ago, an elf with little bells on its hat. Every time we'd brushed against the tree, we'd laughed to hear its tinkling. I moved out to the hall and listened but didn't hear it again. Joopy was quiet at last. Then, after a moment's pause, I heard Auntie's key in the lock. I returned to my task at the grill.

*

Audrey pounced on me at drama class that night, which sounds like a bad thing but not for me. I loved it when she chose me. Even more, I liked showing off my skills to the younger ones.

"Jess, I need you tonight. Will you play the key role for me?"

"Of course, Audrey. You know me. What is it?"

"A scene of conflict among friends. You'll play opposite Susie. She'll be your accuser and you'll be the innocent victim."

"What, like an argument in school, kinda thing?"

"Exactly."

*

"So, last week, guys," said Audrey, "we talked about having empathy and understanding different points of view. We looked at people from different backgrounds and considered how playing diverse roles helps us with problem-solving, critical thinking and conflict resolution."

To break up the theory she immediately went into this weird, drunk character, mumbling to herself, stumbling about the streets, carrying her little plastic bag and tapping the ground with some old stick she'd picked up. The weird thing about Audrey is, she rarely ever uses props. She just performs and you know exactly what the props are. She just gets it, and if you miss Audrey's acting, you feel properly cheated. Sometimes, it isn't even relevant to what we're doing. Sometimes, it's just her way of making everyone pay attention. She's so brilliant.

"This week, we're taking it one step further," she said. "We'll do two different takes on an argument, then you're going to work in twos and figure out your own scenarios. Take One is a full-blown conflict ending with a physical fight. And Take Two will be completely different. This time, the protagonist, or victim, will take a step back and consider why the perpetrator has reacted as they have."

It turned out I was a character called Sammy and my 'friend' was Lauren. We were both reading the same novel by John Green. When Lauren lost hers, she accused me of stealing it. Meanwhile another girl, Kat, was planning a fifteenth birthday party to which the wider group were invited but Lauren told everyone to ignore me and called me a manipulative, lying thief and said I wasn't to be invited to the party. Everyone turned against me and I fought back by shoving Lauren and calling her a lazy, conniving loser. When Lauren slapped me, I flung my book in her face, saying: "Have it then, if it's that important to you." The book's corner landed close to her eye, drawing blood, so a full-on fight ensued.

In Take Two, Audrey made suggestions as to how I could help to diffuse the conflict.

"Show empathy, Jess," she said. "Consider why Lauren is so upset. Perhaps she's crazy about John Green and was loving the novel. Perhaps she has his whole collection, which makes the lost book so much more significant. Maybe she's going through a tough time right now. You can show your empathy in the way you respond. So, rather than reacting, ask if you can help."

It was great because it made us stop and think. And you could see, through each intervention, with some consideration and problem-solving, how the aggression fizzled out and we understood each other better.

In the second half of the class, Audrey went round each pair and said she would pick the best conflict scenario to work into our summer performance.

On my way home, I began to see drama differently. I'd always enjoyed it but I'd never thought about it having an influence on my wider life. All the respect I'd ever felt for Audrey doubled and I smiled at how fantastic she was. I never wanted to stop drama, ever.

*

As I put my key in the lock, back at home after class, I got such a fright when that smoky cat landed on the slabs right beside me. By the angle of its body, it seemed to have jumped from a great height and I was surprised how lightly it landed on its feet. I wondered if it had been on my windowsill again. With my heart pounding, I watched it slink off, leap onto our gate and pour down the other side, then disappear behind next-door's hedge.

I hurried indoors and went straight to check on Jupiter before greeting Auntie. I walked into my room.

"Auntie," I called sharply, shocked to see Joopy's cage door open. "Did you do anything with Joopy while I was out?"

She wandered into my room, frowning.

"No, darling. You know I never do anything with him unless you ask me to. I'm not as comfortable around him as you are."

My eyes were roving all around his crate as I approached but there was no sign of him. The whole thing, which was about a metre and a half long by a metre tall, sat atop metal legs which raised it ten centimetres off the carpet. I peered underneath but he wasn't there.

"Joops?" I called. There wasn't a sound.

Together, we searched my room. He couldn't be anywhere else as we always shut all the room doors when we went out.

I found it hard to concentrate. I reflected on my movements earlier on. I remembered hearing a tinkling sound which I had dismissed as being one of those noises you just can't explain. I picked up one of my boots and put my hand inside. I did the same with the second one. They were empty and anyway I'd just taken them off. I stared at one boot and turned it over and over.

"Jessifer, try not to worry. We'll find him. He must be somewhere in here."

"But how could his crate have been opened? I know I shut it when I put him back in earlier."

"Maybe you thought you had but it didn't quite catch."

"Mm," I murmured. But I knew I'd shut it properly; the catches on the door were not the sort you could accidentally leave undone. I slumped down onto my bed and it was then I saw the dimples on my throw. Perfect little circles in a repeated pattern, like little paw prints.

"Something's been in my room, Auntie," I said, thinking of that grey cat, "look."

"Hm... well the window isn't open," she said. "And even if it were, I can't see an animal getting all the way up here."

"Well, actually..." In my mind's eye, I saw the cat staring in from my windowsill the other night, but Joopy's squeaking interrupted me and he suddenly shot out from under the bed.

"There you are," I said, scooping him up and lifting him to my cheek. His whiskers tickled my nose and I was so relieved to find him I thought nothing more of the indentations on the throw.

9

PINK RIBBON
1863

I WAS WAITING FOR MAMA. WE WERE GOING shopping but she wasn't ready yet so I ran downstairs to see Papa. Mama said he might be busy in his medical room but I decided I would dash in and give him a surprise! But when I pushed the door open, he was shouting at Clementine. She must have been a bad cat because she leaped off his table and there was a fallen-over jar with liquid spilled all over and it had gone on his big brown purse.

"Devil!" he shouted at her. He picked up his purse and some of the papers fell out, so he picked them up, then he kicked Clementine and she flew across the room and hit the wall. Poor Clementine. She howled and she spat and then she saw me and she darted past me in a flash through the door. My poor Clementine.

"Clementine," I called after her and spun around and hurried to catch her and give her a cuddle. But she was so fast and all I saw was her tail disappearing around the corner.

I went and sat on the stairs and put my elbows on my knees and my chin in my hands. My Papa didn't normally do things like that. Clementine would be very cross with him and she would never let him tickle her ears again.

"Adeline?" I heard him say, but I squeezed my eyes tightly shut. I heard him walk across the hall and I put my hands over my ears. I was as cross with Papa as Clementine was.

"Open your eyes, Adeline," Papa said, pulling my hands from my ears. "I want to tell you Clementine will be all right. She's just a cat and she'll forget about it. But she mustn't upset my important equipment or damage my documents. My experiments mean the world to me. They will make me very important. And my documents will show exactly how. Open your eyes now, Adeline, please."

I opened my eyes and looked at Papa. He was clutching his big brown purse with the string fastened around the button to make it closed and he looked sad. But I was still cross.

"Come with me," he said and tried to take my hand to pull me but I folded my arms and turned away and wouldn't look at him any more.

"Adeline, we will do something nice together soon, you and me. You would like that, wouldn't you?"

I didn't answer him and I knew that was very naughty but I would be cross for a long time because Clementine is my friend, not just a cat.

I turned my head away again and I heard his footsteps across the hall and he was saying confusing things, because that's what grown-up people do. They talk in riddles so that it's impossible to understand when you are only six.

"My patience, tried by a tiny child. My own, precious girl... losing her before I've gained her... how can I... ?" I couldn't hear any more confusing things after that because he went back in his room.

"Adeline?" Now it was Mama coming downstairs. "Shall we go?"

*

After our trip to the haberdasher's, I skipped along by Mama's side. We chattered and chattered and my boots clattered on the cobbles of Stonegate. Mama had wanted a new flower, called a corse-large, for her evening gown for tonight's party. The saleslady showed her a pink silk one which was "really now" and would go perfectly with Mama's cream gown.

The saleslady asked me what I thought and when I said it was as pretty as Mama, she laughed and fetched me a matching pink ribbon for my hair.

When we arrived home, Papa came into the hall. He was frowning and his eyes were half closed.

"Jonathon," said Mama, "I wish you'd give up these experiments. They are not good for you. Or for us."

Papa didn't answer at first but when we both kept looking at him, he said in a cross voice:

"I told you, Jocelyn, you should send a woman for your things."

"There isn't any need, darling. I enjoy it," Mama replied. "Besides, it was a little diversion for Adeline. Wasn't it, Addie?" she asked.

"Yes, Father. And look, the lady gave me a ribbon for my hair."

I waved my ribbon in the air. I had almost forgotten how bad Papa was to Clementine because I'd enjoyed my trip out with Mama. But Papa didn't look at my ribbon, which made me feel sad. He went straight back to his medical room. I think he must have been spinning while we were out because he was swaying and he had to put his hand on the wall to stop himself from falling down. Sometimes I spin and spin until I get dizzy and fall down. It's lots of fun but Papa wasn't laughing.

"You shouldn't pand... pander to the child so much," he murmured over his shoulder before he shut the door, "and her name is... Ad... Adeline."

Mama sighed and watched him go and I wondered why Papa couldn't say my name very properly. Mama looked sad but she smiled and crouched down.

"Let's go and see what Cook's got for us," she said and pulled me right along the hall to the kitchen.

*

"Good morning, Missus Howe," said Mama.

"Good morning, Mistress Laythorpe," said Cook. "Good morning, Miss Adeline. May I help you?"

"We are looking for elevenses after our walk, Missus Howe," said Mama. "I know it is an unusual request, but I would like to have something brought to the drawing room."

"And Miss Adeline will be taking her usual milk and biscuit in the nursery, I presume?" said Cook.

"No, Adeline will be joining me in the drawing room this morning, Missus Howe, if you please."

"Righty ho, Ma'am," said Cook, scowling, "though it's more 'n my job's worth if Master finds out. What with the party 'n' all to prepare for."

"Please don't worry, Missus Howe. I will explain to my husband that the request was mine."

When I walked to the drawing room with Mama, Clementine came out of the passage near the kitchen, but she wasn't trotting along. Normally, my ginger cat trotted and skipped. She was always jumping about and running here and there. But now, she was doing a sort of falling-over walk which made me feel sad. I didn't think she'd been spinning too.

"What's the matter with Clementine, Mama?" I asked.

"Let's take her into the drawing room with us," said Mama.

*

In the drawing room, Clementine fell fast asleep. Mama did a funny swirly thing with my long hair then she wrapped the pink ribbon over the top of my head and tied it in a bow. I put my hand on it and it felt special. One day I might grow up to be just as pretty as Mama.

"You can keep it in until the minute before bedtime," said Mama. "That way, you can show it off when you come to watch the guests arrive."

When there was a party, I was allowed to stand on the middle landing as the guests were announced. Sometimes they would wave and call to me. Then Mama would come out of her room and stand at the banister. Everyone would look up at her from the hall and I would watch from the landing. It made me say "Oh" when I saw how beautiful she looked. Mama would wave to me then come down the stairs and stop to give me a goodnight kiss. After that, I wouldn't be allowed to stay any more because I am too little for parties and Nanny would come to take me to bed and tuck me in.

We ate our biscuits then I curled up beside Mama.

"Who is coming to the party, Mama?" I asked.

"Well, Grandmama and Grandfather will come of course."

"Will Uncle Gilbert come too?"

"No. His governess will look after him this evening." I knew that Uncle Gilbert was a grown up but more like a little boy because he had a broken sort of head, even though it didn't look broken to me. Even though he was tons older than me, he still had to have a governess. Sometimes he came to parties but only when they were small parties. I wondered if he minded.

"What about Uncle William?" I asked. Uncle William was Mama's other brother but he lived in London.

"Yes, Uncle William and Aunt Susan are coming too and they will be so pleased to see you, Addie. They will stay here tonight and then on Sunday we will all go together to the big house."

"So, I will see Uncle Gilbert at the big house?"

"Yes, you will."

"Hooray!" I whooped.

The big house was Grandfather's house in the country and if it was sunny we would walk on the lawn and the dogs would run excitedly around in circles and it would be marvellous fun.

"Papa will be able to ride Honey with me too," I said. I loved Grandfather's pony called Honey.

"Hm, I'm not sure Papa will come with us, Addie. He's terribly busy."

"Who else is coming to the party, Mama?" I asked. I hoped Mama's friend Sarah Field would be coming because she always wore the most beautiful dress and she was funny and her laugh was like a big honking goose. "Will Sarah come?"

"Yes, Sarah and Daniel, her husband, and Eleanor and Louise, my cousins, and Dr Anthony is coming over from Leeds…"

Mama went on, listing people including ladies from Sunday School and the Poor Fund and lots more. I thought it was going to be a big, big party and so exciting. I could hardly wait for bedtime to come and it was only morning time still.

10

MULBERRY HALL COFFEE SHOP

It was Saturday and Caroline and I were virtually rolling on the floor, laughing. We were in a hat shop. Caroline's mum had given her extra money so they could share in getting a hat for her dad's birthday.

The shop guy was beginning to get a bit twitchy. We must've tried on three quarters of his stock. With each hat we tried, the situation just got funnier and funnier.

Tears were rolling down my face as I looked in the mirror. A purple fedora with a black and white cowhide band around it almost covered my eyes and I peered at the shining rivulet running down my cheek.

"That one definitely suits your style, Jess. Especially these days, cos you're always so Friesian cold, get it?" whispered Caroline, casting a glance towards the shop assistant.

"You will kindly purchase that particular item now, miss," came a deep voice.

Shocked, I wiped my face and turned to see Lou. We'd told her we'd be in here and she stood behind us pulling a serious face.

"Gotcha," she said and cackled far too loudly.

The shop guy huffed, also loudly, wanting us to hear.

"Ooh, sorry," Lou apologised to him, bold as ever. "Was that too loutish?"

The man turned away but when Caroline paid forty pounds for the first hat we'd tried, he became a little flustered. I'm sure he'd thought we were only in there for a joke.

*

"So, what do you think, Ali?" I asked Caroline's mum, soon after, in Mulberry Hall. We were all huddled around a table, cradling mugs of creamy hot chocolate, bobbing with marshmallows.

Ali considered for a moment and said in hushed tones:

"It's hard to know, Jess, sweetie. Caroline said you've taken a real interest in this but, you know, there are some things we can't explain. I'd hate you to get involved in something we don't understand. It could put you in danger." She paused and looked around the café, then continued: "There is something here..." She gazed through the doorway into the corridor beyond, silent for a few moments, then, she looked at me, stretched her head forward and lowered her voice to a whisper: "We feel things sometimes, especially when the shop is quietening down before closing time."

"So, there… there really is a ghost, Mum?" Caroline asked. She looked troubled.

Ali sighed but she neither confirmed nor denied it. She tapped one finger on the table, thinking, then she said: "There does seem to be an entity, of some sort."

Sensing Lou's eyes on me, I turned to her and she pulled a face, folded her arms across her chest and scanned the room. Caroline just frowned at me then looked down at the table.

"Sometimes, there are noises, too," Ali continued, quietly, "which don't seem to have any origin. The staff obviously find it unnerving." I stared at her. Here she was, admitting that Mulberry Hall was haunted. She noticed the effects of her words on us and sniffed. "I'm frightening you all now." She changed her tone. "Right. Enough nonsense. I need to get back to work. Jess," she put her hand on my arm, "don't get involved. Please."

We finished our drinks and Ali said she'd pay for them. Then, we left the café in silence, but Caroline narrowed her eyes and shook her head at me, then she and Lou, heads together, went, whispering, to the Ladies'. I went downstairs and walked among the many glass cabinets filled with all sorts of posh dinnerware, ornaments and expensive knick-knacks.

I was immediately drawn back to the cabinet with the brass scale in it, thinking over Ali's words and trying to forget Caroline's look. The scales weren't moving now. The weak sunlight from the windows gave the pans a golden-yellow lustre. Something flickered at the back of the cabinet, drawing my focus. A small image of a face was stuck to it and I gasped when I realised whose face it was; not just any little girl, rather, my little ghost. When she smiled, I gasped again; it wasn't a picture. It was her. I squinted then my focus switched back to the scales which had begun to tip. The face drifted forward as if vying for my attention. I stepped back but was mesmerised. Her pale skin was translucent and her long fair hair, swirled up on her head, was topped with a ribbon, which she twirled with her tiny fingers. Instantly, I realised how crazy I must look and glanced over my shoulder to see if anyone was watching me. When I turned back the face had gone.

"Hey!" said a voice from behind me.

I jumped, startled.

"Oh!" I said. "Lou, did you see…"

"What're you looking at?" said Caroline coming up beside Lou.

I decided to leave it for now. "Just the weighing scales. They're so like the ones Aunt Ruby has on the windowsill at home," I said.

My phone pinged. Aunt Ruby, checking what time I'd be back. I peered into the cabinet again.

"Jess?" called Lou from the main doorway of Mulberry Hall. "Come on!"

"Sorry," I said, rushing to join her. "I was miles away."

11

ADELINE SKIPS THROUGH TIME

"CLEMENTINE?" I CALLED AND WAITED.

She came running from the back of the shop.

"There you are, Clementine." I sat on a chair and Clementine jumped onto my lap. I began to stroke her and watched the lady. She was sitting with her friends at another table, along with the grown-up lady who works in Mulberry Hall. They were huddled up as if they had a big secret. My lady didn't see me but when she and her friends left the café, I slid off my chair and followed.

"Come on, Clementine," I said, and Clementine came running after me.

When we got downstairs, I saw my lady go back to the cabinet with the big old weighing scales. I went to the other side and smiled at her through the glass but her friends shouted her and she left, so Clementine and I sat on the floor in the corner. There was a man in the room who was looking at some teapots and he shivered and pulled his coat around him tightly. It is very cold because it is winter. But I don't feel it because I'm a ghost.

"Clementine," I said, "do you think she will hear me again if I sing 'Oranges and Lemons'?"

"Meow," said Clementine. Then she licked my hand, which made me giggle.

"Perhaps she will come to my house and I can show her things," I said. "You can help me, Clementine. Would you like to help me?"

"Meow," she said, again.

"You are such a wonderful friend, Clementine. Just like Tom. We can show my lady all sorts of things. She will love to see all the rooms and the party, too. But perhaps not all of it. We can show her how wonderful Mama is and the things Papa did and Cook and Nanny and Mr Partridge. But I don't like it when Mama and Papa argue, Clementine. And it's all because Mama doesn't like Papa's experiments and Papa doesn't want Mama to stop him doing them. Papa said he was going to be very important and he was but he didn't do it properly and then… well, you know the rest."

I jumped up and Clementine fell off my lap and stalked away. I had to think about what would happen next and I would go back to my living time and then go back, again, to the lady's living time, and then I'd take her with me to my living time and tell her about the bocudents and then go back and go back and go back… ha-ha-ha, that's so funny…"

I started to giggle and the man looking at the teapots looked all around the room but he couldn't see me, so he looked at the teapots again. I started honking with laughter like Sarah Field, Mama's friend, and I watched the man. His head shot to one side, looking for me. I kept laughing and his head snapped to the other side but still, he couldn't see me, then he frowned and dashed out of the shop, setting the doorbell tinkling. Then it wasn't funny any more because I think he was frightened of me and I don't like it when people are frightened.

So, I'd bring the lady back to my living time so she would know about Papa's big brown purse and the bocudents. I liked my living time because there were fun things like running up and down the big staircase, but only when Papa wasn't at home, and chasing Clementine all the way through the house. I liked the in-between living time, too, like watching the people put all their things into carts or the big noisy carriages with smoke coming out of the back, then leaving their houses and the houses getting turned into shops. When my house was turned into a shop, some of the rooms stayed the same but some of them were chopped into smaller rooms and my beautiful staircase was taken away. That was sad. Then long after the Bad Wars, people who spoke different languages came to York to look around and they always seemed to come and look at my house because of all the pretty crockery. And the people from America always said things like:

"My sister's gonna love this coffee pot but I cain't carry it. Do you ship?" or, "I lurve this tea set. Can you ship it to Illynoy?"

Eventually, every house in Stonegate was turned into a shop. There are soooo many different shops and I can go into them and play, because I'm a ghost. If you're not a ghost, you can't do all those things, like going to your own time and jumping into someone else's time. But if you are a ghost, well… you don't belong anywhere. But at least I have Tom and Clementine.

I could show the lady my house and the things that happened. Because, what happened was wrong. My papa was angry when I died and my mama was broken-hearted because she loved me in pieces but I shouldn't have died. And it was because Papa was cross with Mama that the accident happened. But it wasn't an accident. It was a purpose. I didn't fall over the railing like people said. And nearly all the people thought that Papa did only good things because he made some people better and he showed some people how to do special things with a special tool and some medicine.

So, I'll sing my song and bring my lady.

12

MORPHINE

I T WAS SUNDAY MORNING. AUNT RUBY WAS having a good old natter with her friends at church, so I'd given her a wave and said I'd see her at home. It was frosty again and all the normal people were still tucked up in bed. I began walking towards our street but, with that little girl's face ever-present in my head, I changed direction and walked into town instead. I left the footpath and decided to cut through Lock Woods again, taking the shorter route.

When I reached Stonegate, I saw two women going in to Mulberry Hall. The lights were off inside so they were probably about to open for the day. I knew the café normally opened at eleven on a Sunday and the rest of the shop at midday.

I stood and wondered what to do then felt a spot of rain on my cheek. I looked up at the sky. An ominous cloud seemed resolute on blocking out any daylight.

"Say the bells of Old Bailey..." The nursery rhyme 'Oranges and Lemons', in that little sing-song voice again, filtered into my consciousness. Was it in my head or was it real? I couldn't see anyone who might be singing. Neither child nor adult.

The temperature dropped and I trembled inside my thick jacket. I walked round to the side of the building on Mulberry Lane and watched a man enter through a dark wooden door, which he left open. I felt drawn towards it.

I peered inside and heard her:

"When I grow rich…" she sang, then switched to talking. "Perhaps she will come and play with us when you're feeling better, Clementine."

It was her; I knew it. *What's her name?* I wondered. *And who's Clementine?*

"Her name is Ad… Adeline," I heard, as if in answer to my question. It was a man's deep voice. It sounded reprimanding, like when Auntie Rachel insists my cousin is not Olly-Ol, as Steffi and Ellie, my other cousins, call their little brother, but rather, Oliver.

All I could see inside was a blank white wall. I stepped through the door and found myself in a corridor. I looked left and right and saw that it reached a blind end on the left but to the right there was a gap in the wall. It looked like a passageway. I stepped lightly along, reaching the end where a staircase led down, presumably to a basement. A new passageway led to my left and at its far end was my little girl, with her back to me. She seemed to be cuddling a soft orange toy, perhaps her teddy, then I saw it had a tail hanging limply by her side. Perhaps a toy cat or a tiger. Clementine? Her head was tilted down to it and she was muttering soothing words.

Then she had gone, and I heard a different voice and the clinking of crockery.

"Well, I never, Betsy… asking me to give 'er tea in the drawin' room when t' child should be in t' nursery. And now, Adeline's carryin' that cat about as if it's a baby… getting under me feet…"

I scuttled along, my heart hammering. I wanted to turn back but yearned to know more. Immediately on my left was a white door. Seeing it was ajar, I peered in and saw what looked like an office with an examination couch in one corner, like you find at the doctor's. Opposite, in the right-hand corner, stood a huge oak desk and to the left of it, a more solid wooden door. An old, musty smell, mixed with vanilla, hung in the air. The walls were lined with glass-fronted cabinets containing all sorts of jars, bottles and boxes, labelled with Latin names. Everything belonged to the past. A metal tray sat on the desk.

Oh, why am I doing this? I stepped into the room and pushed the door almost closed. Listening for footsteps, I stalked quickly over to the desk. On the wall, a calendar hung. A chill flooded me as I read '1863'. This was too weird. I gasped as the door on my left opened and a man walked into the room. He had hold of the child's fluffy toy by the scruff of its neck. Or, I thought it was a toy. Until, he dropped it and it thumped onto the floor with far more weight than a toy would have. When it opened one eye and let out a horrible attempt at a yowl, I knew it was no toy. It rolled onto its ginger paws and staggered erratically towards the door I'd come in through then bumped its head in its attempt to squeeze out.

"Wha… what are you doing here?" The man had no interest in the cat. He elicited each word slowly as if he were drunk. "If you desire a consultation, you should have c… come to the main door." A thick, probing tongue swept the bristly top of a chestnut beard which hid his mouth even when he spoke. He was of medium height and build. A sweep of brown hair hung diagonally across his forehead and his grey eyes were strangely piercing. He slowly moved his gaze up and down me, frowning. I looked at my purple and green swirly leggings. I must look like an alien to him.

I opened and closed my mouth but nothing came to mind. I realised I had no good explanation for being there.

"Sit," he said, pointing to a chair at one end of the examination couch.

I sat and watched him. He stumbled towards his desk and sat down clumsily, almost missing the edge of his seat. I thought he was either ill or had been drinking.

With his back to me, he opened a drawer in his desk, pulled out a book and began writing. After a while, he seemed to forget I was there. I wasn't sure what to do and wondered if I could slip back out the way I'd come in. Would I be able to get back home? Or would I be stuck here? As I quashed the beginnings of panic, I watched him push his book aside, lay his head on his arms and apparently go to sleep.

I continued to sit for a few moments, not sure how much time had passed. I suddenly realised Aunt Ruby would be looking for me. I reached into my bag for my phone but there was no signal. Though I knew I should hurry home, my mind was burning with curiosity over what lay beyond the big wooden door.

I stood and crossed over to the desk. The man looked white and barely alive but a piece of fluff fluttered on his sleeve in the path of his shallow breath. I had to know what he had written. I held my own breath as I touched the page. A fountain pen lay there. I lifted it and carefully placed it on the desk then read his entries. There was a list of dates and dosages of morphine, the last reading:

'18th January 1863. 10.45 Morphine opiate, weak strength, 2 drops, left brachial vein.'

I tilted my chin and peered into the deep metal tray at the back of the desk. It contained a silver syringe with a needle protruding from it.

This man was injecting himself with morphine. It was obvious. He'd had to enunciate his words carefully when he'd spoken to me, as if trying to overcome drunkenness. His piercing eyes had stood out to me earlier. Now I realised they were affected by the strong drug.

Bloodshot eyes, constricted, pinprick pupils, tremors and slurred speech can be warning signs that your friend is abusing drugs...

I remembered the last tutorial we'd had on substance abuse in PSE. We'd all been discussing who, in our year, might have a problem and we'd secretly scrutinised our suspects for signs. This man's eyes had looked piercing because of the pinprick pupils.

Without thinking, I crept to the door that led further into Mulberry Hall. I opened it and almost exclaimed in wonder at the sight of the imposing hall. Directly opposite me stood an exquisite staircase of shimmering oak. A patterned blue and cream carpet, edged with red, swept up the stairs, with a margin of rich amber wood left exposed at both sides. The bottom of the staircase fanned out in an arc, making a centrepiece in the room. Huge oak doors lined the white-painted walls.

I was so absorbed that I didn't see her until she was right in front of me, grasping my hand.

"Hello," she said. Her big eyes were friendly and earnest.

It's her. It's definitely her. And I'm there: Mulberry Hall. But then. Not now. I'm here but it's different.

All these thoughts rushed through my mind before I replied.

"Hi." My voice sounded mousy.

"I'm Adeline Maria Susan Laythorpe," she said. "I've been waiting for you. Do you want to see my mama?" She twirled her hair ribbon in her fingers.

"Erm, no, it's okay," I said. "I'm Jessifer. Do you live here?"

"Yes. This is our house and there's Father and Mama and Cook and Nanny and everybody. And there's going to be a party tonight. Do you want to come? You look funny."

She began to giggle and then looked pointedly at my leggings.

A woman's voice sounded in the distance.

"Adeline, where are you?"

"I have to go now," I garbled. "How do I get out?"

"You just go through the door, of course," Adeline replied, chuckling again and pointing to my left, where I saw a pair of grand oak doors, clearly the house's main entrance.

"Bye," I said, weakly, and hurried towards them.

"Do you want to be my friend?" Adeline ran after me. "Come back for the party," she pleaded. "It will be fun."

*

I stumbled out onto the street and looked left and right along Stonegate. It was quiet; normal for January. I heard the clopping of hooves and waited for the horse and the bobbing black carriage to pass the street end. The top-hatted driver in his heavy winter cloak stared straight ahead. Quite frankly, he could be a Victorian *or* a modern-day city worker. The tourists loved being pulled around the city in horse-drawn carriages driven by carriage drivers wearing period dress. I spun round and felt relief so enormous I almost collapsed on the cobbles. Someone pushed past me, with a quiet "Excuse me" into the doorway marked 'Mulberry Hall China Shop and Café'. A staff member walked towards the door from the inside and flipped over the sign saying: 'Café Open'. I took a deep breath and hurried home.

13

FRICTION

I TRIED TO ACT NORMALLY. AS SUNDAY WORE ON, Aunt Ruby kept narrowing her eyes at me when she thought I wasn't looking. I could tell she thought something was a bit strange. Boy, was she right! I'd arrived home before she'd got back from church, which meant that while I was inside the nineteenth-century version of Mulberry Hall, time had practically stood still in 2019. How weird was that?

That night I barely slept for mulling over everything. I figured out I'd had seven or eight different ghostly experiences, some more convincing than others. First, the moving scales in Mulberry Hall, followed by seeing the child sitting on our wall, singing nursery rhymes. Then, in the kitchen at home. There was also the boy she was with who I thought I'd seen again the next night in Stonegate, after my night walk through the woods. There was Joopy's crate being mysteriously opened and the weird indents like paw prints on my bed. But the weirdest and most convincing episode, the one that surpassed all the others, was the latest: being in Mulberry Hall in 1863 and meeting the doctor, who was stoned, and then the child herself. Yet, now, I knew her name: Adeline Susan Maria Laythorpe. I wondered if I was losing my mind. Nothing like this had happened to me before. I could still smell the sickly, slightly off vanilla scent in my nostrils. No wonder I couldn't sleep. I'd actually time-travelled to a Victorian house and walked among – and talked to – real, genuine ghosts.

*

In the morning, Auntie really annoyed me.

"Jessifer, darling," she called through the bathroom door, "if you don't hurry you'll be late. It's eight thirty."

"I'm coming," I shot back, roughly. It was her third time-announcement since I'd groaned my way out of bed. I peered in the mirror. I looked terrible. My eyes were bloodshot and my face was pale and spotty. I grabbed some foundation and smeared it under my eyes, scrunched my hair into a clip and made a mad dash into my room for my bag.

"Is something the matter, Jess?" Aunt Ruby asked.

"No. I'm fine."

I felt guilty as I slammed the front door. What had Aunt Ruby done, after all? I'd apologise tonight.

On the way to school, Caroline talked about a get-together she'd had yesterday with her auntie's family.

"You're quiet, Jess," she said eventually.

I was still trying to process my own weekend, so I didn't say anything.

"Jess?"

"Mm… what is it?" I looked at Caroline. She was frowning.

"You're being weird," she said.

"No, I'm not."

"Yes, you are."

I sighed.

"Are you feeling okay?" Caroline asked, her voice softer.

"Yeah. Just… aw… nothing. I'm fine," I said. I'd tell her about it later when I could find the right words. Otherwise she'd go in a huff on me again.

*

I drifted towards English, wondering how I *would* explain yesterday's events to my friends. I felt a vague thrill at the thought of sharing it with them but at the same time, a twist of anxiety spiralled in my stomach. Probably best not to say anything. Mrs Fortiver looked at me quizzically when I walked in the room.

"Come on, Jess, hurry and get settled," she then said, sharply. I suppose she was taken aback. I was usually first to arrive in English.

I struggled to focus on double *Macbeth* and was glad when the bell went for break.

"I'm going to the library," Caroline announced. "Coming?"

"What for?"

"Those books Mrs F suggested. You were there, Jess. What's up? Are you sure you're not ill again?"

"No. I told you. I'm fine. Okay, I'll come."

In the library, I slumped onto a chair and dropped my bag beside it. I studied my fingernails. My cuticles were a mess; I must have been picking my fingers unconsciously.

Caroline came over and placed a pile of books in between us.

"You're keen," I said, counting them. "Six. Any books left for anyone else?"

"They're for both of us," she said and sighed. "Not that you should get your hands on them, seeing as I'm doing all the work here."

"Thanks," I muttered, grabbing the top book and flicking through it, not seeing any words, my head full of how to talk about yesterday.

Caroline selected a book from the middle of the pile.

"I think this one's the…"

"I need to tell you something," I blurted. "It's about her…"

"Who, Miss Botham?" Caroline asked, looking over her shoulder in the direction of our stereotypical library teacher, who, sitting at her desk at the far end of the room, was currently scowling over the top of her glasses at some document. We were never sure if her standard uniform of tweed skirt and waistcoat and her string of pearls was meant to be ironic or if she dressed like that all the time.

"No. Not her, silly. The girl. At Mulberry Hall."

"What girl? Oh no, you're not still on about that, are you?" Caroline was grimacing as if she'd been made to eat curried strawberries or something.

"Yeah," I said weakly. "I saw her." Caroline was my best friend. I wanted to share this momentous event with her but I was beginning to think I shouldn't have bothered.

"Jess, what's wrong with you? You are so obsessed." She snapped her book shut and glared at me. My insides flipped. It was as if she'd changed from friend to fiend in an instant. Her eyes scared me.

"I shouldn't have told you," I said, my voice full of regret, my eyes filling up.

"So, when was this? And what happened?" Her tone was loaded with sarcasm. "Did she appear and play hoop and stick with you in the street? Right down Stonegate? Is she your new best mate now?"

"Aw, Caroline, there's no need to be like that."

"D'you know what, Jess? I think you're stupid. My mum told you not to get involved. She says you shouldn't be meddling in things like this. You don't know what might happen."

"But I keep seeing her. And I've seen other things too. I want to tell you but if you're going to be like this I won't talk to you."

Caroline suddenly flounced out of her seat and swept the pile of books off the table into her arms.

"I'm putting these away," she said. "I think you're just looking for trouble. Either that, or it's just your way of trying to get attention."

I felt my insides hurtle to my feet as I watched Caroline moodily grab her bag, drop two books and march towards the nearest shelf. She plonked the books there, hitched her bag up onto her shoulder and turned back to me.

"Don't tell me any more about your stupid ghost, Jess. If you can't talk sense, keep away from me."

I gawped in shock as my lifelong friend abandoned me when I needed her most. Her hasty strut warned me not to follow her, though I was out of my seat now. She had almost reached the library door when she turned back and tiptoe-ran towards me, halting abruptly.

"And don't talk to my mum about this," she hissed, leaning her face towards me. "You'll get her in trouble."

So that was it. My greatest friend had just turned her back on me for the first time ever. We'd bickered before, like all friends do, but neither of us had ever refused our friendship to the other. I slumped back down on my chair and gazed, unseeingly, at the books Caroline had dropped, angry tears spilling down my cheeks and plopping on the table.

I felt so alone. I'd been cross with Aunt Ruby this morning and now, Caroline hated me. I wished there was someone else I could talk to and I yearned for the big sister I'd had for such a short time. Maybe I should forget this whole crazy, weird stuff, get on with my life and go and ask my friend to forgive me for being a pain. Yet, even as I thought it, I knew I couldn't. It felt like part of me. It would be like leaving an arm behind in the library when I went back to class. I was inexplicably linked with this little girl, Adeline, and I had to find out why.

As I dried my tears, and sucked in a slow, steadying breath, I heard soft footsteps approaching. I looked up and Mrs Fortiver was standing at the end of my table, scowling at me, yet it must've been obvious I'd been crying because her face immediately softened and she asked if I was all right.

"I'm fine thank you, Miss," I replied. "In fact, I'm just going."

I grabbed my bag.

"Jessifer, if there's anything you want to discuss, you can come to me any time. Be assured of that. You know where to find me." She gave me a warm smile and I had to almost run to stop myself from blubbering again. People shouldn't be kind to you when you're already upset.

14

DISTURBANCE

I KNEW CAROLINE WOULDN'T BE WAITING FOR ME
at the end of school and it didn't matter anyway
because I wasn't going to walk with someone who
wouldn't listen or try to understand me. Okay, I got that
she felt silly. She'd insisted the little ghost of Mulberry
Hall was just legend, after all. Now, her own mum had told
her, in so many words, that that wasn't the case. She also
seemed to think Ali might get into trouble over it, though
how, I had no idea. I remembered Ali being a bit hush-
hush in the café on Saturday, though, when she'd said: "We
feel things sometimes..." and "... there are noises..." On
top of that, Caroline was bossy. She was used to people
doing what *she* wanted and, here was I, refusing to comply.
No wonder she's annoyed with me, I thought. Nevertheless,
it bothered me seeing her, Rachel and Lou chatting and
laughing at the school gate. I didn't want them to see me,
so I snaked into the midst of a crowd of kids and, once I'd
crossed the road, I broke into a run. I decided not to go

straight home; I didn't feel like talking to anyone, not even Aunt Ruby. Instead, I'd go and have a coffee and something sweet and sickly to cheer myself up.

Warner's Café was quiet. It wasn't where I'd normally go because it was an old folks' café, but that was better than going somewhere full of school kids. I wanted to be anonymous. I marched straight to the counter and ordered a cappuccino and a big fat Danish pastry covered with maple syrup and nuts.

As I began tucking in to my Danish, I checked my phone. The only message was a reminder from drama group about a change of venue for next week. I pushed thoughts of Caroline out of my head. They were jostling for position with Adeline's voice asking me to be her friend and come to the party and musings over how I'd even got into the year 1863 in the first place, as well as my concerns over Joopy and why he was so unsettled these days.

My head began to pound and I thought I should get home. Then Aunt Ruby messaged me asking where I was. I knew she didn't need to worry but we'd always had a rule about keeping each other in touch over changed plans or delays.

At 4.50, the burly café owner began gathering the battered aluminium sugar pots from the table and wiping down the surfaces with a disgusting grey cloth.

"Four fifty-five," he announced as he reached my table. "Five minutes to closing. Finish up, please." The other customers had drifted off already. I shrugged my bag onto my shoulder and sidled out of the seat. As I stepped outside, my phone pinged again. It was Auntie:

Where are you Jess? Not at Caroline's apparently. AR

I remembered I needed to apologise to her for being grumpy this morning and now would have to double-apologise for not telling her where I'd been. She'd be worried and probably a bit cross. I began dialling her number but as I did, my phone ran out of charge. Oh well, I'd be home soon. I began striding through town to take the shortcut through Lock Woods.

When I walked in, Aunt Ruby was pacing the floor.

"Jess, where have you been?" she said, her hand on her forehead. "I was WORRIED!"

"Just town, that's all. Yeah, Aunt Ruby, I'm sorry I didn't tell you. Oh, and I'm sorry about this morn—"

"Jess, for goodness sake! You must communicate with me. You have a phone; you could have called! You are exasperating."

Oh my God! I thought. *She's upset.* I tried to lighten the situation by being jovial.

"Hey look. I'm here *now*." I did a little dance and a twirl even though my head was thumping like a jackhammer. She brushed past me, to the lounge.

I followed her, talking, desperately trying to recover some good feeling.

Aunt Ruby half sat down, then thrust herself up again, both hands now at her temples.

"Well, look… I don't know what you're getting involved with but… just leave it alone. Ali said you've been looking for that little ghost. Jessifer, listen to me, you don't know what manner of evil you are dealing with."

I stood there with my mouth open. Aunt Ruby had told me, quite clearly, she didn't believe in ghosts. Why would she try and warn me off if she didn't believe in it?

"Just use your phone in future, Jessifer. *Please.*"

"I will and I'm sorry, okay? It ran out of charge."

"Oh, I'm sorry too, Jess. I was worried about you. You weren't well the other day and I suppose, with the cold weather and the dark nights... I just worry about you, that's all."

"Thank goodness somebody does," I said in a grumbly way.

"Oh dear... what's happened?"

I told her about the falling-out with Caroline but not about the hauntings. If she was worried now, how much more would she be if I told her I'd spent part of yesterday in 1863? Never mind the fact that little Adeline had become a regular feature in my weird, disturbing life.

"I'm sure it'll blow over, darling," she said. "You and Caroline have been friends far too long to let a little thing like that spoil your relationship."

"Hope you're right," I said. "She's the closest thing I have to a sister and I don't exactly have much family around me, do I?" Auntie tilted her head and frowned her disapproval at me. She didn't like me complaining. "Or you, for that matter. Neither of us does." She kept frowning. "Well, it's true, isn't it?"

"We have enough, Jess."

But I wasn't sure I agreed with her. I wanted to try and feel okay but my insides felt all tangled and knotted and a scream of frustration was building inside me. Instead, I walked calmly to my room although I couldn't help giving the door a bit of a slam. Why was I so wound up? Aunt Ruby was kind and thoughtful and charitable. What was happening to me? It annoyed me that, despite feeling sad and lonely, I wanted to be on my own and, despite an impossible longing to change the past and have a shared future with my sister, I needed space to think and just be me.

I thrust my coat on the hook on my door and slumped on my bed but soon got up again and crossed over to Joopy's crate. He was squeaking and thrashing. I lifted him out and cuddled him to my cheek where he sniffed and nuzzled. I think we calmed each other down. Nevertheless, I needed to walk.

"Come on, Joops," I said and popped him in my bag. I wrapped my thick scarf round my neck and shrugged on my coat. I left the flat quietly.

*

I was back in Lock Woods, on autopilot, so many thoughts buzzing round my head. I remembered Adeline's voice, singing in a clear, high-pitched tone. Then I walked into town. The last shopkeepers were closing up when I reached Stonegate. Perhaps Caroline was right. I was becoming obsessed with the little ghost. Or maybe *possessed* was nearer the truth.

I looked down at my bag and saw Jupiter's wee nose poking out. I stroked his head and felt him trembling again.

"At least you're my friend, Joops," I said, shivering. "I can always rely on your loyalty, can't I?" But he continued to quiver. I was beginning to think I should've left him at home when I heard her singing:

"… say the bells of Shoreditch…" I looked up and saw that Stonegate had changed.

I was back in the nineteenth century. How was this happening? The dark shape of a horse-drawn carriage was disappearing around the corner at the end of the road. I glanced at Mulberry Hall and saw little Adeline standing there at the front door, beckoning me. She looked so small from a distance. I thought of Judith, curled up with my mum at home that awful day, blissfully ignorant of what would happen. I wasn't sure what to do.

Well, I'm here now. I may as well go over, I thought. But the worry of not being able to get back gnawed at my mind. What if I got stuck here for ever?

"Hello, Jennifer," said Adeline.

"Hello," I said. "Erm, it's Jessifer, actually."

"That is a peculiar name," she replied, "but I think it's pretty." She smiled and the lovely innocence of her perfect little face made me feel kind of peaceful.

"Come on," she said, clearly never doubting I would obey. I followed her inside like a great mute puppy but I was relieved to get out of the cold.

She led me into the vast kitchen and then skipped off, leaving me standing there, unsure. Two women were working with pastry at a big table. They were chattering non-stop. I craned my head to see past the one nearest me. I felt my eyes grow wide when I spotted some huge brass weighing scales on the table. They were just like the ones in the display cabinet in the twenty-first century version of this building.

"Erm, is it okay if I'm here?" I asked. Then, I saw that cat again, the ginger one Adeline called Clementine. Joopy began scrambling about inside my bag, so I held one hand against him, through the fabric, which calmed him a little. One of the women spotted the ginger cat and began chasing it with the rolling pin but it stopped at my feet and arched its bristling back with a ferocious meow before scuttling away from the cook's wrath.

"Out of my kitchen," she scolded, and it scarpered into the hall, its collar bells jingling. I didn't know where Adeline had gone or where to put my hands or how to behave so I twiddled the toggles on my coat.

The women ignored me. Perhaps I should go over. Maybe I should take off my coat.

I stepped forwards but they didn't seem to see me. I wondered if they could.

"Hello?" I said in a big voice. No response. *That clears that up then*, I thought.

I began to tune in to their conversation and looked around for somewhere to sit.

There was a stool tucked into a recess behind the door. As I sat upon it, it shifted slightly and the wooden legs screeched against the slate floor, but the women were so engaged with their chatter they never even noticed. They genuinely did not know I was here.

"They're at it just now," said the older, plumper lady. "Seems to be t' daily ritual. Arguin' and bickerin'."

"'Ope they make up before t' party," said the younger, who looked about my age but had round rosy cheeks and strong-looking arms.

"I feel sorry for Mistress Laythorpe. She shouldn't put up wi' it. 'E spends all 'is time in that medical room or in that laboratory. When 'es not at the 'ospital, anyway. An' I don't like 'ow 'e keeps dosin' up them patients that come 'ere. They come in hurt or wounded an' they allus go out sleepin'. That young fella Tom that came in t' other week… did you 'ear 'e died? Family aren't 'appy about it."

"He didn't ask 'em to pay anything though."

"Doesn't that tell you summat, Betsy? Prob'ly knows 'e caused 'is death with them awful drugs. I bet 'e gave 'im too much o' that stuff. Fella left 'ere lookin' still as a corpse."

I thought of the silver syringe I'd seen on Dr Laythorpe's desk and his entries in the log book. *They're talking about the morphine*, I thought. I wondered if they knew he was taking it himself.

I heard raised voices erupt from somewhere beyond the kitchen. It sounded like an argument in well-spoken English. The row the cook had referred to, still underway? I snuck into the corridor that I thought led both to the basement and the side door out into Mulberry Lane. When I saw the stone staircase leading down, I knew where I was and carried on, right and right again. I was now in the corridor between the medical room and the laboratory.

"You must stop, Jonathon," came a woman's voice. It was clear the argument was taking place in the examination room. "You will lose your position if you continue dosing yourself with this poison."

"I know what I am doing, Jocelyn," came the doctor's voice. "This is essential for my research. I am learning so much about administering the substance by syringe, directly into the venous system. This could lead to great things for us."

"Yet, I fear what you are doing is harming you, and perhaps others too. I worry that what you do may be misinterpreted."

"Jocelyn, I must say, I object to your words. You must remember who you are. That is: my wife. I can achieve great things with this research. For the treatment of neuralgia, for patients recovering from surgery, for so many applications. It will bring me the success I've been striving for. My name will be elevated, at last, in medical circles. It will bring me the respect I deserve and all the financial security we could ever need. So, you must support my work. Rather, you strut off to your women's clubs speaking as only a man ought. Meanwhile, our child expects you to read to her and pander to her incessantly."

I had to strain my ears as Jocelyn lowered her voice.

"I think you must decide what you wish of me, my husband. The work I do is making a difference to the poor of our city. My behaviour is only courteous and gentle. I encourage and educate and have been complimented by many regarding the content and effect of my talks. As regards our precious daughter… well, what do you wish of me? You wish me to stay at home and forget my philanthropic work, yet I am not allowed to raise my daughter myself?"

"We have staff for that. What do I pay them for? Why have a nanny or a governess if you are to do it all yourself?"

"Because Adeline needs my love and comfort, dearest husband. She is a tiny girl with so much love and wonder in her heart. She deserves the warmth of a mother's love."

"She can have your love in so many other ways. We provide a roof for her, an education, books, toys, food and clothing. The child knows what she has. If you do not support my endeavours and if you continue this ridiculous obsession with the poor, I will have to take action."

"I perceive a degree of threat in your words, Jonathon. You should remind yourself why we live in such a beautiful home. My father bestowed such a gift in good faith. Several years ago, you would not have spoken in this way. You are losing your compassion in your quest for medical eminence. It is not my husband speaking, rather the morphine."

I heard the door open and close, followed by Dr Laythorpe's voice, shouting:

"Jocelyn! Jocelyn! I command you to come back into this room and give me your word of support. I tell you now, woman, you will obey your husband! JOCELYN!"

A door slammed and the sound of smashing glass followed. I had an impulse to enter the room and have a look.

I pressed the door handle, cautiously, though I was sure the room was now empty. I stepped inside, leaving the door wide open for a quick getaway. I heard the doctor still shouting after his wife but her only response, which came from a distance away, was:

"And leave Clementine alone. I know what you're doing."

I wondered what that meant as I examined the mess on the floor. A brown bottle lay in smithereens in a pool of golden liquid. A label clung to a large fragment of glass. It read *Dalby's Carminative*. I pulled my phone out of my bag and took a picture of the broken bottle in its sticky puddle. I looked at the desk and saw Dr Laythorpe's book open on the table. A second book sat beside it. I hurriedly snapped an image of the open book. That way, I could read it later.

Next, I scanned the cover of the closed one. It was bound in linen fabric with a label attached dead centre on the front cover. I read:

Morphine anaesthesia for the treatment of neuralgia, and for analgesic treatment post-surgical intervention and post-trauma. October 1862–

The end date was not filled in. I opened the book and flicked to the latest entry. I was rewarded with a double-page spread of notes. Without taking in the detail, I framed the pages with my screen. My hands were shaking and I hoped the image wouldn't be spoiled. I had only just pressed the camera icon on my phone when I heard the squeak of the door handle being pressed. I sent prayers of thanks heavenwards that no one had oiled it recently. I spun and ran for the door, not even checking if I'd been seen. I hurtled along the corridor and made my exit onto Mulberry Lane. I ran the fifteen or so paces it took to reach Stonegate and came to an abrupt stop as an undoubtedly twenty-first century transit van pulled up outside the shop on the corner. I smiled bemusedly as I caught my breath.

"Back in 2019," I whispered, perplexed by the crazy yo-yoing between time periods.

Before I stepped onto Stonegate, I looked over my shoulder at the side door into Mulberry Hall. I gasped, because there, under the dim light from a lamp above the doorway, was the shadowy shape of Dr Laythorpe. He was pointing at me and, though it was difficult to see his exact expression in the dark, I knew his piercing eyes held me in his grip. After a few seconds, he turned, re-entered his home and shut the door. I looked down at my phone clutched in my hand. He must have seen it and though it would look strange to him, he would wonder, wouldn't he? Had he seen me take the last photograph?

My heart hammered all the way home.

15

Books and Pictures

My relief at 'getting out' of 1863 was enough to give me a feeling of accomplishment as I walked home. I was beginning to resign myself to my freaky life and once I had quietly hung up my coat, set Joopy back in his crate and entered the lounge, I realised Aunt Ruby hadn't even known I'd been out.

The fresh air had helped lift my spirits. I decided to text Rachel:

You okay? Didn't see you much today.

Then Lou:

Hey How are you? See you tomorrow.

Neither of them texted back. *What's going on?* I thought. Has Caroline turned *them* against me too?

I called Rachel's number.

She took ages to answer so I was relieved when I heard her voice.

"Hi," I said. "I thought you weren't going to talk to me."

"Don't be daft, Jess," she said. "I was doing trumpet practice. Are you okay?"

"Yeah, just a bit bruised from Caroline's attack this morning. I can't believe she won't hear me out."

"If it's any consolation, Jess, she's not feeling great either. She's quite annoyed about it."

"Well, maybe she should've listened to me and it wouldn't be like this. I mean, it's not as if I asked to be haunted."

"She's got a point though, Jess. You know, you are a bit obsessed. I'm not sure it's normal. I get that you're going through something weird, right, but perhaps you should keep it to yourself. Oh, I don't know what to think. You know we all care about you, Jess."

"Great. Now you as well. I thought friends were supposed to help each other in times of need. Does Lou think the same?"

"Well, I think she's just totally on a grind right now. Her mum's being completely bizarre."

"Okay. I'll see you then. I know who my friends are. Or aren't, rather. Bye, Rachel," I said with finality.

I felt as if there was a stretched rubber band inside my chest and it was about to snap. I'd seen so many girls at school constantly yo-yoing between friendships while the four of us were always constant. Now, they'd rejected me, yet it felt as if it was meant to be all my fault. Three against one. And all because of a tiny girl from the nineteenth century. I ate tea at the table with Aunt Ruby but we barely spoke and I went to bed under a cloud of gloom.

*

The next day at school was the worst day of my life. I knew I was giving the girls the cold shoulder but they weren't exactly making any effort either. I didn't speak to them all day.

At break, I remembered what Mrs Fortiver had said to me yesterday. I stood at her room and peered in the window. My knuckles were poised at the glass, about to knock.

No, I thought, *I can't tell her I've been poking about in Mulberry Hall in 1863. Or, that I've been talking to ghosts. It's not exactly the standard problem you go to your teacher with, is it?*

I scuttled down the corridor and pretended not to hear her calling after me.

*

"Jess, I'm so sorry we fell out," Auntie said at teatime. "I do hate it. It so rarely happens. Anyway, I love you. That's all that matters."

"I'm sorry too, Auntie," I said, frowning.

I climbed into bed and was about to switch off my light when I remembered I'd taken pictures of Dr Laythorpe's record books. I leaned out of bed to reach my phone. What would I find? I'd forgotten to look before. After talking to Rachel last night I'd been in a fury over the girls' campaign against me.

I found the photos and zoomed in on one. It was the book titled *Morphine Anaesthesia for the Treatment of Neuralgia, et cetera.*

I read the latest entry and was stunned to see in writing what I'd heard discussed in the kitchen of Mulberry Hall:

7.50 post meridian. Patient, Thomas Metcalfe, pronounced deceased by myself, Dr Jonathon Laythorpe.

I continued reading the entries in reverse order up the page:

7.30 post meridian. Patient has calmed to a sleeping state although the rate of respiration appears markedly reduced.

7.07 post meridian. Patient remains in considerable distress. Third dose of morphine analgesia given directly into the venous system using new metal syringe and silver needle apparatus.

Then I read again in chronological order.

I wondered about the patient. I remembered seeing the young bleeding man in the street the first time I'd gone to Mulberry Hall at night. Perhaps he was the Thomas Metcalfe referred to here. Just as the cook said, it looked like he'd been given too much of the powerful drug. In fact, so much, it had killed him. It was as if the doctor had simply used him for an experiment. The dispassionate, clinical recording of his death turned me cold.

I looked at the photograph of the other record book.

I was stunned to read from the top of the page:

Overanxious spouse? Fails to understand my use of the drug. Consider treating Jocelyn. A low dose will calm her. Can be discreetly administered at night.

He wanted to drug his wife!

The last few entries showed Dr Laythorpe's schedule of self-injection. The ultimate entry read:

24 January 1863. Seven o'clock in the evening. Morphine opiate, tolerating stronger concentrations, therefore dose increased further. Some disturbance to brachial veins. May need to use...

The handwriting trailed as if he had fallen asleep while writing.

I rubbed my tired eyes and switched off my light. I soon fell asleep and dreamt about Laythorpe holding his wife down to inject her and then seeing me and chasing me away.

It was a relief to wake in the morning and to be back in Aunt Ruby's favour. We talked about normal stuff over our usual hurried breakfast.

*

My phone's vibration startled me. It was eleven fifteen on Wednesday morning and I was in the York Central Library browsing medical history. Of course, I should've been at school really. I'd just selected a book: *Victorian Pharmacology and Medical Practice*. I glanced at my screen. It was school:

Unauthorised absence registered. Please call school office immediately. Parents/guardians will be notified.

Oh-oh. I hadn't thought about being found out. It was the first time I'd ever skipped school. I'd dressed in my uniform but, halfway to school, I knew getting to the library to find out more about Laythorpe was a bigger priority for me. Anyway, I was educating myself, wasn't I? I'd call Aunt Ruby and hope the school hadn't got to her yet. She'd left before me this morning as she was getting the early train to Bridlington to see her elderly aunt.

I replaced the book and left it so that its spine stuck out beyond the others on the shelf, so I could find it easily when I came back in. I hurried outside and glanced about. On the left of the main door, a worker hunched over a cigarette lighter, cupping a feeble flame with one hand, so I went to the right where the library was separated from the Museum Gardens by a strip of grass. It was cold, damp and pungent here, but this shouldn't take long.

I tapped Aunt Ruby's number and felt a drenching sadness consume me when she replied and I lied again, so, so easily. I didn't like the turn my life was taking. Yet I felt I had no other choice. My friends were against me, I'd been lured into a freaky scenario of which I could make little sense, I was deceiving the person I most loved and now I was a truant.

"Jessifer, darling? Is everything okay?"

"It's fine, Auntie." Swallowing hard, I adopted a chirpy tone. "There's been an admin error at school. We've all been asked to alert our parents. The office has mistakenly sent an absence notification to *all* instead of just to the absentees. Crazy isn't it? Anyway, just letting you know not to worry. I'm at school and everything's good."

"Oh, thank you, darling. I haven't had a text anyway."

"Well, you will do. So, that's it. Classes have stopped until everyone's managed to tell their parents about the mistake." I was relieved when the real me dropped in and said: "Did you arrive at Aunt Dora's okay? How is she?"

"Yes. The train was fine and Aunt Dora's very well, aren't you, Auntie?" she continued in a louder voice.

I heard the low timbre of Aunt Dora's husky ninety-six-year-old voice respond vaguely.

"Well, I'd better let you get back to lessons then. See you later, darling Jess."

It surprised me how, even crippled with guilt, my brain focussed on the pockmarks and patterns of the frail, rust-coloured wall. I breathed out slowly and placed my fingertip into a small hollow in the brick and felt its graininess scratch my skin.

She swallowed it, I thought, feeling relief and remorse, strangely mixed. I hated my ruthlessness. I might have preferred it if Aunt Ruby had told me I was a nasty, lying reprobate.

I went back inside and found the book again. It had a big section about addiction to opioids like morphine which were mostly given as pills, gums or liquids, by mouth, and it referred to the curse of 'cocainism'. However, awareness of the addictive properties was limited until the later 1800s. It described the prevalence of 'opium dens' where the drug was smoked. Opium was cheaper than drinking alcohol; it wasn't taxed because it was classed as a necessary drug rather than a luxury drink. Laudanum was a mixture made from the drug and it was found in most Victorian households for treating all sorts of ailments and even for settling fractious babies.

One preparation was called 'Dalby's Carminative'. I turned the page and saw a picture of a bottle of the stuff. It was such a strange name it stuck out in my mind.

I was sure that was what had smashed on the floor in Laythorpe's room when the door had slammed on Monday. I checked the photograph on my phone and gasped. The label on the smashed bottle was identical to the one in the book.

The chapter went on to describe the use of injected morphine during the American Civil War and, though it wasn't really relevant to me, I realised Adeline would have been three or four at the start of the war, so the time periods matched.

There was the briefest mention of Jonathon Laythorpe. The book said he worked at York City Hospital and claimed he was a leading figure in research into injecting morphine but suggested his methods may not have been completely legitimate.

I groaned. It didn't say why! No more mention of him. It just said, even after the hypodermic syringe was invented by Dr Alexander Wood in 1853, syringes weren't widely available and many doctors were suspicious of using them.

I requested a photocopy of the information. I was building up a case of evidence. Everything about Jonathon Laythorpe made my flesh crawl.

At home, I changed out of my uniform and spent the afternoon poring over Aunt Ruby's book, the photocopies from the library and the photographs on my phone. I scanned the information from the library and emailed it to myself for backup. I still hadn't found any useful new information about Laythorpe other than a micro-hint that his practices were dodgy.

It was a while before I noticed the message light flashing on the landline phone. I knew immediately I would have to delete the message.

"Good morning, Miss Stevens. This is the school office at York High. We are obliged to inform you that your niece, Jessifer Jordan, has been registered as absent from school today. Please contact us at your earliest convenience so that we can ascertain the nature of the absence. Thank you."

I wouldn't let myself think twice. I hit 'delete' immediately and was relieved I'd noticed it. Aunt Ruby didn't need to know about it.

*

It was a wonder my phone didn't spontaneously combust during the afternoon. Half the people I knew, Caroline excepted, seemed to have either texted, messaged me or called. I ignored them all. I knew what the general idea was: *Why aren't you at school today?* I eventually switched my phone to silent so I could think uninterrupted.

At three o'clock, I realised Aunt Ruby would be home within the next hour. I went to put the kettle on and, out of habit, picked up my phone and glanced at the list of missed calls and my inbox. One text each from Rachel and Lou, who had both also called, and various other messages, online, from people at drama who also went to my school. (I supposed the disadvantage of being one of the 'always good' girls was that if you did something like this, it was utterly notable.) The text that stood out most, though, was from Mrs Fortiver. I wondered what she wanted and found my thumbs working frantically to the soundtrack of the bubbling kettle. I scrolled down her text and fat, hot tears inexplicably rolled down my cheeks.

Hi Jessifer, hope you don't mind me texting. Am a little worried about you. I know you have had some upsets recently and wish to help. Please come and talk to me in dept. You are always welcome at my door. Anything you say will be in confidence. Mrs C.F.

I wiped my tears away with the back of my hand and made myself a mug of tea, gulping back sobs and nearly scalding myself.

I reached my room, planted my tea on my bedside table and fell, face down, onto my bed.

"Why is this happening to me?" I wailed into my pillow, crying like a five-year-old. My heart was breaking. I was being pulled in one direction by some strange, inexplicable force of history and in another by my friends' distrust, while at the same time, the 'honest' me was trying to keep Aunt Ruby on side and get my schoolwork done.

The only way that felt right and instinctive was the pull from Mulberry Hall and young Adeline. Yet it scared me. Caroline's mum was right. I didn't know what I was getting into and my wailing turned from tears of sorrow, pity and frustration to a cry of real fear.

16

MURDERER OR
MIRACLE WORKER

I KNEW I COULDN'T BE IN WHEN AUNT RUBY GOT home. She'd be alarmed to see me looking like I did so I decided to go back to Lock Woods. It was nearly dark and if I saw anyone I knew, they wouldn't notice my puffy eyes in the gloom.

My mind seemed clearer after my monster bout of crying. The frustration had floated away with my tears but I didn't know what to do next. I needed to know more about Dr Laythorpe. I was convinced he was a fraud. Right away, I knew I was going to skip school again tomorrow. Also, I decided I'd contact Mrs Fortiver. She'd try and persuade me to go to school but I had to talk to someone and there was no one else I felt I could open up to, though, God knows what I'd tell her.

I made my way towards a small clearing in the woods and plonked down on an old graffiti-scored bench. I wore tights, two pairs of leggings, two thick jumpers, my long vintage velvet coat handed down from Aunt Ruby and the thickest scarf I could find. Still, I shivered. I huddled up, my knees squeezed inside my coat. Jupiter slept beside me in my bag.

First, I texted Aunt Ruby and told her I was going to the local library after school and would be a bit later home. I could go in and out briefly and then I wouldn't be lying which would make me feel better. Then I replied to Mrs Fortiver's text. It was four o'clock and school would've finished.

I checked what I'd typed.

Dear Mrs F, thanks for concern Don't know what to do Would like advice please? Can we talk? Not coming school tomorrow but wondered if can meet. Jess J.

It sounded stupid but I didn't know what else to say, so I hit send.

I sat and picked at my nails for a bit and then read through Rachel and Lou's texts from earlier.

I replied:

Don't chastise me Skipped school today Stuff to think about Am ok Won't be in tomorrow but don't tell anyone Aunt R doesn't know Talk soon.

I hit send then checked on Jupiter. I was about to lift him out when my phone pinged back a reply from Mrs Fortiver:

Hello Jessifer. Glad you got in touch. Can't condone absence if unauthorised and urge you speak to your aunt.

But will be very pleased to meet you. How about 1.15 at Conroy's Café tomorrow? Handy for school but not too close if you don't want to come in. CF.

The crying began again. I was relieved at her reasonableness. Her status as my favourite teacher hadn't shifted. I closed my eyes, banishing the tears and imagined sitting across the table at Conroy's tomorrow, looking into her kind face, being soothed by her calm tones. How would I tell her though? *What* would I tell her? What if she thinks I'm lying? *Oh, God, maybe I've done the wrong thing,* I thought. I stood up and began pacing back and forth.

"Oh, what shall I do?" I said. Maybe I should text back and tell her I can't meet her, after all.

I lifted Joopy out of my bag and kissed him deep into his soft, grey fur. His smell and warmth reassured me. I gave him a nugget of granola then slid him back in and began walking through the woods to the small library. As I walked, my resolve firmed up. I trusted Mrs F.

I'll go and meet her, I thought. I'll see how it feels tomorrow and decide what to tell her then.

Our local library was housed in a strangely modern building, nestled right in the middle of a cluster of old stone villas. Once inside, I decided I may as well ask about their history section and if they had anything on medicine in the Victorian age. The librarian said they didn't but recommended I asked at the Central Library where, she said, they happen to have a very good range of books on local history! I felt disproportionately happy I hadn't lied to Auntie again.

In fact, Aunt Ruby was only just home herself when I walked in. I saw her take her coat off as I shut the door.

"Hi, Auntie," I called breezily. "Frozen, need to get changed. Talk to you in a sec." I couldn't let her see I wasn't in uniform. I hurriedly flopped a somnolent Jupiter into his crate, checked my face in the mirror, then scuffled about a bit, opening and closing my wardrobe with a bang. I performed an exaggerated, shivery 'brrr' and emerged back into the hall rubbing my arms. Not only was drama training great fun but there were times when it had the bonus of real-life application.

"Cold, isn't it?" I said.

"Very nippy," Aunt Ruby replied. "The train's heater was broken so the journey back from Bridlington was not good. I must say it's wonderful to be home to a warm house. Egg and chips for tea, Jess?"

"Ooh, yeah, please. But first I'm going to make you a lovely cuppa." I danced over to my aunt, gave her a peck on the cheek and said: "Now, go and sit down, you need to get warmed up with a blanky, you're freezing." If only she knew.

*

Later, I talked to Rachel and Lou online and both told me not to worry about skiving for one day. Lou confided that she'd done it several times out of necessity (none of us had known this! We'd thought she'd been ill), they both hoped I sorted things out soon and told me to call Caroline. I protested that she wouldn't want to hear from me.

*

The next day was dark and frosty. I was up and dressed for school early though all I wanted to do was crawl back into bed. I gave Aunt Ruby the impression everything was normal. I had some warm clothes stuffed in my school bag and I planned to change in the toilets of the twenty-four-hour supermarket, which was wedged between the housing estate near school and the aptly nicknamed 'Mud Moor' which was a big marshland on the edge of our small city. I wanted to have a look around the City Hospital before meeting Mrs Fortiver at one fifteen. The book I'd read yesterday mentioned Laythorpe had worked there and I knew the hospital had two distinct parts: the old red-brick buildings and the new, modern block. If I went to the old bit, I might get a feel for what it was like back then in the 1860s.

I naively thought I would just have a wander round, needing to understand Laythorpe's modus operandi. Being in his space might help to give me a fuller picture. I couldn't comprehend why I felt so drawn into his world.

I didn't feel conspicuous arriving in York City Hospital that morning, at least not at first. The hospital corridors were busy with porters pushing wheelchairs and trolleys; nurses wearing candy-striped uniforms bustling along; frowning patients asking the way; white-coated people, some hurrying, others chatting in corridors; suited men and women carrying thick wads of buff-coloured files, and even teenagers like me, wearing headphones and looking sheepish. Nearly everybody walked with a purpose and there was an entire cross-section of society here. I'd only been twice that I could remember, with Aunt Ruby. The antiseptic smell jabbed at my nostrils and the ultra-shiny floors were almost intimidating, transmitting a subliminal message that this was a place in which you complied with the rules. And yet, I didn't feel out of place. For all anyone knew, I was here to have an X-ray and see a doctor about some mysterious aspect of my anatomy. I smiled. Once again, my drama skills could prove useful.

I didn't know where I was going but I turned a corner and headed for a sign suspended by chains, about thirty centimetres from the ceiling: 'Anaesthesiology'.

I was confused when I heard it. The song; now the line: "When will that be-e…"

I'd begun to link hearing the song with an expectation of seeing Adeline, but here I was at the hospital, nowhere near Mulberry Hall.

The overhead lights flickered and went out. Momentarily, I couldn't see. When they returned to normal, steady again, everything had changed.

"Oh no," I whispered. Two nurses passed me, looking serious. They wore white linen hats, if that's what you could call the concertinaed scraps of lacy origami balancing on looping coils of hair. They had heavy white aprons over crisp blue dresses. There could be no doubt I was back in 1863. Now I did feel out of place. I continued walking but turned and cast a glance over my shoulder to watch the nurses. They took the right-hand corridor at the junction and were out of sight.

I hurried on and reached a crossroads in the corridor. A sign indicated 'Crossley Recovery Ward' on my right. Trying to peer through the frosted glass of the ward doors, I wondered what would happen if I was caught, but pressed on anyway. I had to investigate.

Ghostly-looking beds, draped in white, were lined against opposite walls for the entire length of a long room, which looked nothing like the hospital wards of today. A nurse disappeared from a bedside through an archway in the wall. Many of the beds were occupied but the patients seemed, mostly, to be sleeping. I could hear a conversation taking place in hushed tones from an open doorway and saw a cramped, narrow office, dominated by a large solid-looking desk of dark wood. The desk was covered in piles of papers and books; an inkwell and fountain pen showed this was someone's regular workspace. Two people were sitting face to face. I pressed myself against the wall outside to listen.

A female voice suggested its owner had authority over the ward.

"I will be obliged to document these adverse incidents. They are becoming too frequent." There was a pause. "Even though he has requested I do not."

"I understand your concerns," came a male voice.

"This is my domain and I have responsibility for those who convalesce here under my care."

"Well, I have raised it with the Medical Board and will speak to Dr Laythorpe at my earliest opportunity."

"In the last month, there have been seven deaths following his new regime of injectable opiates. Young Thomas Metcalfe should not have succumbed. He was young and healthy apart from the injury. The wound alone could not have killed him and the infection was minor. The families are calling Laythorpe a murderer. Something must be done."

The male didn't respond at first. I heard a sound like the drumming of fingers on the desk.

"I believe I may persuade him to delay his research for now. If I succeed, would you consider keeping silent on this? Some of his work has been extraordinary."

"I will think upon it. But you must persuade him to abandon the morphia altogether. I trust you know he uses it for himself? I fear his dependence on the poison may already be too deep-rooted." The scrape of a chair being pushed back followed and I scuttled away, back to the main corridor, my heart pounding and a rushing in my ears almost deafening, like the roar of a wind-whipped tide in winter. Through the white noise, I distinctly heard a child's small voice, singing:

"… say the bells of Stepney…"

With my thoughts laden with that innocent little girl and her morphine addict of a father, I stumbled outside into a grey drizzle. A chilly gust of wind hosed a spray of icy particles against my cheek which, along with a screeching ambulance siren, shocked me back to the twenty-first century. I checked my watch. One o'clock. How had so much time passed? I had fifteen minutes to reach Conroy's Café on the far side of school.

*

I jumped off the number seven bus and ran along Apple Garth Lane towards Conroy's. It was one twenty-five. Would Mrs Fortiver have waited for me? Or decided I wasn't going to show?

I needn't have worried. I pushed open the squeaky, condensation-drenched door. It was like stepping into a thick fog of toffee-scented cosiness. I spotted Mrs F across the steamy room. She was sitting at a table for two and was engrossed, both in a doorstep sandwich, which looked divine, and a thick hardback book, which she held open with one elbow. A wisp of dark, wavy hair fell across her face. She looked as if she belonged there.

"Jessifer!" She beamed when she saw me and began apologising for ordering before I'd arrived. "Let me get you a sandwich. This maple-cured bacon and tomato is to die for!" The smell of the bacon was actually making my mouth water despite my nerves.

*

Ten minutes later, Mrs F was looking longingly at my sandwich as if she could eat another.

"Eat first," she said, after I had apologised a third time for being late. "Talk after. Listen, I have some free time this afternoon so there's no hurry for me to be back at school immediately."

*

She listened. It felt like a rare thing. No one else had. Caroline didn't want to know and Rachel and Lou thought this was all a bit weird and were caught between me and Caroline. Basically, they didn't get it. As for Aunt Ruby… well, I suppose she would disapprove of what I was doing and I didn't want to scare her. Too late for that though: she'd totally freaked about me being late home. She'd obviously been talking to Caroline's mum, Ali.

I began carefully. I told Mrs Fortiver how it had all started, with the moving scales and Adeline sitting on our wall, then appearing to me in our house at night. I thought I'd pick out certain details but once I got going, it all tumbled out and she was silent the whole way through. I showed her the photos of Dr Laythorpe's record books and my photocopies from the library. Occasionally, she raised her eyebrows but mostly she just nodded gravely and said things like: "Mm," and "I see."

"Poor thing; I imagine it's been hard for you," she said when I eventually finished. I took a huge gulp of coffee then gazed at her, my mouth slightly open.

"So, you actually believe me?" I said.

"Shouldn't I, Jess?"

"Well, yes, I mean, it's all absolutely true, but don't you think it's weird?" I stretched my neck towards her, my eyebrows arched as high as I could reach them.

"It is a little strange, yes, but these things do happen."

I laughed, spluttering, feeling slightly out of control.

"I'm sorry," I said, "but I suppose I didn't expect this reaction. I mean, what makes you so sure?"

She looked at me quizzically without saying anything.

"That these things happen, I mean. No one else believes me so why should you?"

"Would it surprise you terribly if I told you I've had a similar experience?"

17

CONROY'S CAFÉ

I BLEW AIR OUT OF THE CORNER OF MY MOUTH and shook my head, gazing at the wood grain of the table. Mrs F touched my hand.

"Jess, while we're not in school, why don't you call me Catherine?"

"Okay then," I said sheepishly. I knew it was her first name as I'd heard other teachers calling her it, but it did feel weird, so, to cover my embarrassment, I made a joke.

"And you can call me Jess," I said. It made her laugh and my awkwardness went.

"Well, Jess, I don't want to bore you with the detail, but I think it may help if I tell you a little. First though, how about some sticky toffee cheesecake?"

Over dessert and more coffee, she told me her story.

She had grown up in London and, when she was eight, her family had moved to an old house on the south coast. Along with her new bedroom came a new experience and one which would affect her for the rest of her life. The ghost of a teenager, a prior occupant of the house, had begun visiting her. Marie, the ghost, would sit on the end of Catherine's bed and Catherine would know she was there because she would wake up feeling frozen. At first, Catherine was frightened, but the visits became so regular that she came to accept the friendly Marie, who laid out her story night by night.

It began with a blossoming courtship between Marie and her young man, Lawrence, who was a year older. One day, Lawrence told her he must emigrate with his family to America and soon after the announcement, he disappeared from her life. Marie hadn't been able to bear the loss and jumped to her death from the nearby cliffs. Tragically, death hadn't ended her distress, and her only consolation had been the nightly visits to her old room. There, she had reminisced about the endless times she had sat before her mirror, getting ready to meet her lover on the cliff path just beyond the house. A deep bond developed between Catherine and the ghost. After recovering from the initial fright, Catherine had enjoyed Marie's nightly visits but she had been desperately sad when her father's change of job meant leaving the house for a life up north.

"I worried that Marie wouldn't be able to cope without her visits to me. I knew how much our friendship had helped her and I hoped she would find another friend among the new residents of the house."

My eyes had watered throughout her story. I dabbed them with my tissue.

"Did you ever manage to go back? Or, you know, to see Marie again?"

"I did return but I never saw her again." Her brown eyes looked sad and she lowered them and began contemplating her stretched fingers.

"It was curious but her hands were just like mine," she said, wistfully. "The same squared-off fingertips and broad palms. We would compare them; hers, white and translucent, and mine, pinkish grey in the dark, and solid." She turned her hands over and scrutinised her palms.

"The worst came when I made a visit about ten years ago to find the old house had been demolished."

"Oh, that's awful," I said. It was dawning on me that my lovely teacher had had to cope with this for most of her life. It must have been heart-breaking when she had to move away, leaving Marie's ghost behind to fend for herself. As for Marie… maybe she was still trying to find peace.

"I think she may be more settled now, though." She smiled and continued. "The old house was knocked down to clear the land for a beautiful open-air theatre. The build was completed six years ago. My husband and I go every year in August; sometimes they do a Shakespeare play and sometimes a contemporary one. The strange thing is, I feel a deep sense of peace when I'm there."

She gazed into the far distance as if she could see the place.

"I haven't seen her at all since my teens but I'm sure she's there and I imagine that perhaps she likes the place as it is now; perhaps she enjoys seeing the visitors come and go; perhaps she even sits and watches the plays…"

Her voice drifted off. The café noises became distant and, in my mind's eye, I saw a young woman in an old-fashioned dress, sitting in an open-air theatre with her hair blowing in the breeze. I hoped Marie had found peace.

"Anyway, Jess. That's a long time ago. What are we going to do about you?"

I sighed. "I don't know," I said, sadness washing over me in a huge wave.

"Firstly, we need to find out more and I know exactly who to ask. Mr Lloyd knows a lot about York's history. Would it be all right if I had a chat with him?"

"Mm, yeah, I suppose." I felt a bit panicky. So far, Mrs Fortiver was the only person who had taken me seriously and the thought of telling someone else scared me. Who might they tell? I could become a figure of fun. A walking joke.

"I don't need to tell him about your experiences," she went on. The wrangling in my stomach calmed a little. "I'll say I'm intrigued by the local surge of interest in the story." She drained her coffee mug and pushed it away from her.

"Secondly, we need to get you back in school. I want to see you there tomorrow, Jess." Mrs Fortiver's tone turned from friend to teacher. "You are my best third-year student and I can't have you wasting your school career."

"Okay," I sighed. "I'll be there."

"Who is your guidance teacher?"

Damn. I thought she might ask that.

"Mrs Mills," I answered glumly.

"Oh. Right. I see. Well I want you to go and see Mrs Mills tomorrow. In fact, better than that. I'll try and make an appointment for you today. I'll let you know. I want you to tell her that you've been having some difficulties. It's important she knows of any upset you're going through. It makes things easier in the event anything untoward happens."

"Do I have to, Mrs Fortiver?" I muttered. I couldn't call her Catherine when we were back in teacher–student mode.

"Yes, you must. Please work with me on this, Jess. I'm happy to help you but if I don't do things properly, I could end up in bother. What about your aunt? I'd like you to tell her what has been happening."

"I will, but is it okay if I leave it for a bit?"

"Well, Jess, I'll do a deal with you. If you promise to see Mrs Mills tomorrow, I won't insist that you tell your aunt until you are ready."

"Okay," I mumbled. *She's trying to help you here, Jess,* I thought, and resolved to trust her. After all, she'd been through it too. I raised my head and smiled, feeling much better for having someone to confide in.

"Right. I want you to go home. Your lunch is my treat." Her friendly tone had returned, accompanied by a warm, wide smile. "When I go back to school, I am going to register a late absence for you, to keep us right. Come and see me before you see Mrs Mills tomorrow. Oh, and one more thing, Jess, it might be best to avoid Mulberry Hall for now."

I grabbed my bag and headed away from the table.

"Thanks for listening, Mrs Fortiver," I said.

"You're welcome, Jess. We'll get things sorted out soon. Try not to worry."

*

Sadly, things weren't that simple. I felt so much better but on my way home (I was planning to go via the library again to take me up to the end of school time) I remembered my phone was switched off in the bottom of my bag. I rifled about for it but when I switched it on, my heart hit my feet.

Multiple messages from Aunt Ruby.

I glanced at the most recent:

Where are you Jessifer? Not at school. They called. Also want to know about yesterday. What is going on?

Oh no! For all Mrs Fortiver's good intentions, it was too late. I'd been so wrapped up in Laythorpe and little Adeline, I hadn't considered making a fake absence call to the school office. I was new to this truancy thing. I was going to have to face an angry Aunt Ruby again for the second time in less than two weeks.

*

When I walked in, Aunt Ruby was sitting with her head in her hands. I felt downhearted. I was making my lovely aunt sad. What kind of person was I?

I began to cry. I didn't want her sympathy but I felt overwhelmed at hurting her. She had always loved me as her own, she had given me all she could, and more, and I had disappointed her badly.

"You lied to me, Jess. Why? You must tell me what's going on because you are changing and I am frightened for you. What has happened to my adorable Jess that she needs to lie and deceive and bunk off school?"

"I'm so sorry, Auntie." The tears were pouring down my face. I was amazed there were any tears left after yesterday. "I don't know what to tell you. I'll have to try but I don't know what you're going to think. You'll probably think I'm lying all the more."

"Jessifer," she said, urgently, "darling, you have to tell me what's going on!" She stood and came over to me. She put her hand on my shoulder. "Is it drugs? No, I can't believe it is. Is it someone putting pressure on you? Ah, I know; it's those silly girls at school... Kay-tee what's-her-name and her friends. Are they bothering you?"

"No. It isn't any of those, Aunt Ruby." Kay-tee Short had had a reputation as a troublemaker since she was five, when she used to pull my hair and steal my snacks at break time. Aunt Ruby hadn't ever forgotten, although, no wonder, because the girl's misdeeds usually led her into trouble with the police these days, but the only association I had with her now was being in the same school year.

We both fell quiet.

"I'll try and explain but you won't believe me," I said.

I told her some of what had been happening. I described how I'd felt pulled into a situation I didn't understand: one that had filled my entire waking hours and my dreams. There were some parts I didn't tell, including the bit about Dr Laythorpe chasing me out of Mulberry Hall and the look of sheer hatred in his eyes.

Aunt Ruby listened. She didn't shout or tell me I must have been imagining things. Occasionally, she winced.

She seemed to grow paler as I spoke. I noticed how lined her face was and she kept looking towards the hall door.

"I'm so sorry, Auntie, I can't stop it, I must find out why Adeline keeps appearing to me and I don't know how I'm ending up in Mulberry Hall all the time and in a different era too and it's scary but there must be a way to understand it all." I was breathless at the end of my speech.

"Jess, you are frightening me. I don't want you wrapped up in this."

"It's too late for that now," I said.

"We will sleep on this tonight, Jess, but first we have to talk some more. I can't have you missing school. It isn't acceptable. As for drama, well, you can't go tonight. I forbid it. I know how much you love it but unless you show me that you are going to be responsible about school, you can't go to drama."

"I can't believe this!" I shot back, annoyed that she had listened so patiently and then hit me with this revelation. "They need me. We only have about another twelve rehearsals."

"Well, you have to see that you can't go about skipping school when you feel like it. Phone and tell them you've let them down, sweetheart. You can catch up with things next week."

"I'm not phoning." I twirled around and marched for the door into the hall. "If you won't let me go, you'll have to phone them! Audrey's going to be mad. No one else can do my part."

I flounced onto my bed.

"Oh, and we have to go in at nine thirty in the morning to meet Mrs Mills to talk about your unauthorised absences," Aunt Ruby shouted.

"Aargh," I screamed into my pillow.

I was mortified that I wasn't allowed to go to drama tonight. I'd been looking forward to it; the routines we'd been doing had been great fun and drama took my mind off things. Whenever I was worried or felt lousy, it was an escape for me. Also, Audrey, the drama teacher, was legendary. She was brilliant at her job. I loved being in her presence every Thursday night and she was so fresh and sometimes utterly bonkers. I mean, she was totally hilarious last week when she did her impression of a Shakespearian Minion. Until then I'd never seen anything so funny, but now I just felt bitter.

I was so angry I picked up my phone and threw it across the room. Then I felt mean because Jupiter began scrabbling and squeaking like a loony rat; I must have woken him up. I was shocked by the variety of emotions ruling my body these days. I felt like a touch screen on someone's device. Swipe: depressed; swipe: scared; swipe: now let's make her angry; happy that someone cares; frustrated; I wished I could do a swipe of myself and find 'just bloody normal.'

*

Whether Aunt Ruby called Audrey, I never found out. I'd cried yet more tears of frustration and ended up falling asleep, fully clothed. I woke at two in the morning and found myself under a spare duvet. Auntie must have crept in, found me asleep and covered me up. A note was stuck to my bedside table. It simply said: *Love you x.* I whispered:

"Love you too, Auntie."

I changed into my pyjamas, went and brushed my teeth and climbed into bed. I didn't wake until Aunt Ruby shook me at eight. She was holding a tray with a bacon butty and a mug of milky coffee. She handed me the tray, kissed my forehead and left the room without a word.

18

FAMILY TREE

THIS WAS GOING TO BE A TRULY AWFUL DAY. Apart from anything else, I was being walked to school by my aunty, at the age of fourteen. At least we weren't meeting Mrs Mills until nine thirty so the only people still walking to school were the usual stragglers who'd all get punishment exercises for missing morning registration, so I was in good company.

I left Aunt Ruby sitting in reception while I went to find Mrs Fortiver. She didn't have much time to talk to me but it felt good to have her support.

"We'll get past this, Jess," she said. "You won't even remember it in a few days. Just be sensible with Mrs Mills. It'll go down on your record but your slate has always been immaculate, so it's just a tiny blip. You won't believe how much time some pupils miss from school. Come and find me at lunchtime today and we'll catch up. Okay?"

"Okay then," I said, resigned to the trial ahead. I made my way back to Aunt Ruby.

*

One of the admin staff showed us into Mrs Mills' office, reassuring:

"She'll be with you in a few minutes."

Last time I was in here I was moody and then ill. Apart from that, I'd never stepped inside this room. Aunt Ruby and I had talked, a little frostily, on the way here but right now, we were silent. I looked around the walls. There was all the usual motivational stuff you see in school: posters showing pathways to the career of your dreams, an A5 document describing some sort of support network for vulnerable kids, and an oddly bright advert for Pilates classes for stressed teachers. Then a large framed picture caught my attention. It dominated the rear wall of an alcove at the back of the office. The words Laythorpe–Burton, written in dark green ink in an elaborate script, were the heading for a family tree. My head went on fire, just like that. I jumped out of my seat and strode across to the picture. I had to see this before Mills arrived. Better still, I grabbed my phone. I stood back far enough to frame the entire image on my screen. I could zoom in later to examine the detail. Why would Mills have a family tree for the Laythorpe family in her office? Maybe it was some other family unconnected with Dr Laythorpe. But at least now I had a picture.

Aunt Ruby had been scrutinising her diary; she gave me a questioning glare when I sat back down.

"Don't you see…" I began, but the door opened and Mrs Mills walked in.

"Good morning, Miss Stevens. And Jessifer," she added, scowling. *Great start*, I thought, *she can't even be bothered to look at me so I'm not going to reply.*

"Good morning, Mrs Mills," Aunt Ruby replied. "I am sorry Jessifer was absent from school for the last two days. We have had a long talk…"

"Well, I hardly think you need apologise, Miss Stevens," Mills interrupted.

"Jessifer is sorry for her behaviour, aren't you, Jessifer?" Aunt Ruby said.

I was struggling to focus on this conversation; I could only think about the new photograph on my phone. I had to know why Mills had a family tree of the Laythorpe–Whatever family on her office wall. I glanced over her shoulder, at the picture, trying to make out some detail.

"Jessifer?" Aunt Ruby said, in that 'haven't-I-already-asked-you-once?' voice adults like to use.

"Yes," I said. "I *am* sorry."

"And is that it?" said Mills. "I mean, heavens above, Jessifer! You know, I thought someone of your background and character would have a little more to say than: *'Yes I am sorry.'*" She wheedled this last with a whiney voice, mocking me. "Yet, it seems you are not fully here with us for one thing. I know my family tree may be of great interest." She turned to Aunt Ruby. "My connection with the Laythorpe–Burtons of York is little known in the school. We go back a great way in the city. A long line of eminent medical and legal people. Anyway," she laughed, "we're not here to discuss me, are we?"

"That's fascinating," said Aunt Ruby. "What a great

heritage you have." *This is crazy*, I thought. Exactly what I didn't need was Aunt Ruby, with her interest in history, opening up a friendship with Mrs Mills.

My face was hot. I was beginning to feel ill, like I had the last time I was in here. It must be the same family. How many different Dr Laythorpes could there have been in York? I had to get out of here.

"Erm, Mrs Mills, I am truly sorry." I licked my lips. The moisture in my mouth had gone AWOL and my tongue felt like a curled-up piece of dry, papery bark. "I was having a bad time and I… well, I lied to my aunt, and she didn't know I'd skipped school. It won't happen again."

I watched as she pulled a sheet of paper from a drawer in her desk. She began writing a summary of what I'd said. I could read each word upside down.

"All right, Jessifer. I have noted what you have said. I would like you to sign the document and it will go in your records. I must tell you that if it does happen again, your aunt will be asked to pay a fine. Parents have even been sent to jail for their children's truancy, you know. It is a serious matter. In future, if things are hard for you, you must come immediately to me and tell me what is going on. I am here to listen." She pushed the document towards us and jabbed a scarlet nail at the places where Aunt Ruby and I should sign. She favoured me with a smirk which couldn't have been less friendly and her eyes remained hard and cold. "Remember, I am here to listen. You can tell me anything," she said.

Yeah, I thought. *Like I'm going to do that.*

*

I went to lessons then met Mrs Fortiver in the library at lunchtime. She said she'd spoken to Mr Lloyd at break and he'd promised to see what he could find out.

"He thinks it's an intriguing story. I didn't tell him what has been happening to you, but he assured me if he'd had more time, he would have looked into it before, especially with the interest it has been getting recently."

"What should I do then, Miss?"

"I've been wondering about that, Jess. I think you should let me see what else I can find out and I'll keep in touch with Mr Lloyd on this. Leave it with us for a while. It has clearly taken its toll on you and has even made you unwell. It's important for you to get back to normal."

Her words worried me. I began picking at my nails. I couldn't abandon little Adeline.

"What is it, Jess?"

I squeezed my lips together hard then took a deep breath.

"I have to see this through, Mrs Fortiver." I had picked so hard at my thumb cuticle the nail was welling up with blood. "It's weird but... I don't think I have a choice. I'm just kind of stuck in this. It scares me a bit what might happen if I try to ignore it."

"I understand, Jess. You know I do. Just keep talking to me, all right?"

"Okay," I promised. I needed to be alone for a bit to think. I was going to go and walk outside. "Thanks, Mrs Fortiver," I said and was about to turn away.

"Oh, wait, Jess. Can you show me the images on your phone again? The records you spoke about? Or even better, can you email them to me?"

"Of course."

"And, Jess? Try and make up with your friends. You need them."

I smiled a non-committal affirmation and turned away. I strode past the next section in the library, towards the door but caught a flash of movement. I looked over my shoulder and saw Mrs Mills. She stared at me. Her look was not kind. I knew straight away she'd been eavesdropping on my conversation with Mrs Fortiver.

19

FUNNY LADY

"COME ALONG, ADELINE," CALLED MAMA.

"Here I am, Mama," I said, jumping my boots together in front of her.

"Oh, where were you?" Mama said. "I couldn't see you a second ago!"

"I was just talking to the funny lady," I said. "She's called Jessifer."

"What an odd name. Who *is* Jessifer, darling Adeline?"

"The lady with the peculiar stockings and no skirt. She was here just before. I think she went to see Papa. Then she asked how to get out, so I showed her."

"Well," Mama frowned a little then smiled. "You must tell me more about the funny lady on the way to see Uncle William and Aunt Susan. Besides, sweetheart, she must have been wearing a skirt."

20

RENDEZVOUS

WHEN THE BELL WENT AT THE END OF school, I was relieved it was the weekend. It was as if there was all this traffic buzzing about inside my head. Like, loads of vehicles rushing here and there and I needed to sort it out. Every vehicle represented something or someone significant. There was a big, old-fashioned red bus, like those quirky ones from the 1970s, with a conductor standing in the side doorway. That represented Aunt Ruby. There was a sturdy Volvo with Mrs Fortiver waving from the driver's seat. A bulldozer kept ramming into things and that was Mrs Mills. Rachel was a cute lemon-coloured Vespa meandering through the traffic and Loopy Lou was a kind of run-down, slightly scruffy moped, dashing to keep up with Rachel but with boxes and suitcases teetering, tower-like, on the back. Caroline was a Smart Car primly parked next to a sleek, modern building. An ancient black horse and carriage with a sinister hooded driver appeared from time to time;

that was Dr Laythorpe. And there was a barrier across the entrance to the town and a barrage of cars all waiting to get in. That was school and drama and Joopy, all the things that needed my concentration but weren't getting it.

*

When I arrived home, I was so happy to see Aunt Ruby smiling warmly at me through the kitchen door, I ran straight to her and gave her a tight hug.

"Shall we go out for tea, Jess?" she said, holding me away from her to look at my face.

"Okay then, Auntie," I said, "but I've got some catching up to do tonight and I promised Mrs Fortiver I would get back to normal so…"

"That's my lovely girl back with me," she said, scrunching her eyes at me in a reassuring smile.

*

While we were eating at Paolo's Pizza Place, I switched my phone off. Aunt Ruby and I talked about boring things: the new retail park on the edge of town, jobs that needed doing in the flat and the latest bus service to be pulled from York's transport network. It was great! I think we were both glad to pretend all was normal.

Later, at home, I got on with my work. I'd missed quite a bit and by the time Aunt Ruby brought me a hot chocolate at ten o'clock, I still had some history research to do and some stuff to write up for English.

At one in the morning Aunt Ruby shook me awake. I'd fallen asleep with my face on my English jotter.

*

I got up at half past midday to find a note by my bed. It read:

Didn't want to wake you. Hope you feel refreshed darling. Doing my shopping in town. Will be a while. Get some lunch then come and meet me this afternoon if you want. I have my phone switched on.

I remembered my aunt was doing her usual monthly 'big shop.' Aunt Ruby was such a creature of habit. She would go on the first Saturday of the month to buy things like stationery, tights, new face powder, shampoo and her favourite treats from the health food shop and she would always buy herself a new book. It took her most of the day and this was the first weekend in February, so it was 'big shop' day.

I would get some more work finished and then I would give her a call.

*

I set off into town and called Aunt Ruby on the way.

"Hi, Auntie. I'm on my way in. When shall we meet?"

"How about I see you in... erm... no, actually, *outside* Mulberry Hall at, let's say, three fifteen?"

"Okay, see you then," I said, unsure how I was going to feel about going back to Mulberry Hall.

Soon after, my phone rang and I saw Caroline's name on my screen. My heart lurched. I couldn't believe she was calling me. I'd seen her twice in school yesterday and she'd ignored me completely the first time and later thrown me a frosty glare. I hadn't seen any of the girls at lunch as I'd split my time between the library and walking outside, alone with my thoughts.

"Hi," I said, trying hard to sound cheery. "What's up?"

"Hi." She didn't sound that thrilled to hear me.

"I'm just on my way into town," I said.

"Oh. Right. Actually, I'm in town too. I think Mum's going to meet up with your aunt when she finishes work."

"In Mulberry Hall?" I asked. "I'm meeting Aunt Ruby outside there at quarter past three."

"Right. Mum finishes at two forty-five. I think they're hoping for a quick coffee together. Erm, I was thinking… you know, we should talk. D'you want to meet up just now?"

I checked my watch; it was five to two.

"Great. I suppose. Whereabouts?"

"What about downstairs in the Centre?"

The 'Centre' was short for the Moorhills Shopping Centre which was probably the smallest one on the entire planet but it had a few good shops and some benches around a fountain where you could hang out.

"Okay then. Five minutes, yeah?"

"Yeah. See you."

*

It was strange meeting Caroline. We both sort of hovered, fidgeting, looking at each other, then looking away until finally I said:

"This is ridiculous, isn't it? Are we friends or what? I mean, we've always been friends, since we were tiny and that can't change and…"

"Jess!" Caroline began to laugh and blushed nearly purple. "Stop talking! You always talk too much when you're nervous."

"Sorry." I laughed too. "Why am I nervous? Aw, come 'ere." I put my arms around my friend and we hugged but it wasn't like our old, secure hugs. It felt a bit jangly and awkward but when I stepped back from her, her eyes were so genuinely friendly, I felt better.

We went to the cookie shop and bought a bag of mixed cookies and went back to a bench to eat them.

"What made you call me?" I said, wiping crumbs from my lips.

"Do you wish I hadn't?" Caroline said, frowning.

"No! I'm glad you did. Caroline, I've hated it. I just wondered, why today? I mean, none of you've been talking to me, not properly, and I thought it was for ever."

"I've hated it too. Actually, it was Mrs Fortiver that made me ring. Well, Mum said I should talk to you as well but Mrs Fortiver told me yesterday that she thought you could use a friend just now."

"I talked to Rachel and Lou the other day. They both said I should call you but I couldn't. I've been feeling awful," I said.

"If it makes you feel any better, so have I. And Rachel and Lou are annoyed with me. They say I'm being ridiculous."

I felt quite shocked when she said that.

"Really?" I asked. "I thought you were all together in this."

"Don't be silly. It's not like that. They're huffy with both of us. And Lou said neither of us have a clue what it's like to have real problems, so she just thinks we're both being completely trivial!"

"So, here we are then. We're talking. What shall we talk about? Did your dad like his hat, by the way?"

"Loved it!" she said. "Jess, you should've seen him putting it on. It was so funny, and he hasn't stopped wearing it since!"

"Great!" I chuckled at the thought of her funny dad clowning about in his new hat.

We were quiet for a while, stuck for words. We just watched all the people walking by. Eventually, Caroline spoke again.

"So, did you really skive off?"

"Yeah. Listen, I'm not too proud of that."

"Loopy Lou thinks you're awesome. Do you know she's done it a few times? Like when her mum failed to show up one morning after a date."

"I just found out. Poor Lou. Her mum's terrible."

"So, what was *your* reason then? I can't believe you did it!"

"I just had to find some things out. It was a spur-of-the-minute thing."

"What sort of things?" She tilted her head and looked at me quizzically.

"You know. To do with…" I realised she wouldn't want to hear this. I picked at my thumbnail and then looked off into the distance, thinking. What do I tell her? I can't keep lying.

"Oh, Jessifer!"

I turned to look at my friend. She was scowling again. Her eyes had adopted that suspicious look that had so repelled me before.

"What?" I asked.

"You're not still messing with all that are you? I thought you would have given up."

"Why? I can't give up, Caroline. I'm completely caught up in this. It's too important."

"It's more important that you're all right!" she said, indignation written on her face. "I don't believe this! My mum's worried about you. So am I. *And* I'm worried about her."

"Why? What's wrong with her?"

"Nothing's wrong with her. It's just… her boss is being a pain. The shop might have to close and she'll lose her job. And she loves her job."

"Mulberry Hall, close? Why?" My thoughts were flitting about like trapped bluebottles. What would happen to Adeline if Mulberry Hall closed? Would I still see her? What would happen to the building? A new shop? Or something else? It would be like Adeline's home being disrupted all over again.

"Because, with all the talk of that ghost, the word has spread. All the normal customers are being crowded out by pointless ghost-hunters. They're practically queuing up to get in. And ghost-hunters don't want to buy expensive crystal and china! And it's been bad enough with all the online shopping people are doing. Mum says, some days there are barely any takings. And her boss has said the staff aren't to get involved with ghost-talk."

"Oh… I'm sorry… I…" I drifted off. I'd been trying to get Ali to tell me things. I could've caused her problems at work. No wonder Caroline had been so huffy with me. I remembered how Ali had whispered in the café last weekend. She'd obviously not wanted the other staff to hear her talking about the ghost.

I didn't know what else to say.

"It's not just Mum. You have to stop, Jess. It isn't good for you."

"I'm fine," I said, shrugging my shoulders to make light of it. I smiled at her but I could see she was hacked off with me.

"It's ridiculous, Jess. It's one thing reading ghost stories and watching horror movies but they're not real. This is… this is… well, it's weird and… and, it's scary and… well, well… you shouldn't be doing it."

I wanted to argue but what could I say? She didn't want to hear it. I was appalled when she stood up to leave.

"I thought this was a bad idea," she said. "Mrs Fortiver convinced me to feel sorry for you and Mum persuaded me to call you today but it's not going to work, is it?"

"Don't be like that!" I said. Then, as she began to walk away: "Caroline? Please!"

She looked over her shoulder and said:

"Just leave it, Jess. Sort yourself out!"

21

THE BLACKSMITH'S ARMS

T HERE WAS A HORRIBLE HUMMING SENSATION in my chest as I left the Centre. I couldn't stand all these ups and downs. They call this kind of thing an emotional roller coaster, don't they? Well, that makes no sense; roller coasters are fun. This was no fun at all. I should have thought first before meeting Caroline. Based on her last reaction I could've guessed she wouldn't be happy about what I was doing. What was I meant to do? I'd just got myself (and Aunt Ruby) into big trouble for lying. I wasn't going to keep doing it. I'd trusted my friend, but she wasn't prepared to trust me. All the warm feelings I'd felt when we met had drained away and I kept chiding myself for being so stupid.

"Jess?" The voice woke me from my internal chuntering.

I looked up and saw Lou striding towards me. She was with a woman I didn't recognise.

"Hi Lou," I said.

"Oh, this is my dad's sister, Auntie Mary." Lou had a doughnut in her hand, which she used to indicate her aunt, then she grinned. "This is Jess."

"Hi Jess. We're up visiting from London. Louise wanted to show me round the new shopping centre."

"Auntie Mary," spat Lou, "you totally haven't been around if you think Moorhills is new!"

"Well; it's new to me," said her aunt. "Anyway, speaking of new, we need to get to the Blacksmith's Arms. My cousin's the landlord," she told me, "and I promised I'd pop in to see the new baby before we head back to my brother's."

"D'you want to come, Jess?" said Lou. "You could meet her. She's tiny and so gorgeous."

"She's just three weeks old," Lou's aunt explained.

"Okay then. I'm meeting Aunt Ruby at Mulberry Hall at quarter past three. The Blacksmith's Arms is just over the road from there, isn't it?" I knew of the pub though I'd never been in it. It was popular with tourists for its 'olde worlde' feel but also had a reputation for being the place where dodgy deals were done, scores were evened, and the police were never more than a breath away. Mary's cousin's family lived in the flat above it.

"That's right," said Mary.

On the way, Lou told me all about the baby and her big brother who was two and a half. It was obvious she was mad about them.

We headed into the fusty interior of the Blacksmith's Arms and I wondered what Aunt Ruby would say if she knew I'd been in here. As we walked through the main bar to the stairs at the back, I half sneaked a look at the other customers, some of whom seemed to be disturbingly interested in me and Lou. Their suggestive gawping made me feel ensnared and the sour odour of spilt ale stung my nose. I was glad we were going up to the flat. But when we stopped at the bar to talk to John, Mary's cousin, he told us the family were out.

"Aw, bummer," said Lou. "I wanted Jess to see the babies."

"Another time, then," said John, winking at me. "How about a lemonade, kids?" He didn't wait for an answer and began filling two glasses, which he handed over, then fist-bumped Lou.

Mary installed herself on a bar stool with a glass of wine and Lou and I found a table over near the wall.

"I've never been in here before," I told Lou.

"I'm not surprised," Lou said. "Even Dad doesn't come in unless he wants to see John."

I looked over and noticed John was keeping an eye on us. There was no music but the customers were raucous. Some of them looked well rough but others were just regular tourists with backpacks. I could see the appeal: the low ceilings and oak beams, which were black with age, the wonky walls and floor, all sorts of memorabilia displayed here and there and, the food, which by the burnt cheese and roasted meat smells coming from the kitchens at the back, was rich and comforting.

"Is it true about the dodgy dealing an' all that stuff that goes on here?" I whispered, still watching John.

"Yeah. There's meant to be a bit of that but John's trying to clamp down on it. He's only had this place for a year and he's working with the police to try and clean it up."

"It's old and interesting," I said, looking around and above my head, "but it gives me the creeps a bit."

"You're a laugh," said Lou.

"Why?"

"Cos you're into all that ghost stuff and you think *this* place is creepy."

"Yeah, fair enough. Is it haunted, d'you think?" Though it was warm enough, I pulled my coat more tightly around myself and drew my shoulders in.

"I'm not sure. John tells stories but I think that's to keep the tourists coming."

We talked for a while and I checked my watch, making sure I'd be in time for Aunt Ruby.

"Where's the toilets?" I asked at ten past three.

"Down that way," Lou pointed to a narrow passageway behind me, "turn right at the end and they're at the bottom of that corridor. No, wait, I'll come with you."

We walked down the gloomy passageway, turning right into another that ran a long way back from the street. The walls were covered in morbid purple wallpaper swirled with velour. It was peeling at the edges and torn in places. There was no carpet and our feet slapped on uneven floor slabs. Unlike the bar area, it was draughty and cold and smelt damp. We reached the end of the passageway and stepped inside a poky space to the sound of a leaky tap. The drips echoed too loudly off white-tiled walls.

"Lou, hurry up, won't you?" I urged as we each went into a cubicle, and I was so keen to get out I did the fastest pee of my life.

We retraced our steps but halfway along the corridor, the screech of a cat's yowling halted us.

"Where did that come from?" I said.

"Dunno, sounds close. Weird."

We looked around and Lou began heading back towards the toilets.

"Here, kitty," she called.

"Lou, I'll have to go," I said. "Aunt Ruby'll be waiting for me."

The yowl sounded again, louder, and as I turned back towards the bar, a grey cat sprang out of the wall in front of me, then hurried off towards the main saloon.

"Did you see that?" I asked Lou as she came up beside me.

"Yeah. Man, that was bloody weird," she said. "Oh, come on, it's horrible down here. I'm telling John. Was it just me, or did that cat look like a ghost?"

"Ha-ha," I laughed. "Lou, don't be daft. It was just a grey cat." But before we walked on, I looked at the wall, right where it had come from, and there was not a single hole or space it could have got through. I brushed my hand over the disgusting wallpaper, but it was unbroken.

And when I left Lou with her Auntie Mary, at the bar, I thought of the smoky cat I'd seen recently and wondered…

When I got to Mulberry Hall, there was no sign of Aunt Ruby. I stamped up and down outside to keep warm and blew on my hands. Occasionally, I peered through the windows. But it was too cold. I had to go in.

I watched the customers wandering about and noticed what I hadn't before. Among the normal clientele – you know the type, Burberry jackets, tweeds and pearls – were people with backpacks and tatty jeans. They weren't here to replace their cracked two-hundred-pound coffee pots or buy wedding gifts. Okay, so some were looking at the crockery, but there didn't seem to be much buying going on. I wandered through the compartmented showrooms and it was the same in every section. I found a little corridor I'd never noticed before. It led to a door labelled 'Staff Only' and there was a noticeboard on the wall with fire safety instructions stuck on it. I turned to go back the way I'd come when I began to hear scratching. I wondered if a workman was maybe doing some work on the other side of the wall but then there came a horrific screech, like some creature being tortured. It made me jump and was followed by a snarling, yowling sound. As the scratching became more insistent, I felt as if something was going to come straight through the wall and grab me. I was out of there in a flash.

My heart was returning to normal when I saw Aunt Ruby appear, talking to Ali.

"Hi, Auntie. Hi, Ali," I greeted my aunt and Caroline's mum.

"Hi darling," Aunt Ruby said. "I'm sorry I'm a bit later. I'd hoped you wouldn't need to come in. Have you finished in town? You can help me carry these bags home."

"Yes. I'm done." I took one of her bags from her.

Aunt Ruby and Ali looked at each other and Auntie asked:

"Did you meet up with Caroline, darling?"

"Yep."

"How was it?"

"Great," I said, tonelessly. The atmosphere was unmistakeable and I realised Ali would be having words with Caroline when she got home, so I said:

"Actually, it was really good. I should've said how well we got on."

Aunt Ruby changed the subject immediately, saying we should get home, and we left the shop.

22

PHOTOGRAPHIC

A T SCHOOL THE NEXT WEEK, THINGS BEGAN well. Apart from Caroline reverting to her impression of an icicle, that is, which I'd kind of resigned myself to.

I'd been sleeping well and I'd cracked on with my schoolwork. I'd got a great mark for my English assignment. I'd caught up with Rachel and Lou for a bit and we didn't mention Caroline and I'd seen Rachel and Lou catching up with Caroline and could've bet my name wasn't mentioned.

I was in the library at break on Tuesday when I heard some first years whispering about the ghost again. Then later, in art, the student teacher set us an unusual task.

"Today, we're going to be linking up with the history department by doing portraits of figures throughout the ages," she said. "I want you to choose someone from history, or if you want, someone imaginary from a period you're interested in. How will your figure look? What will they be wearing?"

Her voice droned on in the background and my pencil was busy, all over my sheet of sketch paper, while my mind tried to process all the junk in my head. When she stopped talking and eventually wandered over to see what I was doing, she bent beside me and I could hear her breathing in my ear.

"Goodness, Jessifer," she said. I looked up at her face. She was gazing intently at my sketch, an image of a child. But it wasn't just any child. It was her: a perfect likeness of Adeline in her elaborate cotton dress. I gasped. It was almost photographic. I hadn't been thinking as I drew... it had just happened, and in the space of only ten minutes, I'd managed this. Okay, so I was all right at art. But not *this* all right. This was bloody genius. What the hell was happening to me?

*

When I went down to the canteen for my lunch, that picture really began to annoy me. I was beginning to think I was going completely nuts. I hadn't even known I was doing that drawing. It'd just happened. Caroline's voice echoed in my mind:

You shouldn't be meddling in things like this. You don't know what might happen.

I wondered if I should give it all up. Perhaps Ali was right to say it might be dangerous. Wasn't that what Aunt Ruby had said, too? But it was less the thought of any physical danger that bothered me than the idea that I was losing it. Like, mentally.

That's it, I thought. *I can't do this any more. I'm going to do what Caroline wants and stop it. Then I can have my friendship back. No more deceiving Aunt Ruby, either. And Ali will be happy too. I'll tell Mrs Fortiver I'm giving it up. This whole thing is ridiculous and how did I ever get pulled into it?*

Adeline's face popped into my head but I pushed it away. I needed to live a normal life. And just like that, I made up my mind to stop. I began to relish the idea of telling Caroline.

*

At lunchtime, I went to the library to get some information on our history topic. While I was looking, I found a book of Victorian Britain. It was full of early photographic images. I was amazed when I saw some pictures of Stonegate. And that's when I heard her again.

"… said the bells of Stepney…" I looked around. Some boisterous kids were messing about, being stupid. Mrs Botham sent them packing.

Mrs Mills was standing between two bookcases a few metres away and I felt sure she was keeping an eye on me. Well, she could if she wanted. What did I care? I wasn't the one with anything to hide. A French teacher was working intently at a computer. There didn't seem to be anyone else here. I slid the book back into its place and pulled out one about women of the 1800s. I found an interesting bit about the practice of charitable works by Victorian well-to-do women and the Quaker Society. Although I liked history in general, I felt completely gripped by this period. As I read, I kept seeing mental images of Adeline's mum.

"… I do not know…" came Adeline's voice again. I looked up and it faded. Mrs Botham was coming towards me.

"I'm seeing a lot of you in here, Jessifer," she said, almost accusingly, as if reading was not a commendable activity.

"Yes," I said. "I like it here."

She smiled. I couldn't imagine Mrs Botham in a noisy place. I tried to picture her in the middle of a disco floor, music thumping, and hid my amusement with my palm.

"Please let me know if you need help with anything. However, remember your social time is important. Don't spend *all* your free time studying."

"No, Mrs Botham."

*

I felt a sense of freedom and relief that afternoon. I think it was down to my resolve to abandon the Mulberry Hall stuff, but as I left the school gates, I began to feel awful. My skin prickled and I was tired. Huge floaty snowflakes were skittering down, landing on my eyelashes and shrouding my coat with matted clumps. Reflections of the street lights glittered and swayed in enormous icy puddles. At the kerb edges, the snow was turning to brown-black slush which the passing traffic seemed determined to redistribute onto my tights.

I headed for the woods. I could get home quicker that way although it might be boggy underfoot. Even so,

I couldn't get much wetter. I fantasised about a hot bath and a mug of cocoa and I was looking forward to seeing Aunt Ruby.

It was hard to stick to the path. There was usually a thick carpet of dead leaves here, but now, the leaves were floating on hidden pools of chilled water. It was impossible to tell where the puddles were without prodding the ground with a stick and it was too dark to see properly. My lovely ankle boots, which Aunt Ruby had bought me for Christmas, repeatedly sank into invisible depths. The water began seeping over the tops and through the zips and I could hardly feel my feet, they were so numb with cold.

I knew I was nearly home when I heard Adeline again but this time another voice kept interjecting.

"… I do not know, said the Great Bell…"

"Get out!" came the other voice, a man's. "Stay away! I'm warning you, stay away! Get out!" The last words were hissed, urgently and ominously.

"I do not know…" sang Adeline, though her voice was more urgent.

I was getting so familiar with these ghostly interludes that I knew, with complete certainty, this wasn't a live voice. There was something unearthly about it and it contrasted strongly with Adeline's gentle one. However, as I approached the end of Lock Woods nearest our road, Adeline's voice became more insistent, and louder.

"… said the GREAT BELL OF BOW…"

My body began to feel jerky with cold, then a wave of heat passed from my stomach up to my head. I was going to be sick. The woods began to spin and I had to stop walking. I stumbled and reached out to clutch a tree trunk. Now I felt too hot. I closed my eyes and tried to breathe steadily. My hands gripped each other around the tree and I leaned my face against the rough bark and began to cool down again.

"HERE COMES A CANDLE..." continued the little girl's voice, still louder.

"I command you. Go back! Get out! You are not welcome!" I knew Dr Laythorpe's stern, bitter voice. I was scared. So scared.

I pulled my cheek away from the tree and opened my eyes. Immediately I drew back in shock. It was Adeline's face. So real. Right there. I even felt her cold breath puffing on my face. Yet it barely looked like Adeline. Adeline was sweet, friendly, trusting. This face was not. The eyebrows made a 'V' and the mouth was small and tight. Then, her face began to recede from me as if the back of her head was attached to a tether which pulled her away. My pounding heart began to slow.

"Oh... oh," I heard my own voice and my heart raced painfully again. Adeline's image had been replaced by that of Dr Laythorpe, running towards me, fast. In the dark, there was an eerie glow around him and he was coming right at me. I knew he was dead but I didn't know how this was going to end. I couldn't get away; he was moving so fast, looming, formidable. I was frightened beyond comprehension. I thought I was going to die.

Suddenly, when my heart couldn't hammer any faster, everything went black for an instant, and all I could hear was the traffic noise from Hawthorn Road. I sucked in a big breath and felt my lurching heart slow. I heard the splatter of slush as cars drawled by. I gradually regained my composure as I watched a pair of small prattling boys squelching through the wood close to me.

I looked around. There was no sign of Dr Laythorpe and neither sight nor sound of Adeline. I put my hand to my face, which felt clammy. My bag had slipped down my arm so I hoicked it up onto my shoulder. Then I took a trembling step over a wad of leaves onto the remnants of a gravel path. I looked towards Hawthorn Road and noticed the two boys had stopped. They were watching me. They must have thought I was crazy, hugging that tree.

"You okay?" one called, his expression sceptical.

"I'm fine. Just slipped, that's all." I felt mortified. The pair ran off, joining the main road towards the estate.

Arriving home, the smoky cat which had taken such a liking to our place, flashed by me, yowling. It must have been chasing some poor creature, but I didn't care; I was far too cold and tired. Less than a minute later, I opened the door and felt more relieved than ever to see Aunt Ruby.

23

STUCK

I WAS STUNNED. WHAT I'D JUST EXPERIENCED HAD spooked me properly. I couldn't tell Aunt Ruby for two reasons. Firstly, she'd ban me from my beloved Lock Woods. And secondly, I just didn't know how to put it into words.

Nevertheless, my aunt's face was tense with worry. A good blizzard was building up outside.

"Thank goodness you're home," she wailed. "You're frozen and soaked through. Get out of those wet things. I'll run you a bath and put my herby bubbles in; they're restorative and will help you recover. Then I'll make you some hot chocolate."

A few minutes later, I slumped in a chair in the lounge and listened to the bath taps gurgling while Aunt Ruby rubbed my feet to warm them through slowly. She said I could've got frostbite and I wasn't to get into the bath until they were warm again. I couldn't believe the pain as the feeling came back. It was so bad I cried. Honestly, I was turning into such a baby. By the time I sank through the steamy, aromatic foam, my feet felt better and I lay back in the bubbles and shut my eyes. The old-fashioned scent of Auntie's favourite bubble bath had never appealed to me before but it really did seem curative. I smiled sublimely but my thoughts soon turned to the journey home.

It felt as though Adeline was trying to reach out to me. Her voice had sounded loud and determined. I hadn't heard that before. But then, hadn't I just decided this afternoon that I was going to abandon her? So, this was her way of persuading me not to. I tried to swamp the memory of Laythorpe's image, there in the woods. He was Adeline's father but there was a mismatch between them. He didn't seem like a loving father. Of course, I knew he'd been using morphine. Drugs change people. Maybe he'd loved her once. Maybe he *thought* he loved her. But there was something truly scary about him. I remembered Audrey's words about trying to understand things from other people's points of view and wondered what made Laythorpe act the way he did.

I so wanted to forget about all this. I wanted to enjoy relaxing in the bath, to do my homework and have a great sleep. Maybe school would be off tomorrow if it kept snowing all night. I opened my eyes and, mesmerised by the bathroom light twinkling in the bubbles, I sighed. But the second I closed my eyes, Adeline's face appeared in my mind.

"Don't stop," she said. I opened my eyes again. Everything looked the same, the glistening bubbles, the solid bathroom door, my green towel hanging ready. I closed my eyes. It happened again. Then reality struck. Me. My decision. My preference. All irrelevant. When had I ever had a choice in this? I'd never been the decision-maker. That was Adeline. I realised I wasn't going to have a relaxing bath.

*

For that matter, I wasn't going to have a relaxing evening. When I went to feed Joopy, I saw that his crate was, once again, wide open, and he was nowhere to be seen.

As we searched and searched, calling his name, Auntie said:

"Jess, could you have brushed the latch open as you passed this morning?"

"No, Auntie, look, that couldn't happen." I showed her how firmly the lock shut.

"Well, we've looked under the bed, checked your wardrobe, all through the house... I don't know where else to suggest. We've been searching for over an hour."

I saw by her pinched face that she desperately wanted to find him for me or come up with a suggestion we hadn't even considered, but I knew this was all to do with the ghost. It must be. And that cat, the smoky one, wasn't it chasing something when I got home? I thought about the cat in the Blacksmith's Arms and about Adeline's cat, Clementine. It finally dawned on me – they were one and the same cat. The smoky one was no sleek, cement-coloured cat at all – it was a ghost cat. Loopy Lou had been right. It *had* looked like a ghost. I just hadn't wanted to admit it. Not only that, it was Adeline's pet. So, why did I keep seeing it? And, had it chased Joopy? More importantly, would Joopy be safe?

*

The next day didn't proceed as I'd hoped. I woke, expecting to find a raging blizzard making the windows opaque, and man-height drifts of snow blocking the door downstairs. We'd be snowed in for a week and I'd laze about and wouldn't be able to go anywhere near Mulberry Hall.

Unfortunately, the sun was shining and there wasn't the tiniest hint it had snowed yesterday.

I got dressed for school and then sat on my bedroom floor. My shoulders slumped as I stared into Joopy's empty crate. I loved my rat. He was such a friend to me and always there. I dreaded the day he would die, though I knew rats didn't live all that long. My insides churned but I couldn't give in to losing him. I didn't really believe I had. Something else was happening here. I reached into his paper nest and pulled out a bundle of it. I placed it to my nose and sniffed his scent. As I put it back in the crate, my fingers knocked against something hard, buried deep within the mound of bedding.

"What…?" I said, my fingers grasping something cold and curved. I pulled it clear of the bedding and saw a small silver circle which jingled when it hit the mesh of Joopy's crate.

"Aunt…" No, again, I wouldn't tell Auntie, not yet. This was too weird. I examined the thing and cooed over the curled leaf engravings on the silver band, which was about the diameter of my forearm. It must be a cat's collar. I was sure it was real silver and soon found a hallmark. It was slightly flexible and had holes punched through the metal for size adjustment. Two little silver bells were attached at the front. I gave it a shake and knew straight away the tinkling sound it made was what I'd heard in the flat before. But what was this collar doing in Joopy's crate and who had put it there? It must belong to Clementine, Adeline's cat. No one would put a collar like this on a cat nowadays, beautiful as it was. Somehow, I'd have to make sure she got it back.

I would find Joopy. I must. And I would make sure, the next time I saw Adeline, I would give her back the collar. I dropped the beautiful thing into my bag.

*

I left the house later than normal so that Caroline would arrive at school well before me and we wouldn't bump into each other on the way. A strange thing happened next.

I was having one of my internal debates, trying to decide what to do about Caroline. I checked the time. Five to nine. I'd better get a wiggle on. Then I realised I was in Stonegate. Somehow, unconsciously, I'd walked into town instead of to school.

"… comes a candle to light you to bed…" Adeline sang.

"Oh no. I can't believe this." I turned around and began walking fast. No, I'd have to run. I couldn't be late, not after getting in trouble already. The world began to sway. The street started orbiting round me as if I was the pivot in the centre and Stonegate was a turning wheel. I felt queasy. Clutching my stomach, I folded to the ground, my schoolbag flopping beside me.

Maybe I've got a bug and it's making my vision funny, I thought. Then I couldn't think at all.

Gradually, everything stilled. I put one hand on the ground and pushed myself up to stand, swaying as I did.

I wasn't in the street any more. I was inside Mulberry Hall, the old one. The sense of movement had subsided but I was gobsmacked. I wished I knew how this worked… I was walking to school, I realised I was going to be late, and bam! The world spun and I was inside a building. I didn't know how that could be possible, but it must be Adeline's doing. Something about her having died, then existing as a ghost, made her able to bend things to her will.

In the beautiful hall, I saw her skipping off with her mother, the two hand in hand. Her mother was saying:

"You must tell me more about the funny lady on the way to see Uncle William and Aunt Susan."

I began to wonder when this would all end. I was going to be in big trouble. Mrs Fortiver would lose her trust in me. Aunt Ruby would start treating me like a child and Mrs Mills would say: "I had a feeling you'd let me down, Jessifer Jordan." I felt desolate.

I had to get out of this building and I didn't want to bump into Adeline and her mother in the street. Instead, I'd have to risk passing Laythorpe's office. Hopefully, I could get back to 2019 from Mulberry Lane. I'd done it before. Whatever Adeline wanted of me would have to wait a bit longer; I needed to show my face in school.

I stepped towards the side door but stopped abruptly at the sound of voices. I saw the back of Cook's large figure bulging in the doorway. She was talking to a delivery man in the lane. I turned to go back to the hall. I'd leave the house through the front door instead. But I was too late. Cook leaned back over her left shoulder and looked right into my face.

"Excuse me," I said. I felt myself redden. "I'm sorry, I erm…"

She turned back to the man and continued talking. She'd seemed to look at me, but now it was as if I wasn't there.

"Excuse…" I began again. No response. The Cook hadn't been able to see me before, had she? Even though I'd been right inside her kitchen, probably less than two metres away from her. I'd need to somehow squeeze past her bulky frame. Then I tuned into what she was saying.

"No doubt little un'll be watching from t' middle landing again. Mistress allus lets her stay to watch her make 'er entrance from her room on second floor. Likes to see 'er mama's dress as she comes down t' stairs."

"She's a cracker, that little miss isn't she though?" said the man.

"Awh, she's a right gem. Never any bother. She stays to wave to everyone before Nanny puts 'er to bed and she allus goes off 'appy. The Mistress tells 'er one day she'll get to stay up for the party. Makes 'er beam 'er little face off just to 'ear that. But for now, she's just happy to see 'er mother in her dress and have all o' the guests wave to 'er."

"Just a shame 'is lordship's such an ogre," the man lowered his voice to a whisper. "Never used to be but 'e's changed. People knows it."

"I know. I know," Cook said. "Anyway, best get on."

I was imagining the scene at the party. Mrs Laythorpe, the lady of the house, appearing from her room in a beautiful gown and waving to all the guests from upstairs. Cute little Adeline waiting patiently at the broad square landing. Perhaps Adeline would be in her nightgown, watching her mama descend the staircase, silk skirts swishing all the way down. Mama would kiss Adeline goodnight and continue to the ground floor. Then the guests would call and wave to Adeline who would take Nanny's hand and go sleepily up to bed. In my romantic, imagined scene, the handsome husband would take Mrs Laythorpe in his arms and kiss her and together they would sweep all the guests forward to the ballroom. I didn't think that would happen here.

Dr Laythorpe's raised voice brought me out of my reverie. I heard Cook bid goodbye to the delivery man and she bustled past me, the smell of butter and cinnamon in her trail. I leaned against the wall, hoping Laythorpe wouldn't come around the corner.

"Out! I need you out!" he shouted. Cook must have reached the end of the corridor that took her towards the kitchen.

"Dr Laythorpe? What on earth for? I've a whole kitchen full o' food waiting to be prepared for the party."

"I said out. I have important work to do." I heard his steps retreating into the hall. He continued. "If you can't leave the house you must remain in the kitchen. I forbid you to leave that room until I tell you. If I see you anywhere else, you will not have a job tomorrow!"

Now I was intrigued. I'd read that the Victorian household ran like clockwork and a cook would not be commanded in this way by the master of the house. He was up to something dodgy. I was sure of it. I knew Adeline and her mother were out. He'd told the cook to stay out of his way. I wondered who else he'd banished.

I crept along the staff corridor, nearest the kitchen, towards the hall and peered around the corner. There was no sign of the doctor. I'd be safe to wait here for a bit as Cook had returned to the kitchen and slammed the door. Before long I heard a regular rasping sound. I slipped my boots off, slid silently across the polished wooden floor and crouched down at the base of the staircase, nearest the front door, from where I could escape if required. There was Dr Laythorpe. On the second floor. At first, I wondered why he needed to make repairs to the banister. He was a supposedly eminent doctor, if rather off track. There must be staff to do this sort of thing. Then it dawned on me. He intended to kill his wife.

Suddenly, it all began to make sense. He was damaging the banister so she'd fall to her death at the party tonight. Adeline, so history and local legend told me, had fallen from a high landing in the house, while watching the guests arrive for a party. The story had always implied her death had been an accident but now I knew Laythorpe had killed *her*. He'd meant to kill his wife but had inadvertently killed his daughter instead.

Perhaps that's why Adeline wants my help. She can't rest until the world knows she died as a result of his malicious action. I watched. He worked for a while, removing a large section of the wooden railings. Then he carefully slotted the piece back in place and stepped back to examine it. He considered it from various angles, frowning. Eventually, he dusted off his hands, turned and entered a room behind him. The door clicked shut. I tried to digest what I'd witnessed. Perhaps I had it all wrong. Maybe it was a genuine repair.

I heard the door open again. He seemed to be carrying a long pole. I couldn't see what it was but when I heard the sweeping, I realised he was brushing up the mess he'd made. A moment later, he was descending the staircase carrying the brush and a shovel. I stood against the wall behind the stairs, holding my breath and hugging my bag tightly to my side so it wouldn't stick out and reveal me. Laythorpe reached the hall and hurried to his office. I exhaled slowly, relieved he hadn't come this way. Then I scuttled off to the front door, clutching my boots.

A minute later, from my vantage point in a passageway opposite Mulberry Hall, I watched a baker's cart, laden with loaves and cakes, enter Mulberry Lane and roll to a stop; another delivery for the party. I stood there for a long time. I saw Adeline and her mama return. Adeline was bouncing along, swinging a pink ribbon from her fingers, and I watched many people coming and going. There was a sense of anticipation.

I wondered what I could do. Was there anything? Adeline had sought my help. *Why?* Surely, I couldn't change history. I hadn't stopped Laythorpe from altering the banister. If I'd interfered I think he might have despatched me pretty fast. Maybe I should try and alert Mrs Laythorpe somehow. I felt helpless and scared and had a sense of foreboding.

Now I knew I was in too deep. I wanted to get back to the twenty-first century. I wanted to go home. I wanted to run away but I felt trapped between my own self-survival instinct and Adeline's determination to have me here. What was going to happen to her and her mother? I grimaced. I felt I knew the answer to my question. For now, though, I just needed to see if it was possible to get home. Obviously, Adeline wanted me to do something. I didn't know what it was but I would try and help, if only she'd tell me what to do. Yet, it really bothered me that I'd been flung here against my wishes. I began walking towards Church Road.

There, I saw a normal, bustling, everyday scene. Of the nineteenth century. Not the twenty-first. I couldn't understand it. Usually, when I left either Mulberry Hall or Stonegate, I would be right back in 2019. How far would I have to keep walking? I looked at Lock Woods. They seemed different, more expansive than in my time. The trees were taller, denser. I was frightened. My breathing was quickening and the fluttering in my chest signalled panic. I might be stuck here. I turned and ran back to Stonegate. Perhaps if I re-entered the big old house and then went back to the street, I could trigger my return to the twenty-first century.

Shaking now, I slipped in through the side door, along with some maids, no doubt hired help for the evening's event. Maybe I didn't give it long enough but when I returned to Stonegate and then Church Road, the same thing happened. Carts clattering along, no cars. Women in long skirts, children skipping by, barefoot. I would try again; I would have to keep trying until I could get back because I needed to know that getting back was going to be physically possible when the time came. First though, I had to contact Aunt Ruby. I sent a text:

Don't know what's happening Am back there Scared will never see u again So sorry, so, so sorry Please look after Jupiter I love u XXXX.

24

NOBODY

I RETURNED TO THE TINY PASSAGEWAY. FOR A while, I wept. I felt completely helpless. I flinched as people walked past. I thought they would jostle me but I soon realised they could neither see nor feel me. I began to let them pass through me, feeling the chill of them when they did. A butcher carrying a whole slaughtered pig barged into and out of me, making me hot with annoyance. Bizarrely, the creature's strong dead-animal smell stung my nose and clung there. I wasn't sure, in fact, if I was a kind of phantom or if these folk of the nineteenth century were the ghosts. If I was stuck here, what would happen to me? If no one was aware of my presence, how could I live here? I would just be a nobody, a nothing. It felt as if my soul had been ripped from me. I'd succeeded in wiping myself out.

I wasn't sure how much time had passed. Besides, time didn't matter any more if I didn't exist. I heard a familiar chatter and looked over my right shoulder to see Adeline, stepping out of the grand main door of Mulberry Hall again. This time, she was with a sombrely dressed lady, who I assumed to be her nanny or governess.

"The funny lady is going to be my special friend," Adeline was saying in her chirpy voice. "She is going to help me and get the big brown purse," she added. I watched the pair walk down Stonegate then my gaze fell to my feet.

She means me, I thought, and I have no idea how she thinks I'm going to help her. And what the heck is the big brown purse?

25

TYLER

I RAN ALONG BESIDE NANNY, CHATTERING AND chattering. I told her about my special friend, Miss Jessifer.

"She is going to help me and get the big brown purse," I said.

"Is she really?" Nanny asked.

"Yes," I began, but I saw something strange and stopped to watch.

There was a dirty boy sitting in a brown floppy box made out of paper and he was talking to a lady and they were wearing funny clothes like Miss Jessifer. I began to listen to them.

"Is that you, Mrs Mills?" said the boy.

"Yes, Tyler. I've seen you here a few times since you left school. I see you're still wasting your life. Living rough, are you?"

"Got to live somewhere, Miss. We're not all fusty old brainboxes like you, with fancy houses. Some of us have to graft hard on the streets to get anywhere."

"Is that what you're doing now, Tyler? Grafting hard?"

"Takin' a break, right now, but later, yeah, I've got a few jobs to do."

Then, Nanny tugged my hand. It sounded as if she was talking to me through a towel and it felt as if time was all sort of mixed up.

"What are you looking at, Adeline?" she said.

"That boy and that strange lady, Nanny."

"There's no one there, Adeline."

And she tugged again but I pulled away and squatted down next to the boy to listen.

"Adeline, for goodness' sake, we don't have time for silly games," said Nanny.

"Actually, these jobs you do…" The strange lady put her head on one side. "I might have one for you."

"Oh, yeah?"

"There's a girl at school. She's in some trouble. We think she's been… well, that doesn't matter… suffice to say she's causing me a problem…"

"And what do you want me to do?" The boy's eyes grew wide but his skin was all white and spotty.

"I need her phone."

"Not asking me to steal it, are you, Miss?"

"It's for a good reason, Tyler."

"Who is she, then?"

"Her name's Jessifer Jordan. This is her."

The lady took a little piece of paper out of her bag and it had a picture on it that looked just like Miss Jessifer. She showed it to the boy called Tyler.

"Yeah, I recognise her from school. Hangs about with that Louise What's-er-name. She's a good 'un. What d'ye want her phone for?"

"I've told you. She's in some trouble. That's all you need to know."

"And where am I supposed to find 'er?"

"Well, she's spending a lot of time around here: Stonegate, Mulberry Hall. If you're about, you'll see her."

"So why should I do it? What's in it for me?"

"I'll pay you thirty pounds."

"Fifty," said Tyler.

"Fine."

"What if she puts up a fight?"

"I need that phone, Tyler. Do what you need to do."

Nanny bent down and tugged my hand harder and suddenly, the boy and the lady disappeared.

26

CONNECTING, DISCONNECTED

I MIGHT NOT EXIST. MY SOUL MIGHT HAVE LEFT me. Nevertheless, my stomach was rumbling. I remembered there was a chocolate bar in my bag. I ripped off the wrapper and began eating the real, reviving twenty-first century sweet. I knew it was supposed to contain chemicals which made you feel good. Those chemicals did it for me. I didn't exactly leave that passageway smiling but my determination was back. I could do this. I was here for a reason and I had to find out why. I'd get back home once I'd done whatever needed to be done. Of course I would.

A large cart loaded with dozens of potted trees, flowers and greenery was parked at the front door when Adeline and her guardian returned from wherever they'd been.

"Wow!" I whispered. "This is going to be some party." The pair entered the house via Mulberry Lane, so I crossed Stonegate and watched them. Adeline turned and waved at me. I wiggled my fingertips in tentative response and watched her disappear through the side entrance. I began to rack my brain. There must be something I hadn't thought of. Some way I could help this little girl. Moreover, some cross-era pathway to get me home afterwards. Maybe there was a sort of time delay that had to pass before I could return to my own century.

My phone pinged, breaking my focus.

"Aunt Ruby?" I murmured hopefully.

I looked at the screen: *Message failed Resend?*

I had to force down any thoughts of despair. I wouldn't be defeated. I'd always had a strong conviction that I had to follow this chain of events, which seemed to be linked somehow with my own grief. I didn't know where it was going to lead me but one thing was certain: Adeline had called on me and she wouldn't give in.

I flicked to my gallery and looked at the photographs I'd taken of the documents in the Central Library. It was strange reading them right here, just off Stonegate, standing outside Dr Laythorpe's house, in 1863.

I scanned the first. An article by an American medical historian who wrote about the development of narcotics.

There remains some doubt about the methods of the British doctor, Jonathon Laythorpe of York, England, but in the absence of evidence to oppose the view, he has always been hailed as a pioneer in the field.

Maybe that's what this is all about, I thought. Someone needs to provide evidence. Evidence that he was a fraud.

Somehow, Adeline knows about something that I can bring to light. I flicked to my photographs of his journals. I looked over his regime of self-administered morphine. A fraud and an addict, I thought.

As if to complement my thoughts, a voice called to me. My little friend.

"Good afternoon, Miss Jennif… Jessifer!"

I looked up, gave Adeline a wave and plunged my hand into my bag, dropping my phone in amongst my jotters and school text books.

"Come along," she called, grinning.

I began to cross the lane. About halfway, it was as if I passed through a wall of invisible jelly. The sounds from the street grew louder. Adeline reached out her hand to me. I clasped it, thinking my hand would close on air but it didn't. Her hand was firm and real, tiny, but warm, just as a six-year-old's *should* be. Not cold, as it had been in the china shop. She gave mine a surprisingly strong tug and led me into the house.

"I am so happy you are my friend," said Adeline, stopping in the hall. "My best friend is Uncle Gilbert," she said and looked at the clenched fist of the hand that wasn't holding mine. She stuck up her index finger and continued talking while also counting with her fingers. "And Tom is my next best friend and you can be my other best friend! That's three friends."

"Well, that's… that's pretty cool," I said, stuttering.

"I'm going to show you my whole house. It's big but not as much as Grandfather's. But first, I have to tidy my things. You can wait here." And she belted off at speed, her feet clattering on the wooden floor. I was in the corridor at the side of the house, right beside Dr Laythorpe's rooms, his medical room on my left, his study on my right. I didn't want to be there. I had a real horror of the man but would have to wait for Adeline's return in this quiet part of the house.

Yet, quiet was not the word, because, as soon as Adeline had left me, I heard the same yowling I'd heard in the shop. It was coming from the study on my right. I sidled up and saw that the door fitted the frame poorly. A gap in the wood gave me a slender view inside. I'd never been in this room but I could see a table and a chest of drawers. The doctor was right there in the centre, holding Clementine upside down by her tail. Clementine hissed and tried to scratch him but he was wearing long leather gauntlets and held her at arm's length. I saw that her collar was missing and slid my hand in my bag, feeling the ornate silver hoop I'd dropped in there this morning. Instantly, she stopped yowling and her green eyes turned to me and blinked. I shot back from the doorway thinking Laythorpe might guess I was there. But he continued to curse Clementine.

"Foul creature. I can't imagine why Adeline likes you. Do you dig your claws into her, the way you do to me? Now, I am satisfied I have given you just enough opiate to let you sleep for an hour. Then you can wake to enjoy the full effect of your eternal life trapped inside a wall."

I held my breath and gulped. What was he going to do? I turned back to the gap in the doorframe and watched the battle between doctor and cat; the cat flipping and twisting in its attempt to be free and the doctor callously provoking her. Eventually, he let her go and she landed with grace and shot across the floor. But the door was shut and I knew he wouldn't let her out. I couldn't see her now but I heard his words.

"Enjoy your sleep, little witch. In ten minutes, you will be safe in your tomb." He turned to the wall behind him and lifted a panel of wood away. Behind it was a hole, just about forty centimetres square. Then he picked up a hammer and some nails, which he jangled in his hand before putting them down again. This man was barely human any more.

Adeline's voice heralded her approach.

"Would you like to see my nursery first?"

"Oh. Erm…" I looked at the study door. "Do you know Clementine is in there… with your dad… your Papa?"

"Oh, that's where she is!" And she was at the door, her chubby hand on the handle. She pushed the door open.

"Papa?" Adeline said. But the door slammed into her, making her trip backwards a little. I caught her and pulled her away so that her fingers wouldn't get trapped.

"Out!" yelled her father and the door closed with a bang.

"Ow!" Adeline's hand was at her nose. She turned to me with a wrinkled face and I thought she was going to cry.

"Aw. You're okay," I said, peering at her nose. "There's no damage." And, just like that, she buried her head into my tummy and placed her arms around me. I hugged her back and we stayed like that for a minute. I stroked her head and thought how vulnerable she suddenly seemed.

"I think you were going to show me your nursery," I said. "I'd like to see it." I spoke with that kind of enthusiasm you use when you talk to small children and she pulled away from me, encouraged.

"Would you?" she said, frowning. But in an instant, she brightened. I guessed the moods of children her age could be quite changeable. "Come on then. Follow me," she said.

I did and imagined she was my sister; sometimes she did a little skip between footsteps and I wondered if Judith had done the same at that age. Now and again, she'd stop suddenly to tell me something. She'd stand with her tummy sticking out, watching for my reaction.

"You know my friend Tom, don't you?"

"Well, not really, no," I said. She frowned again. "I know who he is though," I said, and it was the right thing to say because she beamed.

"He's the boy who Papa tried to make better but he didn't get better and Papa only made him worse instead. And he talks to me. And he is sad because of what Papa did. And I said I was sad too. But I said you could help and Tom said yes. And then we won't have to be sad any more. And you can talk to Tom, too."

"Oh, right, okay, okay." But her speech was so fast, I wasn't entirely sure I followed.

Without warning, she pulled my hand again and we were off. I tried to put Laythorpe out of my mind and I couldn't stop thinking about Clementine. Maybe I could get back and release her.

I almost tripped in my efforts to keep up with Adeline. I couldn't keep up with her chatter either, which didn't stop. She seemed excitable.

"We're nearly there now," she said, pulling me up the stairs.

"Where?" I said, glancing around nervously. No one seemed to have noticed me with Adeline. "The nursery, do you mean?"

"No, silly, not the nursery. There. At the end, of course."

I had no idea what she was talking about but I felt conspicuous.

"Erm, I don't think I should be here," I said. "People might not want me here." However, in the next instant, I found I needn't have been concerned.

"Now, young Miss Adeline." A gentleman wearing pinstripe trousers and a silver waistcoat stopped on the middle landing. "Don't you be tripping on these stairs. Rushin' about like you are. What's the hurry anyhow?"

"We're going to see my nursery, Mr Partridge."

"An' who might we be, Miss?"

"My friend and I, of course."

"Oh, yes, very well, your friend!" said the man, shaking his head and grinning as he continued down the stairs past us. He clearly thought Adeline's friend was imaginary. I began to relax a little.

"Who is Mr Partridge?" I hissed.

"That man there," said Adeline helpfully pointing at Mr Partridge.

"Yes, I know but... well, what does he do?"

"He's the butler." She giggled at me then said: "You're funny!"

*

We reached the first floor and Adeline hurtled through the open door of the nursery. Her hand slipped from mine and she suddenly stopped when she saw her nanny.

"Adeline, please stop running. If your father hears you clattering about, he will undoubtedly show me the door. Remember to behave with decorum."

It seemed like an odd way to speak to such a young child but I supposed it was normal for then.

"Yes, Nanny. Look, here's my friend, the funny lady. Do you like her?" Adeline began to run back towards me but thought better of it and slowed to a 'decorous' walk.

"I can't see… oh yes, she's lovely. Now Adeline, your father has asked me to stay late tonight because of the party. I've to bath you at the usual time."

"Yes, Nanny. How long is it till the party?"

"Well, it is almost six o'clock…"

I gasped. Adeline looked at me in surprise and giggled. I wished I could understand how time worked in my life these days. It didn't seem to follow the normal rules. I'd left home for school this morning and since then, apart from standing about crying, and tagging along with Adeline, I hadn't done anything all day. I wondered what had happened in school. I wondered how Aunt Ruby was doing. She'd probably called the police by now. I thought about Joopy and imagined his little brown body nestled against my forearm and chest. Would I ever cuddle him again? I remembered he'd been missing this morning. I didn't even know where he was. And I thought about my parents and Judith. If this ghost was real, and now seemed to be living, and if I was in the nineteenth century, then surely, there really must be a heaven because up to now I'd doubted it, even though I faithfully went to church with Auntie most Sundays. And if there is a heaven, are Mum and Dad and Judith there? And if they are, will I ever see them again? Because I could be stuck here for all eternity. So, what if I was never to die and never to be released from 1863? I didn't know which was worse: the thought of dying one day, or the thought that I'd be here for ever and ever and never reunited with my family.

"… and the party begins at eight, so you have an hour or so to play."

"Come on, Jessifer," Adeline said. "Come on," she tugged on my hand again and I realised I'd been staring at the floor, lost in thought.

I stumbled after her and tried to ask her what she wanted me to do.

"Adeline," I said, "please can you stop? Please, tell me what you want me to do."

But she just giggled again and, still running, said:

"You'll see."

She gave me the full tour. Wherever we went, she introduced me to people who couldn't see me. There was only one person who argued with her that there was no one there. Clearly, Miss Betsy, the girl I'd seen before, in the kitchen, didn't have much imagination.

"Miss Adeline, there isn't anybody there."

"Oh, Betsy," said Cook, exasperated with her. "Just because ye can't see owt, it doesn't mean t' little 'un 'ant got a friend. She's yer special friend in't she, Miss?"

"Yes, Cook," said Adeline and giggled.

I'd seen bathrooms, guest rooms, her own bedroom and her parents' rooms on the second floor.

"Hello, Addie," said Mrs Laythorpe, who was resting on a chaise longue. Her complexion was fair like Adeline's and her eyes sparkled when Adeline sprang into the room. "Remember to save some energy to greet the guests when they arrive. They will all love to see how much you have grown, my big girl."

Yet, Adeline still didn't stop. She had me running up and down the stairs in her excitement. I realised she was on her own as a child in this big house. It must be nice for her to have a companion at last. I got the idea she didn't quite understand that I wasn't a grown-up but at the same time, she recognised I was more like her than all these stuffy Victorian adults she spent every day with. There didn't seem any order to her tour. My lungs were heaving from the effort and I began to lose track. We'd seen the large library on the ground floor as well as the drawing, morning and grand dining rooms. There was a small saloon (I heard a maid call it that), the secretary's and the butler's rooms and a music room. The most beautiful was the ballroom, which blazed brightly with perfumed flowers.

"One more room," she said, "and that's Papa's secret room."

"Oh, actually, I've already been in there," I said, thinking I'd better explain myself. "I went in by accident before. It's where he keeps his medicines and things, isn't it?"

"No," she said. "That's his doctor room, not his secret room." She flung her head up and down with each word, emphasising my mistake.

"Oh," I said. I felt a bit stupid. "Silly me. What's his secret room for then?"

"It's where he puts his bocudents but he doesn't let me go in. Once I was a ghost, he made a hole in the wall and put them in there. I watched him. You can get them."

What was she saying? "I was a ghost," she'd said. She was *here, now*, in 1863. With me. How could she talk about being a ghost? But, then, how could *I* be here, in 1863? That really set me thinking. If I was here, at Adeline's calling, she must have known things after her death. Things like: her dad was a fraud; her death wasn't an accident; her dad had been commended for his work but he shouldn't have been. So, now she was trying to lead me to the truth. She must be able to rerun her past so that I could see what happened and understand. Yet, it was all too weird for me to make sense of. Well, I was getting used to weird, like, the weird with a capital 'W' kind of Weird.

One thing *did* finally make sense to me though. She'd also said: "You can get them." At last, she'd told me something useful. She wants me to get something.

"Jessifer?" she put her hand on my arm and shook it. I realised I hadn't been keeping up with her speech.

"Sorry, what were you saying?" I asked.

"And once, when I *wasn't* a ghost, I crept in and hid behind the curtain." She opened her eyes wide and clapped her hand to her big O-shaped mouth, seeming to enjoy the idea of her naughtiness.

I sucked in my breath in mock horror and she laughed.

"Did you get caught?" I asked her.

"No. No. No." She thrust her neck from side to side.

"Adeline? What did you say he keeps there?"

"His bocudents," she announced. "In a big brown purse. Come on. You can get them." She darted off again.

I was stunned by the size of the house. It seemed larger than the china shop and café of my own century.

"Here you are," she said, showing me a small square room on the first floor. "This is Papa's secret room. I'm not allowed, but you can go in. I was cross with Papa because he was mean to Clementine, and I'm still cross with him because he pushed the door at me. Now I have to go and get her."

I was so relieved to hear her say that. But I wondered if she'd be able to save the cat. No doubt her father would stop her.

"She's got a little face and a pretty collar with silver bells on it."

"Oh," I said, "I know." I took a deep breath. I should give her the collar. I dug in my bag and pulled it out.

"Is it like this?" I asked, offering it, but she didn't take it.

"Yes, yes," she said, clapping her hands. "But you can keep it. Clever Jessifer."

Then she turned and ran off, laughing. There was something odd in the way this little girl behaved. I would've thought she'd have wanted the collar. Or asked me why I had it. But, despite her small size, she seemed in the know. And I felt bossed around by her. I liked her though. There was a connection developing between us and I could feel a hard stone of grief inside, knowing the inevitability of her death. It was as if this was all a big puzzle she'd set for me and I had to solve it. Yet, before she died, how could she know? I first met her when she was a ghost – I think – but she didn't seem to be a ghost now. She seemed real. I was more like the ghost. The ghost of the not-born-yet Jessifer? I had no idea how this worked. It was all just truly bizarre. Yet, Adeline not only had a strange way of talking, as if she knew things… it seemed as if she could make me come here, into the past, manipulating me, manipulating events. Like her past and my future were all wrapped up in some weird time warp.

My next question was, why had she brought me to this room? Was it to find her Papa's big brown purse? What was in it?

I pushed open the door and stood, clenching and unclenching my fists. What if *he* came?

First, I clicked the door shut. I turned and saw a long sideboard against one wall, with a wooden chair squeezed into the corner. The other three walls were lined with bookcases, the only gaps being for the door and one small window which looked onto Mulberry Lane. There were heavy, floor-length curtains, drawn open. A small desk and chair sat in the middle of the room. I turned full circle, trying to pick out the titles of the leather-bound books, but I didn't know where to begin.

What was the word Adeline had used? Bocud… something? What did she mean? And Papa's big brown purse. What was that? A purse… could it be a wallet or some sort of bag? Bocuden…? I kept saying the word over and over and then it hit me. She was talking about documents. I felt like such a dunce. She was only six and she got her words wrong sometimes. Of course. I stepped towards the sideboard and touched one of its brass-handled doors. I pulled tentatively but the door wouldn't open. I tried a drawer. The wood stuck but my determined effort brought it open with a screech and I saw it was stuffed full of papers. I began rifling through them and my fingers felt something soft and smooth. There at the bottom. I lifted the piles and underneath was a large brown document file, fastened with a loop of black cord encircling a brass button. Adeline's 'bocudents'? In Papa's big brown purse.

I heard footsteps, not a child's. A hurried pace, now slowing. In fright, I let go of the brass handle, which rattled loudly against the filigree plaque it was mounted on. I shoved the drawer back in and looked for somewhere to hide. The curtains. Exactly where Adeline had hidden. I was much bigger than Adeline. I sucked my breath in and held still. The door opened and closed again, with a small click.

"Need to get the key and lock this room. Child's been in here again, I fear." It was his voice.

My heart was hammering. What if he locked me in? There'd be no escape for me. I heard the brass handle clatter again. He was at the drawer. It squeaked and I heard the rustling of papers, then a shifting sound. He was removing the leather file. His file of secrets. I heard the door handle clunk as if he'd tried to grab it and missed. I peered out from my refuge. He stood in the doorway, the file in his hand. Dammit. I needed to look in that file. He pulled the door closed. A small click again. I waited for his footsteps to recede down the hall, my heart slowing gradually. I felt bad. Adeline had wanted me to get that file, I was sure. She'd said: "You can get them"; the documents. What was in them?

Perhaps I could come back another day. Then I remembered. I'd tried to get home today and failed.

By the time I'd slipped back downstairs and slumped near the front door, unnoticed, the tears were once again rolling down my face. Only a day had passed but the rawness of missing Aunt Ruby made it feel like a year. Would I ever see her again? I realised how much I needed her.

27

TOM METCALFE

I RECOVERED MYSELF AND THEN I REMEMBERED Clementine.

"Oh, no!" I had to get back down to the study and see if the doctor was still there. If not, perhaps I could free Clementine. But it was no good. As soon as I walked into that corridor, I heard his voice, still ranting and cursing.

I leaned one elbow against the wall, my head in my hand. I felt hopeless. Maybe I could get back later and try again but, for now, I had to move. I felt unsafe being so close to Laythorpe. I began to wander through the house. Everyone I passed was oblivious to me being there. The evening moved into night-time. There was a sense of order and calm, different from the bustle of earlier. Everyone was in their place getting ready: Cook and Miss Betsy, along with other help, in the kitchen; Mama in her room; Mr Partridge going between the ballroom and the dining room; Adeline, I heard, was in her bath. I flinched when I saw Laythorpe pass through the hall and I tried to hide behind a large planter bearing a huge bay tree. The man stumbled, muttering:

"Must dress for dinner."

He looked absolutely stoned. No doubt he was on a fresh trip, just in time for the party starting. I think he must have heard my movement for he looked right at me and scowled. He was peering hard. I was only partially hidden by the tree. However, the effort seemed too much for him and he clutched at the wall, muttering, again:

"… dress for dinner."

The clock in the hall chimed the half-hour: seven thirty.

I felt awful. Sadness was pressing down on me like a heavy weight. My tummy churned like a rolling barrel of cream with big clods of butter thumping the sides. Tonight was going to bring bad things. I would need to keep out of Laythorpe's way, especially if he was drugged up to the eyeballs; he was a liability and there was no knowing what trouble he might cause. But I knew I needed that file, too.

I slumped by the bottom of the stairs and waited.

*

Mr Partridge and two other suited men appeared in the hall. Partridge barked orders. This party was going to run smoothly as far as he was concerned. Other staff appeared.

Suddenly there was a commotion upstairs. I heard a raised voice.

A door banged. I craned my neck and looked up. Adeline had appeared on the stairs and was running down them as far as her long nightgown would allow. Her nanny appeared and the door banged again.

"Adeline! Come back this instant!"

My earlier impression of Adeline as a strong-willed six-year-old was confirmed. She ignored her nanny's pleas and ran all the way down to me. She kissed me on my cheek and said:

"Goodbye, Miss Jessifer," then ran all the way back upstairs. I chuckled and placed my hand on my cheek. This little girl had a place in my heart. I wondered why she'd said goodbye. Had she meant 'goodnight?'

Soon after, the first guests began to arrive. Rapidly, a trickle turned into a crowd of bustling, chattering people, flowing in, eager for a good time.

I saw Adeline and her nanny appear on the middle landing, halfway between the first and second floors. I was entranced by the costumes of the guests. There was so much silk and lace on display in the women's clothes and the men looked distinguished, removing top hats as they arrived. My little friend beamed and waved. I'm sure she would have squealed and shouted if that had been acceptable; but this was a well-to-do Victorian household. Adeline knew that, at this moment, she must conform to certain rules. I was relieved she stood at the middle landing. She was safe. Under different circumstances I'd have found the night incredibly exciting. This was a different world from mine. A fascinating, thrilling other world. But I was on edge. I wasn't here for fun.

A maid trotted downstairs, her face serious. She didn't acknowledge Adeline or Nanny. When she arrived in the hall, she whispered to the butler, Mr Partridge, who asked for quiet. A hush descended. Mrs Laythorpe appeared on the second floor. I almost forgot my plight when I saw her. She was dazzling; the embodiment of feminine beauty. I'd only seen her in dark clothing before. Now, she was like a wisp of magic. Her cream silk dress clung to her slender figure and her skin glowed like peach blossom. She smiled generously at her guests below and began to move along the floor, soundlessly.

I remembered with a lurch what was supposed to happen next and willed her not to lean on the banister. Perhaps my being here could change events and neither Adeline nor her mother would be harmed tonight.

Mrs Laythorpe stepped carefully, seeming to glide but she gazed at the floor and something caught her eye. A line of puzzlement creased her face, but she looked up, smiled and walked on. She didn't stop at the banister.

Her guests began oohing and muttering. I scanned their faces and picked out Dr Laythorpe. He was leaning against the door to his treatment room. He seemed more sober than he'd been earlier and he, too, was looking up at his wife. He watched her continue along the second-floor corridor. Then his expression changed. He should have been smiling with pride but, instead, unmistakeable anger described his features.

I switched my gaze to Mrs Laythorpe as she approached the middle landing, where Adeline was now jumping up and down with excitement.

"Mama, Mama," she cried. "You look beauuuuu-tiful!" Her mother kissed her and said goodnight, bidding her to be a good girl for Nanny, and then progressed on down the stairs.

The party had begun. When Mrs Laythorpe reached her guests, she turned back to her child and blew kisses and the guests joined in. Adeline waved and giggled until Nanny led her up the remaining stairs to bed. The last thing I heard her say was:

"Nanny, please may I keep my pink ribbon in?"

*

For a while, I stayed at the bottom of the stairs and watched the guests. Black-suited waiters wandered among them with trays laden with canapés and glasses of wine. The smell of the food was tantalising. The noise level in the hall died down gradually as many of the party-goers made their way to the back section of the house where the dining room and the ballroom were situated.

I sighed with frustration.

"How am I going to get that file?" I muttered. I drew up my knees, crossed my arms upon them and lay my head down. I wasn't aware of drifting off but when raised voices disturbed me, I understood how tired I was.

"What the hell are you doing, Jonathon? You'll be thrown out of the profession!"

I pushed myself up, wobbling with fatigue. Hanging onto a staircase strut, I peered into the central portion of the hall. A middle-aged man had his hands on Laythorpe's shoulders; he'd spoken in a harsh, breathy whisper.

"Don't be ridiculous, Anthony," Laythorpe responded in a calm, clear voice. He was trying to placate the other man. "The results will show. You'll see. We will give our patients a much-improved experience. I understand so much more about venous-injected morphia. You should try it on your patients in Leeds. They'll thank you for it." He smiled and shrugged away Anthony's hands.

"I'd rather stick with standard practice, actually. Anyway, I promised Jocelyn I would speak to you, as a friend. She is extremely concerned about you. You have to stop injecting yourself."

"I might have known she would interfere," Jonathon replied. It may have been subconscious, but he looked up at the top floor railing as he spoke. "She should keep her mouth shut!"

"Oh, I won't speak to you if you're going to be like this. It seems you won't listen to a word I'm saying. You'll go on and do your own thing even if it hurts all around you." Anthony huffed and walked off towards the rear of the house.

I wondered if Laythorpe would follow him and forgot to be on my guard. He turned and looked right at me. Surprise lit his face. I had to run!

I grabbed my bag. I had the advantage of being closer to the front door than him, but he didn't hang about. I heard him give chase but smirked when Partridge began shouting at him. Of course! The butler couldn't see me.

"Dr Laythorpe? Sir? What on earth?"

I scuttled down the steps onto Stonegate and heard Laythorpe's voice.

"That girl, man! Stop that girl!"

"What girl, Dr Laythorpe, sir? There isn't anyone there."

I ducked into the passageway opposite the house and pressed my back to the wall. Then I watched and sighed with relief as Laythorpe jabbed Partridge angrily in the chest.

"I told you to stop her," he growled.

He went back inside. Hopefully, he'd remembered he was meant to be hosting a great party. Yet, I was surprised he didn't just stay out and hunt me down.

My heart was pounding. *What if he'd caught me?* I breathed deeply and weighed up my options and realised I didn't actually have any. I had to go back in and try and get the file. I didn't want to let Adeline down.

"Miss?" came a male voice, close by.

I stepped out of the passageway and felt as though I'd collided with an arctic wind, a chill so penetrating. The feeling subsided and I turned and heard the same voice, chuckling now.

"Oops-a-daisy!" said the guy. "Beg yer pardon."

I blinked and wondered if I was seeing things. Then he spoke:

"Still here!"

I was face to face with a ghost. A grinning one. In fact, his blue eyes were sparkling and all I could do was grin back. I knew this boy.

"You're Thomas Metcalfe," I said.

"That's me!"

"Hi... erm... my name's Jessifer. Jessifer Jordan."

"Pleased to meet you, Jessifer," he said, offering his hand.

I tried to respond but my hand just kind of slid through his. That set him off laughing again. I couldn't help but join in.

"Actually, we 'ave met before, 'aven't we?" he said.

"Yes. It was here, that night I saw you were injured. You were bleeding."

"Yep. I died," he said simply. "It was 'im that killed me." He pointed at Mulberry Hall. "Was meant to 'elp me, an 'e did, but 'e gave me too much o' that stuff. It right took pain away but it took me life wi' it!" He smiled again. He didn't seem to mind too much. I guessed he'd got used to his new status. Of being dead, that is.

"I'm sorry." What else were you supposed to say in conversation with someone who was dead? I already knew he'd died because I'd heard his death mentioned *and* seen his name in Laythorpe's records. I looked at his neck and saw that he still wore the spotted necktie, although the colour was all bleached out.

"I was *'oping* to see you tonight," he said, running a hand through his thick, shaggy hair. "You've got a job to do, eh?"

"You know about it, then?" I asked.

He nodded.

"I'm not sure exactly what, but there's a file. In a room, in the house. I found it. I think Adeline wants me to get it but he came in and I had to hide, then he took it before I could... and, anyway, I don't understand how it'll help anything. Maybe I should've asked her to tell me what's in it but she's so little…" I realised I was rambling so I stopped talking but he nodded again, with raised eyebrows.

"Go on," he said.

"Well…" I said and laughed at the memory of her chasing up and down stairs in her enthusiasm to show me the house, "she runs about and keeps talking and telling me things. I mean, she's so cute and funny but I don't belong here and I… I…"

"Carry on," he said and pulled his big, twinkly smile.

"If I'm honest, I'm scared. I don't like it. I kind of know what's going to happen and I wish I could stop it… and on top of all that, her dad terrifies me."

He nodded along with me.

"Is any of this making sense?"

"Oh aye," he said. "'E's scary all right. Aye. She said ye must get the papers. Says she knows ye can. 'Ard to imagine what's in 'em but she 'as a knowin' way about 'er. It'll be tough for ye tonight, but we believe in ye. Don't lose 'eart will ye?"

I saw that his outline was starting to fade and I panicked. I didn't want him to leave me. He made me feel safe somehow.

"But how can I get the file?" I asked. His body was patchy as if it were dissolving. I knew I wasn't going to get the answers I needed and I knew my connection with this lovely boy was going to be broken, just like all my other connections: my parents, Judith, Caroline and Adeline. I wanted to know so much more about Tom.

"How old are you?" I asked him.

"Sixteen," he said, fading out.

"Don't go!" I said, clutching at his shoulder but simply making a fist in the air. My voice was trembling. As he faded out completely, I heard his soft voice:

"It'll be all right. Trust me. An' see what ye can do."

He'd gone.

28

HISTORY UNFOLDS

I couldn't believe he'd gone. Tom. His eyes were so kind. His was the friendly voice I needed in a place where I was a complete alien. He was the line of reasoning in my confused mind. And he was the ordinary person I could relate to amongst all the opulence, luxury and status inside Mulberry Hall, a world so different from mine. Even if he *was* dead. Dead or not, I felt like I needed him right now.

I didn't want to go back to the party, but I knew I had to try and get my hands on that file.

I slipped back in and slowly closed the door to a soft click. The doorman jumped back, ready to welcome a latecomer to the party, then stared at the door, which to him – unable to see me – must have seemed to glide open and shut of its own accord. He crossed the hall, checked around, glanced upstairs and went back to the door, opening and closing it twice. His scrunched face and arched brows actually made me smile.

The first thing I did was return to Laythorpe's secret room but when I tried the door, it was locked. So, he certainly did suspect Adeline of sneaking in. I could hear the clatter of knives and forks on plates and all the chatter coming from the dining room and went to have a nosy. I peered around the doorway and saw Laythorpe sitting at the far end of a long table; the people sitting on either side of him were leaning forwards, chatting across him, but he was staring sullenly at a fixed point on the tablecloth, chewing as if the food tasted bad. Now was my chance to look in his medical room for that file, but I was nervous; he scared me and all I wanted to do was keep away from him. I had to do it though. It was what Adeline wanted. Maybe I could get into his study too and free Clementine. The chattering clatter of dinner-party noise receded as I scuttled towards the medical room. I was still fascinated by the fact that I could move openly where other people were and not be seen. How was it that Adeline and Laythorpe could see me but, to everyone else, apart from Tom, I was invisible? Was it through Adeline's intervention, or even to do with the good versus bad forces of nature? Maybe it was just that they were motivated to see me, whereas no one else was.

I let myself into the doctor's room and shut the door quietly behind me. I darted towards the desk but was immediately dismayed. The only thing on the surface was a metal dish with a really ancient-looking syringe inside. Not even the record books I'd previously photographed were here. I checked the shelves on the walls and found more drug paraphernalia and medicines including a fresh bottle of that liquid called Dalby's Carminative. So, I tried the two desk drawers. Again, I was disappointed. There were a few bits and pieces in there but no file. I gritted my teeth and growled. There was nowhere else in here to look. I stepped across to the far door, opened it a crack and checked the corridor. The last thing I needed was to have kitchen staff seeing doors mysteriously open and close, unaided, like the doorman had. The corridor was empty, so I darted across to the study opposite. Its door was unlocked. The most awful thing on entering the room was the silence. I'd hoped I'd hear Clementine's caterwauling, but, either she was asleep, or he'd moved her, or she was no longer in the land of the living. I didn't know what to do first: see if I could get to Clementine or try and find the file. If I checked for the cat, I'd know whether it was worth my while trying to free her.

Laythorpe had been at the left side of the room when I'd spied him lifting a panel away from the wall earlier. A framed picture of a landscape hung there now. It was small enough for me to lift so I took it down carefully and placed it on the table. My heart fell when I returned to the wall. The panel was fixed in place with rows of deeply embedded nails. How could I ever get this off without being disturbed? It would take me forever. I didn't know what to do and felt helpless. Without thinking, I began tapping on the wood. Maybe if she was still alive, I could come back at night, when all the house was sleeping, and use a kitchen knife to work away at the nails, bit by bit. But there was no sound from inside and I feared the worst. I could search for the file and perhaps she would wake up and start scratching at the wall. I looked at the table and saw some text books but no documents and no brown file. So, I went to the chest of drawers. It was a large, solid piece of furniture with brass handles like curled-down tongues. Each drawer had a rectangular brass frame containing a label. There were drawers for: Cases, Research, Accounts, Finance, Pharmacology, Letters, Receipts and Private. I pulled them open one by one, searching through piles of papers, looking for Adeline's 'bocudents'. At least I knew what the file looked like now. But it wasn't there. I checked and checked again. No big brown purse. It must be in his 'secret room'. I had failed Adeline and I had failed Clementine.

Now I had a problem. If I couldn't find the file or save Adeline or even save her pet cat, what was I doing here? I left the study. I chewed my lip and twisted my hands; I walked this way and that, pacing the corridor; eventually, I found myself in the kitchen, where I was apparently invisible again, so I ate some food from the table. I sat on the stool I'd used before. By reflex action, I took out my phone. I could try Aunt Ruby again and if that failed, I'd look through my photos. I doubted I could access the web. Haha-ha! The thought made me laugh and brought to mind the advert of an internet provider: "… keeping you connected… twenty-four hours a day… fast and reliable…" Except, my crazed sense of humour added: "across 140 years!" But my phone wouldn't even switch on. The battery must be dead.

I began wandering the house and watched the guests disperse from the dining room as the dinner was finished. The hired staff were bustling between the kitchen and dining room with empty plates and dishes, cloths and brooms. I went to the ballroom and watched the dancing for a bit. Then I slipped into Adeline's room and gazed at her sleeping face. I returned to the kitchen and picked at the leftover cakes and sweets, wondering how I could possibly be eating, a century and a half before I was born. Only Adeline knew that, and I doubted she could explain it even if she were awake. Throughout, though, I was tired and restless.

"How can I get that file if Laythorpe's got it locked away?" I muttered. "How long is this going to last? Hanging about, waiting, always waiting." *Maybe I won't be able to get the documents*, I thought. Yet Tom had said, "It'll be tough for ye tonight, but we believe in ye." He'd also told me not to lose heart. Did he have any idea how tired, confused and grumpy I was? I'd just have to keep going back to the 'secret room' upstairs and try again, or somehow find the key, but I was sure Laythorpe would have that stashed away in a pocket. Perhaps he'd leave it lying somewhere and I'd strike it lucky.

The guests wandered about, sometimes dancing, or lounging together, chatting, then joining other groups. I listened to parts of conversations, then grew bored and moved on.

"Isabella, have you met Anthony Richardson?"

"This is Violet and Samuel, neighbours of my mother and father."

"When were you last in London, George?"

After dinner, the guests moved between the rooms. I latched onto different people to pass the time and noticed that Laythorpe appeared now and again, no doubt to fulfil his duty as host, but returned to his medical room frequently, and each time seemed to spend longer and longer inside. Was he topping himself up with morphine? Probably. Every time I saw him come back out, I tried to sneak in to see if he'd left the key to the upstairs room on his desk, but his appearances at the party grew shorter and shorter. One time, I'd managed to get in, but he'd only been gone a minute, if that, when he came back. Luckily, I heard the door handle and in a split second I was at the other door. I got out and was sure he hadn't seen me, but it was close.

Then I hung about in the hall. Jocelyn, Adeline's mother, was talking to her brother, William. They were sitting on a chaise longue, next to a huge potted palm tree. It was clear Jocelyn had noticed her husband's recurrent visits to his room. She sighed.

"Don't worry about Father," her brother was saying. "He will never withdraw his support as long as you and Adeline are here."

"I know that, William." She smiled at her brother then sighed again. "It makes me feel so ashamed. We were all proud of Jonathon once. You know, William, he wanted to make things better for his patients. He really hoped that he could be the one to bring them relief and healing. And, for a time, he did. He cared for them so well but that wasn't enough. He wanted success too badly and now…" She didn't seem able to finish her sentence and she wiped her eyes. I could see she was fighting to control her emotion.

The sound of a door banging came from upstairs. It was followed by laughter as two women appeared at the back of the hall.

"Jocelyn, dearest," one of them called. Jocelyn looked over her shoulder at them. "You must come and dance!"

My attention was caught between Jocelyn, in the hall, and the noise upstairs. I looked up again and saw that Adeline had appeared at the railing on the second floor. She was wearing her nightie and was rubbing her sleepy eyes.

"Oh no!" I gasped. "This is it." I hurtled towards the steps. I had to stop her!

As I took the stairs, two at a time, I could see she'd climbed onto a stool which had been pushed up next to the railing. Perhaps a maid had left it there and forgot to tidy it away. Suddenly everything made sense. It was what Jocelyn had frowned at when she emerged from her room at the start of the party. It had prevented her from standing right up at the railing, so rather than move it, she'd descended to the middle landing.

Now, Adeline, who looked as if the noise of the party had disturbed her sleep, had found it a convenient step from which to view the events below. I couldn't get there fast enough.

"Mam…" she began but a creaking, shifting sound interrupted her voice and the railing had slipped forward. Adeline's hands slid from the polished wood and her body tumbled through the air. In less than a second, she lay crumpled in an awkward position on the floor. A split length of wood from the banister lay beneath her, protruding like an extra limb.

Jocelyn was screaming. Then her head was nuzzling Adeline's, her face obscured from view. Her back began heaving up and down; she was sobbing wretchedly. People came running.

I was stunned. I stood there on the stairs looking down. I didn't want to look but I couldn't turn away. My throat filled with such a lump I could hardly breathe. But no tears came.

"Where is Jonathon?" someone shouted.

Jocelyn's brother, William, was in shock, frozen where he sat, staring at his sister and his niece.

"Get Laythorpe!" someone shouted again. Then William stood and ran to Laythorpe's room. Other people were shouting and wailing, while the two women who had called to Jocelyn seconds ago, clung to each other, their faces pale with fear.

Jocelyn's plump mother appeared in the hall. She began to fire instructions at the crowding guests. Partridge, too, appeared and began ushering people towards the back corridor, away from Adeline.

I slumped to the top step at the middle landing and doubled over in pain. An animal sound came from me and I tried to bury it in my knees. I knew how this was to end. With a vivid little life extinguished. Just like when Judith died. There one minute, alive, full of hope and promise. Then, gone, finished, never to be again. Not physically. And then the unfairness of Judith's and my parents' deaths hit me like an explosion. I knew *this* death was not the end of Adeline. Yet, what had happened to my sister and my mum and dad? They had died in a most awful way. And that was it. And my anguish over the loss of them felt magnified by the unfairness of Adeline's death, which was an abomination.

And then the tears did come and they overwhelmed me and I felt more alone than I'd ever felt before. I broke my heart, there on the stairs. And all the shouting and wailing and barking of orders went on below me and I cried and cried and cried. For Adeline. For Judith. For my parents. And for myself. I cried because I felt helpless and alone. And I cried because I was so afraid I was going to lose Aunt Ruby. What if I got home eventually and something had happened to her while I'd been gone? What if the flat had blown up like our house had, so long ago? What if she got cancer? Or got killed in a car accident? And then I would be left with no one. No one at all. And I became anxious and agitated. I began pleading with God. Did I even believe there *was* a God?

"Well, if there is, please, God, don't let Aunt Ruby die. Please, keep her safe. I will never skip school again. Or be unkind to my friends. Or have a single cross word for my auntie, but please, God, don't let her die."

I twisted on the stairs, looking for a way out of my misery, looking for someone who could help me. But I was in this alone.

Eventually, weary with exhaustion, I plodded downstairs and watched as Adeline's body was removed from the house. I followed Mr Partridge, who carried her tenderly to a waiting carriage. A second carriage took Jocelyn and her father, and I heard people say they were taking her to the morgue. As the carriages trundled off down the street, with the only sound their rattling and the horses' hooves on the cobbles, I stood and stared, my arms limp at my sides.

And then the anger hit me. I tried to quell it.

You knew this was going to happen, I thought. *And you've failed her. And you still have to get those documents. That's what she wanted.* I was angry with myself and I kept repeating the words in my head: *You've failed her, Jessifer.* I paced between Mulberry Lane and Stonegate. But it didn't take long for my anger's direction to change.

People were leaving the house, silently. What a horrific way for a party to end. I went back in, through the side door. I hunkered down in the corridor and shivered. And I heard him.

"It should have been her. It should have been HER!" he shouted.

I erupted.

"HOW DARE YOU?" I yelled, jumping up. I didn't care now. He'd killed Adeline. He'd wanted to kill his wife. People thought he was a leader in his field. He would later be hailed a pioneer, but he was a murderer. Just an evil murderer.

I sprang into his room, hot tears welling in my eyes.

"You killed her! She was just a little girl. You're a fraud and a lunatic. All because of that disgusting drug!" I pointed at him. A newly loaded syringe full of poison shook in his trembling hands. His sleeve was rolled up.

He dropped the syringe, which clattered on his desk. He lunged towards me, grabbed me then began shoving me towards his treatment couch. I tried to push him away, but he was too strong. Then I felt a staggering blow to my head and sank to the floor, submerged by blackness.

29

DRUGGED

I CAME ROUND. I WAS LYING ON MY BACK, FEELING awful. I opened my eyes and found myself in near darkness. I rolled onto my side and promptly fell what seemed like a great distance. I groaned. My right shoulder had crunched against a hard floor and felt bad. This wasn't my room with its soft carpet. I put my fingers to my chin and they came away feeling sticky.

"Where am I?" I groaned. "Aunt Ruby? Are you there?"

I knew it was ridiculous to ask because I knew I wasn't at home, but my mind was fuzzy. And when a familiar noise caught my attention, I grew more confused. I also knew that sound: squeaking. As it grew louder, I felt something tickling my face.

"Joopy?" I said. I rolled over and there, right in front of my face, was my rat. Weird, blurry memories flitted across my mind... Jupiter had been stolen, no, he'd escaped, no...

The sound of talking broke through my confusion but I couldn't make out the words. Then, fear skewered me as the volume increased and I recognised Laythorpe's bitter tone. I lifted Joopy, who was squeaking and trembling, and held him close.

"She was my child as well. You are not the only one grieving!"

"Now, Dr Laythorpe," came Partridge's deep tones.

"I don't know who you are any more, Jonathon," Jocelyn said, her voice cracking.

"Aargh," came Laythorpe's distressed wailing.

I sat up and began retreating under the medical bench. I felt trapped and vulnerable. But it was hopeless. He flounced into the room and immediately began looking for me. He squatted to peer at me and his eyes met mine. He yanked me out by my arms. Pain wracked my shoulder and I cried out. He pushed me flat to the floor. Joopy scuttled off and retreated to the corner. I saw that my sleeves had been rolled up. With one hand, Laythorpe held me pressed against the tiles and with the other he reached into his jacket pocket. I don't know why I was surprised by his strength. I suppose I hadn't expected it in an erudite doctor, a drug user at that. He pulled out a loaded syringe and before I could react, the needle was in my thigh, through my tights. He withdrew it and flung the syringe through the air onto his desk, then he stalked out, slamming the door behind him.

Now, I was terrified. A minute ago, I'd woken, feeling woolly-headed and confused, but with enough sense to realise he'd injected me. With my head spinning, I raised myself again, peered at my arms and saw the place where he'd first injected me. A lumpy purple bruise in the crook of my left elbow gave it away. Now he'd injected me a second time but not into a vein. I knew about the dangers of strong drugs and this was no twenty-first century, refined morphine. I could die from an overdose of opiates. Nevertheless, I also knew that an injection into the flesh of my leg would take longer to take effect than one into a vein. I had to get out of this place. Somehow. I must. It could be the only way to save my life.

*

I found my bag and coat bundled up on a chair. Grabbing them, I called Joopy, who came scuttling back to me. I threw on my coat, slid him into my pocket then stumbled through the side door and along the corridor, feeling worse by the second. I reached my hands out to the walls on either side of me. When I opened the door into Mulberry Lane, I gulped the fresh air, which made me feel sicker than ever and I threw up the food I'd stolen from the kitchen last night.

I rummaged in my bag for my phone but couldn't find it. I'd have to go back. If Laythorpe had been through my things, I bet he'd have taken it. He'd seen it in my hands before and he'd have been curious about it. Barely keeping upright and knowing I was risking everything by putting myself in his way again, I staggered into his room and tried to focus my blurred vision. I couldn't see it anywhere. I tried the drawers. It wasn't in either. I swept my hands along the shelves. It wasn't there. Maybe it was in his study. I practically fell through the door and as it opened, I saw him sitting at the table, with his head down. He heard me and looked up. Despite my lack of coordination, I knew he was properly drugged up now. His eyes were bloodshot and his pinprick pupils bored into me. Simultaneously, we looked at the surface of the table. And there was the phone between us. At once, we both pounced on it as if we were playing a violent game of snap. But I was quicker, and I had the advantage of being closer to the door. I fell against it with my phone in my fist but managed to escape before he was even round my side of the table.

Seconds later, I was back outside. I dropped my phone in my bag and felt my way along the exterior wall of Mulberry Hall until I reached Stonegate. Although it was dark, I guessed dawn was approaching, as I could hear the chirps of birdsong echoing off the buildings. If I could put some distance between Laythorpe and me, I would stop and try to call Auntie.

The street was empty. I lurched like a drunk. My vision was bad but I knew I was heading in the direction of Church Road. I hoped I'd be able to get home and I remembered Tom's words:

"It'll be all right. Trust me." And I did. I truly trusted that boy with his wide smile and honest, round face. I kept him in mind as I stumbled along, occasionally tripping, falling and scrambling to stand again, trying to keep up my momentum towards home and Aunt Ruby.

I could see Lock Woods in the distance, not far away. I was nearly there. This time, I'd get back to the twenty-first century. This time, it would work out. This time, I was going to see Aunt Ruby. I smiled, still trusting Tom, still keeping his face in my mind's eye. I reached into my bag and pulled out my phone. I'd call home. Oh, how I wanted to hear my auntie's voice. Then I looked at my phone and my heart sank. It was completely dead. Despair threatened to overwhelm me but I wouldn't give in to it. I kept moving and the further I got from Mulberry Hall and the evil Laythorpe, the stronger I felt. Nevertheless, the thought of him still made me shake.

"Have to get away from him," I said, stumbling on. "I'll be home soon. I will." But the drug was affecting me, even though some of my thoughts were clear. It was like being in that half-and-half state, when you know you're dreaming but you've also got some wakeful consciousness. Waves of confusion kept washing over me. Wasn't I lost? Or stuck here? Yet, there were familiar buildings ahead: the shops of Stonegate with their red bricks and white-painted window frames; St Helen's Square; the Mansion House, solid and grand. *I'm in the city*, I told myself. *I'm in York. I'm going home.*

"STOP!" he yelled, and I heard footsteps slapping the pavement. Getting louder.

"No." I couldn't believe this. He'd destroy me. He'd drugged me. I hoped he was in a worse state than me, but *he* was accustomed to narcotics, I wasn't. The sound of his coordinated slap-slapping feet, eating up the gap between us, made me weak again.

I tried to run but tripped and fell, grazing my knuckles. Again, I scrambled to my feet. I pulled my bag onto my shoulder and began tilting forwards, my centre of gravity all out of kilter. I had to get to the woods.

"You can't get away from me. I *will* stop you before you ruin me." He wasn't shouting any more. He was too close…

He yanked me backwards. My bag slipped to the floor but I hooked my ankle through the strap. I felt myself being pulled along on my back. My muscles were floppy and far too slow but being ensnared focused my mind again. I could see him, stalking sideways, back towards Stonegate and Mulberry Hall. He groaned with the effort of dragging me.

"Wait!" I yelled at him. The cold air was sharpening my thoughts and Audrey's voice, at drama, cut through: "Consider why Lauren is so upset," she'd said. "Show your empathy… rather than reacting…"

He stopped dragging me and leaned down. His eyes bore into me, his face growing in both size and anger as he got closer.

"Just… just let me go. You're hurting me," I said. "I know about the work you've been doing. I just want… want to tell you that." My mind was scrabbling to make sense of Audrey's advice. If I could find the right words, then maybe he'd release me. "I know you really care about making things better… at the hospital, in your… your work… making patients better and helping them and…" What had Jocelyn said? If I didn't get it right, I was dead. My mind wanted to burst into panic.

"What do you know? Where did you come from? You're spying on me. Tell me, who sent you? WHO?" he yelled. I flinched, thinking he was going to hit me, but he turned away from me again and started to stride forward, pulling me with him.

I gulped. I'd have to try again.

"No... wait," I said. If I could keep talking, perhaps I'd buy myself time. "Please just listen to me. Please." Then louder, I screamed: "PLEASE? PLEASE?" Even if he continued to drag me, hopefully someone would hear and come to help. Then I remembered that no one else could see or hear me in 1863 and desperation drove my determination on. The words began tumbling from my mouth again:

"I know you're a good man. You love Adeline and you didn't want her to come to any harm, your little girl, your daughter, your... I know she loved you and looked up to you, an important doctor, her father..." My voice trailed off. He'd stopped to listen but didn't respond. I hoped it would make him think.

"I have to help Adeline," I began again. "No... I mean..." I was saying the wrong things. Things which would anger him. "But I know your work started out as something important... a difference... to science... to helping people..." Again, I trailed off.

He stooped and tried to pick me up, but I forced myself downwards to stop him.

I thrashed and tried to twist from his grip, but he clung on tightly. I put my left hand to the ground to try and get some leverage to pull away from him, but it just scraped along, gathering grit, but was barely sore at all with the effect of the drugs. He stopped for a moment and punched me in the side of the head.

I must have blacked out.

Then I came round and saw that we'd barely moved. I dug my heels in and twisted my whole body in one huge effort to stop him from taking me back.

He turned and glared at me, his face distorted, rippling like an image on a flag blowing in the wind. I knew I was going to pass out again. But before I did, he suddenly let go of me. He was moaning and I saw him running away, which made me feel so gleeful, I could have laughed, but I had to gather myself and get home. I got to my knees and my head whirled like a waltzer in a fairground. Someone was coming towards me. A boy, wearing a red tee-shirt with a football logo on it. He might help me. Then I smelled his stagnant breath and my heart sank. His face loomed towards mine.

"Jessifer?" he said.

His eyes were bloodshot with specks for pupils, and his teeth were brown and I was drowning in waves of confusion and exhaustion and my eyes were drifting closed. Then I felt a massive smack to the back of my head and collapsed.

30

GHOST SO SMALL

MY LIP WOBBLED WHEN I WATCHED MY mama screaming and sobbing. I wondered at first what was wrong and then I remembered whirling through the air. I think the wooden railing must have broken. There'd been a loud thump and my head had hurt lots then not at all.

Now, it was like floating. It felt funny.

*

I jumped forward to Miss Jessifer's time and I didn't like watching them take me away. This was my house. Where were they taking me? Oh, yes, I remembered. They were taking my body to the cold room at the hospital because I was dead now, wasn't I?

Then I saw my friend. I drifted down to the ground and ran after her.

"Miss Jessifer! Miss Jessifer!" I called but she didn't hear me because of the nasty medicine Papa had given her.

I followed her outside. She was taking big, big strides and I tried to catch her. I put my hand out.

"Oh!" I gasped. Miss Jessifer walked straight through it.

I stopped and remembered when I first became a ghost a long, long, long time ago. I had looked at my hand. Then I'd looked at all the people leaving the house. They were sad and quiet. Their clothes were red and green and blue and yellow and black. I'd pulled the ribbon from my hair and wondered where all the pink had gone. My ribbon had turned white and my skin had turned grey.

I'd looked down at my grey feet. I'd looked at my grey legs. And my grey hands.

"I must have a ghost in me now," I'd said. I wasn't sure I'd liked it.

But now it was Miss Jessifer's time, so I scuttled along to Mulberry Lane and watched her go through the side door.

I followed her inside. Poor Miss Jessifer. She began to shiver. I tried to touch her head, to lift it up so she could see me, but she just trembled and trembled. She didn't know I was here. I would have to work hard to make her be able to see me.

Then I heard Papa begin shouting inside the house. I remembered he had done bad things and I got very cross with him. Then I got even crosser when he smacked Miss Jessifer. He gave her some of his horrible poison medicine.

*

I had to look after Miss Jessifer now. I tried to wake her up but she wouldn't. For probably a lot of minutes and hours, I tried to wake her and so did her rat. He kept squeaking, but she was too fast asleep to hear. It was clever of Clementine to bring the rat to my house.

Eventually, Jessifer woke up but she fell off Papa's couch onto the floor. I listened as Mama and Papa shouted at each other. Papa came back into the room and he was very bad because he dragged Miss Jessifer out from under the couch and stuck a nasty medicine needle in her. I stayed beside her when she went back outside and I was just drifting along with her when, all of a sudden, I saw my cat.

"Clementine!" I called. And I remembered how she'd trotted straight over when we were first ghosts a long time ago and how funny she'd looked. My Clementine was supposed to be orange but, instead, she'd turned grey, like a puff of smoke. "We're both ghosts now, Clementine," I'd told her, and she'd meowed and drifted along with me.

Jessifer went along Stonegate. I frowned. She was all stumbly and she was sick. I felt sorry for her because I'd hated nasty sick when it had happened to me.

Together, we went along, me drifting and her wobbling about. After a while, I felt better because I saw Tom. He waved his red spotted necktie at me from St Helen's Square at the end of Stonegate. I waved back as I followed Miss Jessifer. She was going the other way, out of town, towards Lock Woods.

I looked at Miss Jessifer's face and saw her cross mouth. She began talking to herself. Then she looked at the funny black box in her hand.

"You can't get away from me," yelled Papa. He was running.

Miss Jessifer fell down. She got up again.

Papa kept shouting. He wanted to stop her.

Miss Jessifer fell again. Papa was dragging her. I tried to stop him, but it wouldn't work.

"Just let me go!" Jessifer said.

Papa seemed to want to take my friend all the way back to Mulberry Hall.

"Stop it, Papa!" I yelled. "Stop it! She's my friend. She doesn't want to go." I began sobbing. Then I got angry with Papa and I ran at him and shoved him.

He looked frightened as he stumbled backwards, and I was glad. I ran after him and pushed him again.

"No," he said, covering his face with his hands. "Adeline... no, no, no, no, no!"

He could see me. I ran at him again and pushed him. He ran away. Then I turned back to my friend.

"Oh no," I yelled. Miss Jessifer was fighting someone. It was that dirty boy called Tyler. Then he hit her head and she dropped back to the ground. Tyler got down on his knees and rummaged in her bag. He grabbed her black box and ran off towards St Helen's Square.

I chased him and saw the stern lady he'd called Mrs Mills, waiting for him. Her legs looked shimmery black and she had shiny red shoes on with tall, spiky heels. Her lips were covered in bright red lip rouge and some of it was on her teeth. She scowled at Tyler through puffy eyes.

"Did you get the phone?" she said.

He pulled the black box out of his trouser pocket and gave it to Mrs Mills. She gave him some money and then he ran off. I knew the black box was Miss Jessifer's and not hers so I rushed at her and went:

"Boo!"

She jumped back, saying:

"Heavens above!" and ran away. Her spiky shoes clicked on the pavement like a horse's hooves. She kept looking back at me as she ran. I scowled at her.

When I rushed back to Miss Jessifer, a man with black skin was crouching down to her. He was puffing and puffing. I think he'd been running. Then I saw him take a black box, just like Jessifer's, out of his pocket and he started talking to it. Miss Jessifer was lying very still and her head was bashed in. She wouldn't wake up. I didn't know what to do, so I just sat next to her and watched the man and patted Jessifer until the funny, noisy carriage came with blue flashing lights. Two nice people in funny green overalls wanted to help her so I didn't mind.

*

After that, I went back to my time. *My time*, when I first died. I thought I should feel sad especially because I couldn't seem to walk properly any more. It was more like I was blowing along in the wind, but it felt a bit funny. Then I saw the boy who came to our house a bit broken and he was doing the same thing and he had a ghost in him too, just like me and Clementine.

"Hello, Adeline," he said, and he smiled a big curvy smile. "My name's Tom. You and me can be pals, if ye like. It might 'elp cheer us up, after all that's happened, eh?"

"Yes, please," I said, and he took my hand.

That was when Tom and I made friends with each other.

31

Aunt Ruby's Secret

THE NEXT FEW DAYS WERE CONFUSING AS I tried to get a sense of place and time. When I woke, the light stung my eyes, my skin prickled all over and my arm ached where an intravenous drip was attached. Fuggy scents cloyed in my nostrils and it felt as if someone had emptied a bucket of sand into my mouth.

I turned my head to find Aunt Ruby, sitting beside me, stroking my hand.

"Hi," I rasped. "What day is it?"

"Darling, have a drink first." She held a glass with a straw to my lips. "It's Sunday."

"What happened? Why am I here?"

"Jess, you were missing for over twenty-four hours," she told me. Her face was pale and more lined than I'd noticed before and her eyes were dull. "The police said you were probably sleeping over at a friend's, despite my protestations that you wouldn't do that without asking me. I called the hospital in case you'd had an accident and been brought in. When you eventually were, they phoned. What a panic I was in." She sighed deeply and continued.

"We think you were mugged, and your phone was missing. Darling, I'm so relieved you are all right. Do you remember anything?" she asked, twisting her hands.

I told my aunt I'd been attacked by Dr Laythorpe. No more selective telling of the facts. The memories flooded back like a deluge. I remembered wrestling with him and knew he'd hit me several times. The last thing I remembered was someone wearing red who I thought had come to help me. Then I must have passed out.

"I don't even know how I ended up in Mulberry Hall that day, Auntie. I was going to school; it just got weird; I mean, *well* weird. But now I know what happened; I know exactly how Adeline died and why."

Aunt Ruby's eyes were wide yet hooded.

"It's all right, Aunt Ruby."

"We were so worried." She took my hand. "And, darling, what do you mean you know what happened?"

"Well, it was her father… he caused her death. It wasn't an accident. And I know he really meant to kill his wife, because…" I tailed off. The pain in Aunt Ruby's eyes was too much.

"I tried to let you know I was there. I thought I might never see you again," I said, and began to cry with relief.

Then I remembered I'd found Joopy at Mulberry Hall. It felt like weeks since I'd found his cage open and him missing.

"Oh no! Jupiter… Auntie, I found him – and now – now, I've lost him again." I sat forward and began looking around the room. "D'you know what happened to my bag? He was in my bag when I got out of Mulb…"

"Jessifer," Aunt Ruby said, firmly. "It's fine. He's at home. Apparently, the nurses got quite a fright when they found a rat snuggling up against your arm. He got a fright too, I heard, when they screamed, and he promptly shot off down the bed frame and wedged himself behind the bedside locker." She began to laugh. "I called Louise and she came and collected him."

"Oh, phew." Brilliant Loopy, she wouldn't have hesitated either.

I slept on and off throughout the day, and that night, Aunt Ruby slept beside me, on a fold-down bed. We talked lots and I was shocked when I found out she'd kept a secret from me, too.

"I have to be honest now, Jessifer," she'd said. "It's probably all a bit fuzzy to you, but…" She paused. "You see, there was an incident at home. Two and a half weeks ago."

I tried to remember back then. The last few weeks felt more like a lifetime. My God, how much my life had changed. But I did remember that Aunt Ruby had been weird. She'd had a phone call from Lynn, her friend. Then she'd walked back into the lounge, looking spooked. Not only that, she'd acted a bit weird from then on, always scuttling through the hall, using any excuse not to spend time lingering there. And she'd been downright weird about the drama tickets too. I remembered thinking at the time, she was talking too much. As if she was trying to keep her mind off something.

"What happened, Auntie?"

"I'm rather embarrassed to admit it now, Jess," she said, looking at her feet, "but… and I was so firm with you about not getting involved in all that unearthly nonsense… well, of course it's not nonsense…"

"Auntie? What is it? Just tell me."

She kept looking at her feet, so I touched her arm.

"Aunt Ruby?"

"I saw her, Jess." Her grey eyes looked into mine and softened. "Such a sweet little thing. And, do you know?" she asked, then continued: "She looked so like Judith." I nodded. "But, I didn't like it." Her eyes filled with tears.

"It's okay, Auntie." I shuffled out from under the bedcovers and bent over her chair to hug her.

"It scared me, Jess. *She* scared me. Such a little, helpless thing too."

I laughed, even though my eyes had filled up, and saw that Aunt Ruby was shocked at me.

"Adeline… helpless? I don't think so, Auntie. I think Adeline knows how to get exactly what she wants. She *is* little and she *is* cute…" I imagined her in my mind's eye and smiled. "Yes, definitely cute, but not helpless."

We spent ages after that just talking about Adeline. I told Aunt Ruby all about her determined, bossy personality and the funny way she talked and skipped about. I felt I'd remember every word she'd ever said to me for the rest of my life.

*

Caroline came the next day.

"I'm sorry, Jess," she said and began to cry, which made me cry all over again. "Your auntie told me what happened. We were really worried. I should've helped you. I've been really mean."

"No. Don't say that, Caroline," I said. "You were worried, that's all. And no wonder. I should've thought more about how it was affecting you. But, I hope you understand… I had to do it."

"I do. I do, Jess. I'm so relieved you're okay. I was a complete cow to you."

I shook my head through my tears and Caroline's eyes filled up too, which made us both laugh and cry together. Actually, the crying was sort of washing me clean of Laythorpe, but I knew I still had work to do. Nevertheless, now wasn't the time.

I lay back against my pillows and Caroline talked about school. My eyes drifted shut. I woke and apologised then did the same thing again.

Rachel and Lou came the following evening and Caroline came again, so all four of us were together. Then Mrs Fortiver arrived. Aunt Ruby shooed the girls out so I could talk to her on my own.

"You've been so brave, Jessifer," she said. "I admire your determination. I just wish I could have carried some of the burden for you."

"But you did, Mrs Fortiver." I paused and smiled at her. I wanted her to see how much she'd helped me. "You know, I thought I was all alone and I just didn't know how to handle it. I couldn't tell anyone. I felt like I was cracking

up. But when I found out about Marie, your ghost, well…
it made me think about how hard it must've been for you,
when you were so young."

"Well, you're young too, Jess, and I must say, you've
handled yourself exceptionally well. And you didn't turn
your back on Adeline. You should feel proud of yourself."

We were both quiet for a moment.

"I feel as if I've let Adeline down though," I said.

"Why?"

"She asked me to get something. Well, at least she told
me about a file, of her dad's, and she said a couple of times,
I could get it. I think that's what she wanted me to do…
what this was all about… and I failed her."

She was quiet for a moment.

"I could try again. I think I know how."

"Now, Jess…" she began.

"No, it's okay, it won't put me in any danger this time."

She didn't look happy about it though.

I decided to change the subject.

"It makes me wonder how someone like Loopy Lou
manages. She has to look after her brother and sister
before she can even do her homework and she's living
between two houses, and she has to do that almost every
day. Normally, my life is so easy compared with hers."

"Well, of course. Now you've been in such a challenging
situation, you can feel a new admiration for Louise."

We were both quiet again.

"I have news, anyway," Mrs Fortiver said, eventually.
"It's about Mrs Mills. She's given her notice at school
and has been absent for the last two days. I feel sure she's

connected with the Laythorpes, as you thought. And to think that ridiculous family tree has been in her office all these years." She gazed off into the distance for a few moments, then continued. "But you know, I do feel rather sad for her."

I wasn't entirely sure what she was getting at and didn't feel comfortable talking about Mills. I remembered her earwigging on my conversation with Mrs Fortiver and watching me in the library. How much did she have to do with this?

"I want to write it all down, Mrs Fortiver," I said. "Do you think I could send my story to the local paper or something?"

"Yes." She clapped her hands together in surprise. "What a great idea. You should. In fact, I think this is the story we've all been waiting for. I have a feeling we can let your little Adeline rest at last." Her warm smile reflected the joy she felt, and I understood how important this was for her after her worries, long ago, about Marie, her teenage ghost.

Then she came back to the idea of me doing more searching.

"What you were saying before, Jess, about this file… you seem to think you can get it. Is that right?"

"Yes. I can. I'm sure of it." I paused. "Because if I don't get it, people might think I've made everything up. I mean, those documents I took pictures of, well, I could've forged those myself, couldn't I? Without the actual record books or something *real* to show, I can't expect people to believe me."

"*How* sure are you though, Jess? You really can't put yourself in danger again."

"I'm pretty sure. Cos, it feels different now." I'd thought of little else for the last three days. I'd seen Adeline's face in my dreams. She'd grinned. Sparkle shone from her eyes. It was a happy face I'd remember forever. Not only that; as well as singing 'Oranges and Lemons', just the title, over and over, she'd also sung: "Papa's secret room". I remembered her showing me the upstairs room: "One more room," she'd said, "and that's Papa's secret room."

*

The next day the doctors said I could go home. I was so happy. Despite Aunt Ruby trying to keep me calm, I sprang into my room to see Jupiter and cried all over his fur. I don't think he was too impressed at getting wet.

*

I looked at my battered face in the mirror. There were greenish purple splodges and a cut over one eyebrow which I think came from the final obliterating punch. My chin was crusty where the scab I'd picked had bled and thickened. At least my spots didn't stand out so much now. I gazed into my own eyes and resolved:

"I'll write who he really was. For you, Adeline, and for me." It was like we were one and the same person just now, despite the age difference. Her little, smiling face, framed by her pink-ribboned braids, swam into view and then quickly faded. "And, for your mama too."

*

I called Caroline's mum. I had a favour to ask.

"Hi Ali," I said.

"Hi Jess. Are you home now?"

We chatted for a bit until Ali said, "Anyway, what can I do for you?"

I explained how I thought there were still documents hidden in Mulberry Hall. I described my images of Adeline, showing how they'd changed. I told Ali how she only said the words, "Papa's secret room."

"She wants me to find the documents," I said.

"I see what you're suggesting, Jess, but I'm not sure I can help. Although…" I waited as the silence on the phone stretched out.

"Give me a couple of days," she said, eventually. "I might have an idea."

*

I strolled into the lounge and collapsed in a chair, puffing out my breath. I was so tired.

"Jessifer," Aunt Ruby said, walking in, "look what I've just found in my bag. I'd forgotten all about it. It was sitting on your bedside locker when I came back from the tea machine, the day you were found. Someone must have delivered it to the hospital by hand. There isn't a stamp."

She handed me a white envelope. It was blank, apart from my first name.

I wrinkled my nose. Who would hand-deliver a letter to me at the hospital? Who could have known I was there? My finger tore a ragged line along the envelope's top edge and I pulled out a small sheet of blue paper. It read:

Jessifer Jordan,

I know you think things. You have it all wrong. Jonathon Laythorpe was a world leader in developing new medical treatments. You are a child. You do not understand. The ghost-child you have become obsessed with is a figment of your imagination. I warn you: do not go any further with this. The Laythorpes of York are an esteemed family. My ancestral family. They have a reputation for prestige and respectability you can only wonder at.

Leave well alone.
Mrs Mills

I stared at her handwriting. So, she *was* connected with Laythorpe. I guessed her pride had been badly hurt. I know we all mocked Mrs Mills at school, but I hadn't ever really minded her that much. I just felt pity for her most of the time. She seemed like she had something to prove, strutting about in clothes meant for someone half her age, accessorised to the hilt with loads of jewellery and always heavily made up. We knew she'd lost her husband years ago and didn't have any children. Maybe the idea that her ancestor's reputation was a sham was too much for her to bear. Perhaps the beliefs of her entire life and the pride and honour she felt were all crashing down around her. So, basically, I was a threat to her status, with my mission to dig up the truth.

*

I'd been told to stay off school for a week. Apparently, I'd been badly concussed and should rest. I was good with that. Also, my blood had shown high levels of morphine.

I recalled the doctor's accusatory tone and the way he'd looked pointedly at the bruise in the crook of my elbow:

"Are you sure you don't remember taking something, Jessifer?"

He'd come back later the same day accompanied by the female consultant. They'd played 'good cop, bad cop' with me. She'd stood there, just smiling, while he'd frowned at me.

"You can tell us. You know, if you've remembered. We won't tell your auntie. Just tell us what it was and where you got it." When I'd remained silent and scowled at him, he'd continued, more brusquely, his voice raised slightly.

"Jessifer, we can give you the best treatment if we know what we're dealing with. Was it someone at school that sold it to you?"

I'd lost my rag at that one.

"I told you before, I didn't take anything," I huffed at him. I needed to show my annoyance because he was implying I was a user and I wasn't. How could I tell them the truth?

Well, you see, I went back in time. To 1863, actually. It was really good. You should try it. I got to meet this guy. A bit like you: a member of the medical profession who thinks he's superior to everyone else. Except, he was addicted to morphine. And he decided to give me a shot too. How nice of him, huh?

They didn't believe me now, but somehow, I suspected they'd believe me less if I told them the facts.

Eventually, 'good cop' had spoken in a soft voice:

"Perhaps the trauma has blocked the memories. I think your attacker maybe gave you a spiked drink? Before you passed out? And then injected you with some crude form of morphine?"

Her raised eyebrows and gentle smile told me she wanted me to agree with her.

"Perhaps," I said. I turned to face the window and heard them leave the room.

*

For the parts of Monday when I wasn't sleeping, I read. Auntie wouldn't let me out of the house, but she went to the library and brought me a stack of books and I enjoyed her own collection too. I couldn't get enough of all things Victorian. There was a great book called *Folklore and Fairy Tales from the 1900s*. I was amazed by the superstitions those people had and they didn't even live that long ago. I mean, it was a long time to me, but in the history of the world, it was like, no more than five minutes, and yet they believed in so much rubbish. When I came across the subject of superstitions surrounding cats, I nearly fell off my chair. I showed Caroline when she dropped in after school.

"Look at this," I said, smoothing a double page flat. "Remember I told you what Laythorpe did to Clementine?"

"Ugh. Sealed her into the wall, poor creature. Cats aren't my favourite thing, but burying a cat alive? No animal deserves that."

"Well, it was a thing they did in Victorian times, although some people say they only put in cats who'd already died."

"So, why would anyone do that?" Caroline was scowling at a gruesome photograph of a mummified cat.

"It was to protect the household against evil spirits. Look here." I pointed to the part of the passage that explained the reasons for the bizarre custom.

A practice which had been prevalent in Europe from the Middle Ages, the purpose of entombing the family pet was to ward off evil, bring good luck to the residents and protect against witchcraft. It is not uncommon for mummified remains to be discovered during renovations to old houses. Image, p57.

"The irony is, Adeline's dad did it out of spite, not for protection. Boy, their house could've used some protection from evil spirits. Or from *him*, more like. But no! He used poor Clementine and when he'd finished with her, he chucked her in that hole and left her to die."

"And you saw all that?"

"Yes." I sighed. I still wished I'd been able to get her out before she suffocated.

*

On Tuesday, I began to write about my experiences. It was funny how I became a bit more detached from the story. I began seeing it from the view of a bystander more than a participant. And I felt as if I could let go of Judith more. I'd never forget her, or my parents, but spending time with Adeline seemed to have satisfied that craving in me to experience again what it was like to have a sister. And it made me think a lot about my relationships with all those – still living – that I loved. Most of all, I totally doubled my love and respect for Aunt Ruby. I'd never take her for granted again.

I didn't get my phone back but at least I'd emailed everything to Mrs Fortiver last week. I shuddered when I thought about the mugger and wondered what he'd done with my phone. Probably sold it to fund his next fix. I found it hard to separate the mental image of the guy with the red tee-shirt from Laythorpe, as if they were one and the same.

When I went back to school, I went to see Mrs Fortiver at lunch and together, we looked over the documents we had. We talked about my article.

"One more thing," I said. "That's all I need. Something that will prove what he was doing. I *will* get it. I know I will." I hadn't ever felt surer of anything.

32

MULBERRY HALL
CHINA SHOP

"HI ALI," I SAID INTO THE PHONE. IT WAS Tuesday evening and I was feeling tons better.

"Hello Jess. I've got good news but there *is* a catch, okay?"

"Okay," I said.

"I have to do an out-of-hours stocktake for my department. So, I've asked my manager if Caroline, and all of you, can come in and help, to earn a bit of money. Sort of a mini work experience."

"Right," I said, not quite understanding how this was going to help. "Is it because of problems with sales at Mulberry Hall?" I felt partly responsible, even though it was nothing to do with me. Nevertheless, the ghost-hunting bug had affected business and I'd been hunting – and finding – my own ghost.

"Partly, Jess. The owners are running viability studies. There's a risk the shop'll have to close. But it's also the time of year for stocktaking. We need to list the existing stock before we order up for the new financial year."

She must have detected the worry in my voice because she added:

"Jess… listen… it isn't to do with what's been happening to you. And before you ask, I haven't said anything to my boss. He doesn't know any more than anyone else. Just that a teenager was mugged in the street. No connection with Mulberry Hall."

"Okay. If you're certain then."

"So, about the job… I'll show you all what to do and we should be able to get it done fairly fast. Caroline thinks Rachel and Lou'll agree to help. Then, once we're done, we can go and look for your evidence. The storerooms and the office all open from the same master key. What do you think?"

I was so relieved. We might not find anything but at least I'd be trying. For Adeline.

"That's amazing, Ali. Thanks. Really, thanks so much. You're brilliant!"

Ali laughed.

"When do we do it?"

"How about Friday evening?" she said.

"Great."

*

Ali had promised to take us all for pizza after, so we were motivated to work efficiently. It was actually interesting.

Ali's department was glass and crystal which was sold along with all the varieties of china. I'd never known there were so many different types. There were wine glasses, decanters, plates, fruit bowls and ornaments. The stock lists were meticulous and we got through the work quickly.

Then Ali suggested we check the cupboards in the upstairs storerooms and the filing cabinets in the office. I'd never been in the eaves of the building before and it was amazing to see all the old furniture up there. Touching the items, even smelling the sweet, yet fusty, aroma of the wood, made me feel close to Adeline, as if I were back there with her. While I didn't want to go anywhere near Laythorpe ever again, that closeness to Adeline made me feel calm, fresh and happy.

"Why is all this stuff shoved away up here? Lou asked. "Wouldn't people buy these cupboards for, like, loads of money? They must be antiques." She ran her hand along the intricate carving of a sideboard panel and sniffed the musty air.

"Probably, Lou, but the company's focus is tableware and that sort of thing," Ali said. Then she looked warily at me. "They say some of these pieces date from when the house was a family home." She was twitchy and began to hurry us. "I think we're done here, Jess. We'll check the office but I'm not feeling very hopeful, I'm afraid."

So, we searched the office on the ground floor, which I thought roughly matched the part of the house where Laythorpe's medical room had been. There, both in folders on shelves and sorted in filing cabinets, everything was immaculately organised. It didn't take long for Ali to recognise it all concerned Mulberry Hall tableware. Absolutely nothing from Laythorpe. I would have gone through it more systematically, but Ali was doing me a favour and she soon ushered us out and locked the door. It was clear she felt uncomfortable about the whole thing, but I knew this was my last chance to incriminate Laythorpe. I tried to get a mental picture of the rooms as they'd been during Adeline's short life here.

"Ali, is there a small room on the first floor? I think that's where the documents will be. Remember, I told you about the room Adeline called Papa's secret room?"

"Er, yes, I think so," she said.

"It was at the right-hand side of the building, nearest Mulberry Lane."

"There is a poky old room there, but I think it's empty," Ali said, grimacing. "And I think we should go. Come on girls, get your coats on."

I was stunned. That was the one room I really needed to look in.

"But, Ali, can't we just go and have a quick look?"

Ali began looking about her.

"Jess, we need to go, honey," she said.

I chewed my lip.

"Would it be okay if I catch you up? You can leave me the keys and tell me how to set the alarm. I'll go and have a quick look and meet you all in Paolo's."

Ali laughed, a bit hysterically.

"Jess, I can't do that! Come on, girls, coats on."

"Yeah, I'm starving," said Lou.

I put my face in my hands and groaned. I couldn't leave without finding Adeline's 'bocudents'. And then I realised what was wrong with Ali.

"Oh my God; I've just realised… Ali, you've seen Adeline, haven't you?"

Ali turned white. Caroline's head snapped round and she glared at her mum.

"Mum? Have you?" she said.

Ali shut her eyes and nodded.

"We don't go up there. That room has such a strong presence. I saw the child once, in the café, and still can't accept it, even though her image is stamped on my mind. I was scared, yes. But the child isn't the problem. It's that room. Everyone avoids it. That's why it's virtually empty. Even the owner doesn't go in there. And I don't think you'll find anything." She glanced around at us all. "Aren't you hungry?" she asked. "Wouldn't you rather go and have pizza now?" Again, I could see how uncomfortable she felt but I couldn't give in. Adeline's voice drifted through my mind again.

"Please, please let me go up on my own. If I don't find anything, I'll settle for food. You can all wait for me down here." I peered hard at her, grimacing. I had to show her how important this was.

Ali sighed. "All right. You need to go round the back of the café kitchen. There's a narrow corridor. Turn right and the door's just along there."

"Thank you, thank you," I said and ran up the stairs.

I was at the top step when I heard Lou.

"I'm coming with you. You're not doing this on your own, sister."

Then, they were all upstairs, even Ali.

"Jess, I'm sorry," she said. "I really don't like it up…"

"It's okay, Ali," I said. "We're all together. What can happen?"

We headed up the narrow staircase and into the corridor along the far side of the café, which was shut up for the night. I shuddered. This was one section of Mulberry Hall which seemed unchanged from the nineteenth century.

"Oh man, it's freezing up here," Rachel said, hugging herself.

This corridor did feel ten times colder than the rest of the building.

"These old buildings tend to be pretty draughty," Ali said, her voice shaking. "This is the room." There was the door. It looked just as it had.

Then I heard Adeline singing again, but this time, I wasn't the only one to hear her.

"… and here comes a chopper to chop off your head."

I caught the look on Caroline's face and felt sorry I'd dragged her into all this.

"Blimey, Jess. I can't b… bear it; the things you've gone through," she said and clutched my arm, her grip so tight, it hurt. Rachel was clutching her too, and we were almost moving along as one, in a huddle.

"My God, is that Adeline?" said Lou, scowling darkly. "Is that why it feels so cold… and, urgh, bad up here?" But I thought it more likely that Laythorpe was the one providing the evil presence in this corridor.

Ali pushed open the unlocked door. She fumbled around the wall, reaching for the light switch.

The light came on but was dim. It felt different from the other rooms. Sombre. I hadn't liked it in 1863 and I didn't like it now. I glanced around and spotted the small window which looked onto the lane.

"This is his secret room," I whispered. "I recognise it and the window's the same as it was." I scanned my friends' faces. They were all frowning at me. I think they were worried all the bad things would start again.

There *was* a presence here, like Ali said. It was like an indecisive breeze, fluctuating, as if competing forces of good and evil were vying for position. The room was mostly bare but there was a small square desk, a bookcase containing some books about pottery, and a sideboard with nothing on it. It had two cupboards and three drawers.

"It's the same sideboard," I said.

I was starting to tremble and my teeth began to chatter.

"You've gone pale," Caroline said, pulling her coat around her more tightly.

"Jess, are you all right?" Ali asked, putting her arm round me.

"Yeah. I think so," I said but I just stood, staring at the sideboard, my feet glued to the floor.

"Right," said Lou. "I'm going in. I want outta here. Pizza here we come!" She plunged forward and began yanking open the top drawer with two hands, pulling on the same brass handle I'd touched in 1863. The drawer screeched and the entire sideboard shook with the effort of getting it open.

"I'll do this cupboard," said Rachel, pointing at one, "if you'll do the other one, Caroline."

"I'll check the bookcase then," said Ali.

"I wonder if there's anything in these," said Rachel, pulling cardboard files out of her cupboard, but they seemed to be mostly full of data sheets about different types of pottery. Dull as anything.

"Look at this!" said Lou and held a brown leather document file up to her nose and sniffed it. It was old; the cover was soft and worn. She opened it and two sheets of paper fell out.

"These are definitely old, Jess," said Caroline, lifting one from the floor just as the lights flickered. "Look at this: 1853… seems to be his degree… University of Aberdeen… and this…" She picked up another. "Blimey, it says *Marriage Certificate of . . .*" She peered at the tiny, looped writing. "*Jocelyn Margaret Eden Bulmer married Dr Jonathon David Laythorpe. Saturday the sixth of September, 1856.* Wow."

I stepped beside her and touched the leather.

"A big brown purse," I whispered. But what we'd found wouldn't help at all. These were old documents but there was nothing incriminating in them.

"There's nothing but books on these shelves," said Ali. "I've opened them all in case there are any papers slipped inside but, nothing. Sorry, Jess. Are we done? Can we go now?"

I sighed.

"These aren't going to help prove anything, are they?" I said. Caroline placed them on the sideboard and my heart plummeted. What should we do now?

Without warning, I heard Joopy's squeaking and he scrambled out of my bag and down my leg, then scuttled across the floor to huddle in the corner.

"Joopy!" I gasped. "How did you get in there? I left you in your crate..." I looked around at the others.

"Oh, yeah," said Lou, scrunching her face in doubt.

"I did. Really, I did. I couldn't bring him back here after..." But I couldn't finish my sentence. Before our eyes, curling like smoke, threading between us, followed Clementine, sleek, determined, predatory. Of course, Jupiter spied her coming and shot from his corner. He scurried up the far end of the sideboard, over the open cupboard door and into the dark interior. Clementine flashed after him in full chase and she, too, disappeared inside the cupboard.

"Jess, it's that cat we saw in the Blacksmith's Arms. It *is* a ghost cat after all," said Lou, her mouth hanging open. And there wasn't any doubt. My live rat was being chased by a cat-spirit. Accepting the impossible without question, we all bent forwards and examined the inside of the cupboard.

"I think we should get out of here," said Ali. "This is too strange for words. Come on, Jess, please."

"I have to get Joopy," I said, kneeling in front of the cupboard. There were a couple more cardboard files, empty ones, which I swept onto the floor. Then I reached all around, expecting to find a fluffy mound in one corner.

"Here, Joopy," I called but the cupboard was empty. My heart sank lower. I'd lost him again. Perhaps, in the dim light, I'd failed to notice that he'd scuttled back out of the sideboard. As I twisted around to look, Clementine burst back out of the cupboard, seeming to spring from my very flesh. We all gasped as we watched her glide towards the door and slink into the corridor beyond.

Turning back to the cupboard, I could hardly see anything in the gloom, yet, my fingers caught on something at the back.

"There's a hole in the wood," I said. I hooked my fingers inside. The hole was the size of a small apple, just big enough for a slender rat to squeeze through. I began tugging, and with a crack, part of the back panel of the cupboard came away.

I pulled the splintered wood out carefully and Rachel took it from me and placed it on the floor. Back inside the cupboard, my hand flicked into a large free space beyond… a hole in the wall. Just like Adeline had said. My skin brushed against gritty stone or plaster and as I lowered my hand and patted about, I felt, first, something dry, rough and creased, like fabric, a package of some sort, then behind it, something warm, furry and trembling. I let Joopy smell my hand then gently lifted him free. I cradled him to me and then stood and turned to Loopy.

"Lou, will you hold him for me? There's something else in there." Lou took Joopy and began cooing to him. My heart was thumping.

I knelt back down and reached inside, this time with both hands. My fingers pressed against the rough fabric and I was just about to reach further in when a distant jangling sound came from downstairs. I turned to look at the others. They'd all heard it too.

"The shop door," gasped Ali. "I must have forgotten to lock us in."

"What shall we do?" asked Rachel, querulously.

I watched Ali chewing on her lip and I brought my hands back out of the cupboard. By now, we could hear someone thumping up the carpeted stairs. Whoever it was, they weren't worried about being heard because mumbling accompanied their progress. I gulped when I realised I knew the voice.

"Quick!" I said. "It's Mrs Mills." I reached my hands in and heard Ali say:

"Come with me, Caroline. Lou and Rachel, stay here with Jess." They stepped out into the corridor and headed towards the stairs. I had the package now and moved it forwards easily. It dropped from its secret hiding place into the cupboard. Pulling it out, I saw a cream-coloured linen bag.

"This *must* be it," I said, turning to Lou and Rachel. "Hidden in the wall." I reached inside the bag and pulled out a pile of linen-bound books and another brown leather file. Dropping the bag to the floor, I knew I was right. The books were Laythorpe's record books, the very same ones I'd photographed in 1863. I opened one and began peering at the words when Ali's raised voice burst along the corridor.

"You can't be in here, Mrs Mills. I should have locked the door. I'm in the middle of a stocktake and my daughter and her friends are helping. I'm afraid you'll have to go back downstairs and leave."

"I'll do no such thing," barked Mrs Mills in response, her voice getting closer.

"How did you know we'd be here, anyway?" Ali asked.

"Because your manager told me," said Mills. "I called at the weekend. I wanted to come and have a look around, before the shop closes." She appeared in the room, ahead of Ali and Caroline.

"How do you know about that?" asked Ali. "It's meant to be private, at least for now."

"You'd be surprised," said Mills. "When one has a connection with the family that used to live here, it brings certain privileges. I happened to mention to your manager that I teach your daughter. He told me you were doing a stocktake tonight."

Ali shook her head in disbelief.

"So, you won't mind if I look around. Hello Jessifer. Fancy seeing you here." She completely ignored Lou and Rachel and her eyes burned into mine. She gave me a look of such hatred, I should have felt afraid of her, but I didn't. I held the books tightly to my chest. Her eyes dropped and she saw them.

"What have you got there?" she said and lurched towards me on silly, tottering heels.

Suddenly the light flickered then went out altogether. Someone shoved me and the books and papers fell with a thud to the floor.

Lou and Caroline screeched, and Rachel grabbed me in the pitch black.

"Girls, try and stay calm," said Ali with a wobbly voice. "It's the old wiring system. This room wasn't updated like the others." I heard her stepping towards the light switch. A blast of chilly air blew against my face.

"Rachel? Is that you?" I said. "You're tugging my arm." I heard the flick of the switch as Ali tried, in vain, to dispel the darkness.

"Rachel?" I said. "Wait till the light comes back on or…"

"I'm not touching you," came Rachel's shaky voice from the other side of the room.

"Who is it then?" I said. "Stop pulling me!"

The lights suddenly responded to Ali's incessant flicking and everyone screamed.

"Oh, no, please," said Ali, her face masked in shock, her eyes wide, focused just above my head. The others were huddled around her. As the lights flickered off again, my bones felt as if they would crack from the force of his hand. Then his hold switched to my waist. I glanced down and saw his skin, grey, somehow ethereal, but so strong. I twisted my neck, daring to look him in the eye. His face was full of menace. I thought I'd choke because my breath was stuck. I couldn't draw it right in but I couldn't get it out either. His animal stare drilled into me, leaving pain and fear so strong I thought I'd buckle to the floor. As he pulled me backwards, my feet scraped the boards, but he seemed to lose his grip a little and I slid down, my legs wobbling with fright. But his strength fired up again and he began pulling me in the opposite direction.

"No!" I cried out, thinking he would drag me off and obliterate me. Though, where could he take me? This was the twenty-first century. He didn't belong here.

"NO!" I screamed, again, into the blackness of the room. "Not now! You're not getting me. I *will* show the world who you really were."

"No… no… no… surely not," I heard Mills say, her voice tremulous. "Dr… Dr… Laythorpe? Is it… is it really you? I'm Margaret Mills… your brother was my great…" Her voice cut out as the lights flickered on and off, continuously.

But she began again:

"This gentleman was an… is an… esteemed…" Again, she stopped short and the room filled with a tearing, ripping sound which turned to a fluttering, as if we were surrounded by a flock of vicious paper demons.

He's destroying them, I thought. *The documents.* Anger screamed in my head. *Let him shred them. However long it takes me, I will piece them all back together.*

As the fluttering settled, his voice clattered out:

"I will not let you shatter my reputation. Adeline is only a child. What can she possibly understand? I tell you, I will make you regret your actions. Leave alone what does not concern you."

His grip intensified and I couldn't understand how he could tug so hard. It felt as if I would split in two. As the lights flashed on, I saw his arm again. He yanked me backwards and then hurled me away from him but tugged me back. Away, and back again, like rope in a tug of war. I was powerless to fight him. How was he doing this? My neck was flipping from side to side and I felt winded.

"Leave her alone!" came Ali's voice, commanding, then my friends' voices, more panicked. Now the light was flickering persistently, on, off, on, off.

"Dr Laythorpe… if you will let me deal with this… I will… I will protect your name. I have almost persuaded the council to make a plaque, a commemorative plaque, for the building, with your name…" tried Mrs Mills, seeming, in the flickering light, to grasp at his arm, trying to gain his attention, but Laythorpe silenced her with a loud:

"NO. Be quiet. You are nothing to do with me."

In another flicker, I saw Mills still trying to grasp his arm, desperate for his approval.

Suddenly, I fell to the floor and felt the strong grip around my waist. But it wasn't him. It couldn't be. Laythorpe's arms were pale and thin. This arm was muscular; the arm of someone used to physical work out of doors; not someone who worked in a hospital; or someone who kept careful record books; or someone who injected himself frequently with opium. This was the arm of Tom Metcalfe and it was supporting me, firmly, to stand. I realised why I'd felt tugged in opposite directions. It was because Laythorpe had pulled me one way and Tom the other. Tom, with his superior strength, had won. I raised my eyes and what I saw left me feeling more conflicted than I could have imagined. With my back to the door, I saw Laythorpe's figure, diminishing, like a dying rainstorm, as if he was passing through the far wall. And, hanging on to him, still, was Mrs Mills. Her eyes were wide and her mouth was open but mute. As the sweetest sound of a six-year-old's laughter rippled through the room, the pair disappeared and the light came back on, dim but steady.

"Haha! Hahahaha!" Adeline had come back. And Tom was with her. As he let go his grip of me, Adeline took his hand and the pair drifted to the door. There, they turned to face me.

"I knew you could do it. Thank you, clever Jessifer. And Clementine too, my brilliant cat." She beamed and turned to smile at Tom, who grinned back at her.

Then he looked at me.

"I told you it'd be all right, didn't I?" His eyes twinkled at me and then, together, they turned and left the room. Adeline began to sing the nursery rhyme but this time she just kept singing:

"Oranges and lemons…", repeating the phrase over and over, the sound fading as she went down the corridor, until we couldn't hear it any more.

I stepped back against the wall, panting. I looked around. The light stayed on and warm air filtered into the room. I saw the papers, scattered everywhere, some ripped. My friends stood in silence for a few seconds, staring, shocked.

"Let's gather these and get out of here," said Ali, taking charge.

We moved like clockwork, fast and efficient. They handed me their bundles and Ali switched off the light.

*

As we stepped into the main office, I hugged the big bundle of papers, books and torn documents to my chest and sucked in a huge breath. I felt exhausted and triumphant yet confused. *What had just happened to Mrs Mills?* I watched Ali take her bag and scarf from a hat stand. She put them on the big table in the corner which also bore a kettle and a tray of mugs.

With pinched eyebrows, she scrutinised the room. I knew she was trying to locate the weird clacking noise, like a regular tick-tocking, but she seemed to dismiss it and stepped over to me.

"Jessifer? How do you feel?" she asked.

"I'm okay."

Ali narrowed her eyes.

"No, I am, really. But how about you all?" I tried to keep my shaking voice even. "I've been getting used to this stuff. I'm so sorry I got you involved." I coughed, trying to cover the awkwardness I felt. I looked at their faces. Apart from Ali, none of them had said a word since we left the 'secret room'.

Lou was the first to respond.

"Awh, we're okay, aren't we troops?" Her voice was strained.

"We're good. I think," Caroline said, shrugging her shoulders.

"I can't believe it," said Rachel. "It's awful." Her face was white.

"It's over, Rachel," I said, stuffing the leather files and all the papers into the cream linen bag. "*Now*, it's really over." I'd seen what the documents contained. "Let's get out of here." I looked at Ali, who smiled. No one mentioned Mrs Mills.

"Go Jessie!" said Lou, air-boxing with her fists, though slightly half-heartedly.

I indicated for them to leave the room ahead of me. I wanted to be the last out before Ali locked the door. As they went, each of them looked back at the table in the corner. Gazing there, too, and seeing nothing but the dark shapes of the kettle and mugs, I backed out of the room and smiled. Click-clack. Click-clack. Click-clack.

33

HAPPY GIRL

TOM SAT ON THE TABLE NEXT TO ME.

Miss Jessifer had found Papa's bocudents. She was happy and I felt like summer. I smiled at Tom. He smiled back.

I sat on my hands and swung my legs. My boots were like a locomotive engine, click-clacking, click-clacking, down a railway track, all the way to the seaside for a lovely holiday. I liked what Lou said, so I copied her.

"Go Jessie!"

"Go Jessie, go!" said Tom. He laughed a big, noisy laugh.

I slid off the table and ran to the door. I heard the key click in the lock on the other side.

"Come on, Tom," I said, "let's find Clementine."

Tom followed me through the door.

"What a little cracker, you are, Adeline," he said. "You did right good."

We walked towards the hall and the lights came back on and we were in my house, how it used to be and that was nice, because I liked my house a lot better when it was that way. We sat on the second-bottom step of Mama's beautiful staircase and Clementine came strolling over, curling her tail like a question mark.

"Good job, Clementine," said Tom. Then she jumped on my lap and Tom and I stroked her. She purred and purred.

34

RIGHTING WRONGS

WE WALKED QUICKLY AWAY FROM Mulberry Hall. As we approached the shimmering lights of Paolo's Pizza Place, my mind buzzed with anticipation. We shrugged our coats off and talked about other things for a while but by the time the waiter brought our food, we'd recovered enough to go over what had happened.

I passed Laythorpe's books around the table and the others pored over them.

"God, he was a right nutter, wasn't he?" said Rachel, working her way down a page with her fingertip. "Imagine giving yourself that junk in order to test it out for your patients."

"Yeah, I'll just try this myself… oops, I seem to have developed a bit of a drug habit!" mocked Lou.

"Phh," sighed Caroline. "I feel so sorry for his wife, don't you?" She looked at Ali.

"Yes. She must have worried terribly when he was taking the drugs. What was it doing to him? From what you've discovered, Jess, he was quite deranged, really, but his physical health must have suffered, too. I'm sure Jocelyn would have tried to shield Adeline from it but, in private, she would have been in turmoil. The shame of it would have been awful. A doctor, in his position, ministering to patients and not fit to practise. No doubt, she'd have tried to keep it from the servants and the public, too. But these things usually come out in the end. Especially in cases of addiction. People just know."

I remembered the conversation between the ward sister and the doctor in the hospital, when I'd eavesdropped. The sister certainly knew and tried to do something about it because it was affecting patients. Big time.

"Jocelyn tried to get him to stop," I said, watching their faces. They still didn't know how much I'd seen and heard but Ali continued:

"She must have been so embarrassed. But, in the end, she lost her child. What did that do to her?" Ali's gaze dropped to the table. "We can't begin to imagine how awful it must have been." Her hand drifted across to Caroline's. Caroline gave it a squeeze and we were all silent for a few minutes. Eventually, Ali sniffed and looked up again.

"Is it enough?" she asked me, indicating the books and papers. "What you've got there? Because that man destroyed his family."

I looked at her face, which was creased with concern, and thought how generous she'd been, taking us along, asking us to help with the stocktake. I could imagine, with all our chattering *and* searching for the documents, it had probably taken us twice the time it should have.

"Oh yes," I said. "Thanks so much, Ali. I'm sorry for putting you through all this. I'll make it up to you, I promise."

"No need for that, Jess. If it helps, that's enough for me." She smiled broadly then put her other hand on mine.

I scanned the document I was holding. It was written in Laythorpe's looped handwriting. I'd had to match the pieces to read it as it was one of the pages he'd torn. It was a description of his development of the morphine solution and how he began to use it on himself and his patients. All the results were there. But it wasn't a scientific document. It was littered with profanities against those who didn't support his experimentation: Jocelyn; his doctor friend, Anthony; his brother, Hobson. His threat to kill Jocelyn was there: '*If she doesn't stop interfering, I'll have to silence her ...*', as were his vows to continue his work. It was exactly what I needed: an autobiographical account of that terrible time in his life.

"And look at this, Jess," said Rachel, who'd found the bottom half of a torn page, which she'd matched with its top. We read:

Partridge thinks he can have me investigated. Seems to think I orchestrated Adeline's death. He even brought a policeman in to examine the balustrade upstairs. But guess who they believed? Unlike Partridge, they are not deluded. Partridge no longer has a place in this house.

"He did orchestrate Adeline's death! Well, at least, Jocelyn's. The guy was completely deranged. He deliberately messed with that banister so she'd fall to her death. And that's why Adeline wanted me to sort things out. Because he was a murderer. Not just that, but the fact that he's meant to be this amazingly talented doctor, who brought a great service to the world. Huh! As if!"

I flicked to the bottom of the pile of documents.

I'll go to America, he'd written in dramatic style. *They won't bother me there. Jocelyn has gone off to her father's house and they do not understand the importance of my work here. I'll be appreciated in the war effort. I can treat the wounded and they'll see . . .* It ended there.

The others were all huddled round, peering at the sheet, reading along with me.

"He was a disturbed man, Jess," said Ali. "It's hardly surprising that he thought it was okay to attempt to kill his wife like that. I don't suppose he was thinking logically."

*

"Jessifer?"

It was the week after the stocktake and I was on my way to meet my friends in the canteen. I turned to see Mr Lloyd rushing towards me.

"Yes, sir?"

"I've got news for you. You'll know I've been doing some research into Dr Laythorpe?

"Er, yes, sir."

"Well, I kept coming up against a wall until I heard about an American historian with an interest in the development of narcotics. I emailed her and she wants to meet you."

"Okay. What exactly for, sir?"

"Well," and he began to smile widely, "well," he continued, "you might be surprised by this, but she's been researching Laythorpe too."

"No way," I said, my jaw hanging.

"Well, how about that then?" He seemed really pleased with himself, still smiling, hands on his hips. Everyone liked Mr Lloyd. He was lovely and a more camp guy you'd never meet. Although, he said 'well' far more than was healthy for anyone.

Then his face fell suddenly.

"Oh, Jessifer, you're not very happy about this? I haven't given her your personal details, I promise."

He must have noticed my straight face. It was just that I was deep in thought.

"No. It's not that. It's just a shame she's in America."

"Well, well, don't worry about that. I actually spoke to her online on Saturday," he rushed to say. "We can arrange another internet chat. Well…" His eyes were bright and I couldn't help returning his smile. "How about I have a chat with your aunt, and we can arrange a time to call? I can be in on it too, if you want."

*

So, that's what we did. We made a video call. The historian's name was Clare and she was lovely. I couldn't believe all the facts she'd found. She had details of Laythorpe's arrival in New York and she'd mapped his movements west, towards Pittsburgh. Actually, he didn't last long. He'd applied to work as a doctor in the American Civil War but a festering wound of his own (said to be from a deep scratch, possibly sustained by a cat) led to septicaemia and he'd died in agonising torment, unable to gain any relief from the morphine treatment they gave him because of his tolerance to the drug. At that point, his brother, Hobson, had had his body repatriated to Britain.

By then, his misdemeanours were forgotten by the authorities. Nevertheless, Clare had found letters from Jocelyn to Partridge and vice versa. It was true that Partridge had tried to have Laythorpe convicted. When Adeline died, Jocelyn's anger had pushed her to blame the staff at Mulberry Hall. She'd accused Partridge of not looking after things properly. He'd investigated the damaged balustrade and thought it had been tampered with, so he'd contacted the police. An officer had come and heard him out but said there was no evidence that it was anything but an accident and Partridge had detailed all this in his letter to Jocelyn, who was, by then, living at her father's house. The police had refused to investigate further.

"The only thing I don't understand is why he did it," said Clare.

"He was trying to kill Jocelyn," I said, and I told her about his resentment at Jocelyn's interference. "He mentions it a couple of times in the documents I have. At one point, he was going to give her morphine somehow, without her knowing, to quieten her down. I don't know if he ever did, but he threatened to. And then, he said he was going to silence her for good, because she was trying to stop his work."

"Okay, well, that makes sense," said Clare.

"But why would they have dropped the case so easily?" I asked. "Wouldn't the police have had to go into it a bit more?"

"Not really," Clare said. "Policing was different then, Jess. With domestic crime like that, and particularly in a wealthy household, they would only have investigated at the wishes of the homeowner. And, of course, the word of a woman wouldn't have stood for much, which is probably why Jocelyn didn't take it further. She'd have known she wouldn't be taken seriously."

"Wouldn't they have brought detectives in, though?" I said. "Or something like that?"

"No. Victorian policing was much more basic and criminal investigation wasn't a thing until later. Into the twentieth century, really. Not only that, corruption was very common at that time and it's possible that Laythorpe might have bullied the police."

"Yes! Yes!" I said, jumping up from my chair in front of the laptop screen. Clare raised her eyebrows.

"It sounds to me like you know something." She smiled.

I rifled through my documents till I found the one.

"Here, look." I held the page up to the screen for a few seconds and then I turned it round and began to read: "*Partridge thinks he can have me investigated. Seems to think I orchestrated Adeline's death. He even brought a policeman in to examine the balustrade upstairs. But guess who they believed? Unlike Partridge, they are not deluded.* Doesn't that sound like he influenced the police?"

"It certainly does. You've done well, Jess. Maybe you can scan and email those documents to me."

"Sure, I'd be glad to. I think you'll find his record books interesting."

So, between us we filled in the gaps and concluded that Laythorpe had got away with it all: his shocking treatment of patients, his lack of professionalism, his own addiction, and most of all, his daughter's death.

There was a letter Clare had found that showed how Hobson, Laythorpe's older brother, who was a lawyer, had protected Laythorpe, and it seemed as though he, and some medical supporters of Laythorpe, were responsible for promoting his work as commendable. The weird thing that came across in that letter, which was dated September 1863, and sent to Laythorpe in Pittsburgh, was that Hobson had loved Adeline and had continued a positive relationship with Jocelyn. '*Jocelyn*', he wrote, '*struggles badly with grief for Adeline.*' The same letter described a conversation between Hobson and the director of the hospital, in which the director referred to Laythorpe's compelling results.

I was really pleased when Clare told me she'd found records indicating Jocelyn's later remarriage. I wanted to believe Jocelyn had found happiness eventually.

*

A week later, I was thrilled with the article in the local paper. The editor had called Mrs Fortiver to let me know it would be in. Mrs Fortiver had been a great help, showing me how to redraft it and make it really good. Aunt Ruby and I huddled together on the couch with the paper between us. We snapped the pages over, scouring every headline. It was like unwrapping a giant sweetie.

There it was.

Teenager Unravels the Truth.

I'd met with and liked the editor. She'd been warm and attentive. I'd given her my permission to change my work a little to make it better for the paper but she'd hardly changed anything.

Of course, I missed out all the parts about meeting ghosts. Mrs Fortiver had said that was something for the future. A novel. My story. For now, and for the paper, it was best to stick to the back story of the little ghost of Mulberry Hall.

So, I wrote about Mulberry Hall and its residents. I described my own 'imagined' image of six-year-old Adeline Laythorpe. I painted her as a happy, energetic little girl. I showed her mother, Jocelyn, as the philanthropist she was. Mostly, though, I described the doctor who became so wrapped up in his research into new ways of administering morphine that he became addicted to the drug himself, ruining his future, splintering his family and killing his daughter. I explained how morphine was both a blessing and a curse of the time and listed the evidence I had to prove Laythorpe was not a pioneer but a fraud and a murderer.

The editor loved it and said what Mrs Fortiver had predicted: it was the story the whole city had been waiting for.

35

A Play, a Tree
and a Bench

"WOOHOO! WE DID IT!" LOU KNOCKED MY bag to the floor in her excitement.

"Loopy!" I gasped. "Do you have to always do that? I take it, you've won again? Do you ever *not* win?"

"Not much," she said and grinned. "Anyway, how's the play coming along?"

"Great," I replied. "You coming?"

"Try and stop me."

"Try and stop you what?" asked Rachel, as Lou and I joined her and Caroline in the canteen.

"Coming to the play," I said.

Audrey, my drama teacher, had suggested doing a drama about my experiences. She'd seen my article in the paper and got in touch with Mrs Fortiver and together, they'd written the play during the summer holidays. Now, almost a year after I'd first met Adeline, our drama group was ready to perform. We'd booked the local amateur theatre and the show would run over three nights. The first performance was less than a fortnight away. I couldn't wait.

"Are you going to mention about the tree then, like you said?" asked Caroline.

"I think so. Audrey said we could ask for donations after each performance. Oh, I forgot to tell you. My uncle's friend is going to make one of those circular benches to go around it. Maybe we could get a plaque for it."

"Aw, that's a nifty idea," said Lou, wrinkling her nose in approval.

Caroline and Rachel's faces fell.

"What's wrong?" I asked. "Don't you think so?"

"Oh, yes," said Caroline, her eyes brightening but her mouth drooped again. "It's just sad, that's all."

"I know. She was so young, wasn't she?" Rachel said, her eyes fixed on the table.

I glanced at Lou. Even she now looked downcast.

"Hey, don't be glum," I said. Unconsciously, we all held hands across the table. "She was happy at the end. She just wanted it all known."

"I think it's a great thing to do, Jess," said Caroline. "You're really kind. You've been through so much for her. As for her father, what an evil monster." Her eyes narrowed.

"Yeah," said Lou.

Rachel snorted her agreement.

I was quiet. I pictured him, after the death. He'd been in despair, like everyone else. He *was* her dad, after all.

That must have meant something to him. And his research had started with good intentions.

"Jess? You're not saying anything," said Caroline.

I sighed. "He was good once, you know. He did love her, I'm sure of that. He just made some bad decisions."

"Too right, he did," spat Lou.

"What I mean is, I think he wanted the good family life, with his wife and little girl. And I think, maybe he wanted to show Jocelyn's family that he could be successful. Maybe he was intimidated by her father's wealth and wanted to prove he was a suitable husband. It just didn't work out that way. And when he became addicted to the drug, well, it all went badly wrong."

"Yeah, duh, he killed his daughter," said Caroline.

I chewed my lip and looked at the table.

"You'll always have a special place in your heart for Adeline, won't you, Jess?" said Rachel, returning the conversation to happier things.

"Mm-hm," I said, feeling a huge lump in my throat.

*

The play was a success. We got a good crowd every night and we collected enough money to pay for the tree and the plaque. There were loads of people from our school and practically all the staff from Mulberry Hall came.

*

A month later, we were in the woods for the tree-planting ceremony. Aunt Ruby had asked permission to plant a little birch sapling in Lock Woods and our minister from church had agreed to preside over the ceremony. Now, here it was: a bright little tree with a cage of wire to protect it until it grew bigger and stronger. A perfect memorial to Adeline's short life. And surrounding it, a beautiful, circular oak bench with a brass plaque:

Our small friend, Adeline, 1857–1863.

"You know, Auntie," I said before the ceremony, "this is really for Adeline, but every time I come and sit here, I'll remember Judith and Mum and Dad too, so it's for all of them. It's so peaceful here. And, for the first time, I think I can finally accept that they're not coming back."

"Oh, Jess," said Aunt Ruby, and she gave me such a big, tight hug. When she let go, she said: "And I agree. I've been thinking the same thing. It's a beautiful little spot, isn't it?"

*

The ceremony lasted about ten minutes and I was with the girls after, while Auntie was saying goodbye to the minister. The photographer, Mike, from the local paper, was trying to make us relax and smile for the camera.

"What was she supposed to have been like then, the little girl?" he asked.

"A bit of a rascal, I think," I said. I couldn't help grinning as I thought about her running up the stairs, pulling me by the hand, giggling. "They say she was cute and funny."

Mike didn't miss it. My smile, I mean. *Whirr, click,* went the camera. The others caught on and began to laugh, so the camera clicked again.

"Do you want to see?" he asked, when he'd finished.

We gathered round, looking at the shots he'd taken. Aunt Ruby came and peered at the screen too.

"Look at that one, Jessifer," she said and laughed. "You look like the cat that got the cream." It was true. I'd felt so pleased with how well everything had gone, I'd beamed from ear to ear. Mike was a good photographer.

"Speaking of cats," he said, "that's a lovely grey one." He pointed to the trees on the other side of the clearing and I spun round.

There, strolling off, with her tail flicking like an earthworm, was a familiar smoky cat.

"That's Clementine," I said.

THE END

About the Author

PAULA HAS BEEN A NURSE, A MIDWIFE AND A crafter. She began writing stories when she was five but didn't become a *proper* writer until 2012. She used to be a dormouse and has always been a fidget. She grew up in North Yorkshire, lives in Glasgow with her 'Weegie' husband and grown-up children and loves cooking, gardening and the outdoors.

ACKNOWLEDGEMENTS

To KAREN KING: THANK YOU FOR encouraging me to put Jessifer in a book. Thank you, Keith Grey, for your feedback on an early version of my manuscript. I enjoyed sharing writerly chat with you at the Scottish Association of Writers. Thanks to my Moniack Mhor friends from July 2017 and especially Jenny Valentine and Melvin Burgess, whose guidance helped shape this story into something more book-like. To all my friends at Strathkelvin Writers' Group, thanks for helping me believe I am an *actual writer*. To my readers: Jean, Simon (middle), Pat F, Liz, Pat P, Miriam, Angela and, most importantly, the fabulous Molly, I am grateful for your generosity. I appreciated everything you said (particularly the best bits) and I hope I have carried out your advice. Special thanks to Jill Calder, illustrator extraordinaire, for the amazing cover design. Thank you to all the team at Matador and… Thanks, finally, to my wonderful *Four Family*: your patience, love and support are endless.

ENDNOTES

O RANGES AND LEMONS IS A WORK OF FICTION set in the beautiful, historic city of York. While some of the buildings, places and names are real, others were created for the purposes of Jessifer's story. Mulberry Hall, on Stonegate, is a Grade II listed building, dating from the fifteenth century. It was, at one time, a Tudor townhouse. It was later used as retail space and became a china shop – with a delightful café – in the 1950s. In 2016, the china shop closed permanently. Since then, it has been the York home of a Kathe Wohlfahrt Christmas shop.

The Victorian episodes of *Oranges and Lemons* take place during 1863, the year *The Water Babies*, by Charles Kingsley, was published. For the purposes of the story, I have assumed it was already published and on sale by the time Adeline's mother was going to read it to her, though this may not have been the case.

All characters within the story are fictitious and any resemblance to real persons is coincidental.

If you are interested in learning more about the hidden cats of York and completing 'The Fabulous York Cats Trail' please visit:

https://www.visityork.org/explore/york-cat-trail-p801381